# NO MATCHA FOR MURDER

## A WITCHY, COZY MYSTERY

### LE DOUX MYSTERIES
#### BOOK EIGHT

## ABIGAIL LYNN THORNTON

# UNTITLED

"No Matcha for Murder"

**Le Doux Mysteries #8**

*To my oldest daughter.
You enthusiasm for books and
support in my work makes life a joy.
Thank you for all you do.*

# ACKNOWLEDGMENTS

No author works alone. Thank you, Mariah.
Your cover work is beautiful!
And to Laura, for your timely and thorough editing!

# CHAPTER 1

Wynona hummed in contentment as she spun a slow circle. "It's perfect," she cooed.

Violet snorted and wrapped her tail a little tighter around Wynona's neck. *It could have used a few mouse sized tables.*

Wynona rolled her eyes. "I only have one mouse guest," she told her familiar as she walked toward the kitchen. "I don't think I need an entire area dedicated to it."

*I can get you guests.*

Wynona laughed softly. "Are you trying to get me shut down? I just barely got Saffron's Tea House back!"

Violet grumbled under her breath but didn't argue more.

Walking slowly through the kitchen, Wynona let her fingers trail along the stainless steel countertops. She'd taken the opportunity to do a little upgrading while the rebuild was going on. After all...when a building burns to the ground, it leaves a lot of wiggle room for starting over.

The dining room, however, Wynona had built in almost an exact replica of what she had before. She loved the cozy, kitschy feel of the old, original building and didn't want to lose that. The hardwood floor was new, but distressed, and the antique cupboards displaying her growing collection of teacups and pots were intentionally aged.

An eclectic array of pillows and afghans were displayed artfully around the space, much to Celia's disappointment. If Wynona's sister had had her way, the entire shop would have been metallic and sleek, but that wasn't Wynona's dream.

She did have to give her sister credit though. The floral and colorful decor was much better than it had been the first time around. Instead of looking like pieces picked up at a flea market, Celia had brought in a touch of contemporary by using modern colors and shapes mixed with the antique objects.

"She's good," Wynona murmured, walking down the hall to her office. "You have to give her that."

Violet's grumbling increased. *I don't have to give her anything, thank you very much.*

Wynona's smile never budged. Celia and Violet didn't get along and try as Wynona might, she was positive that wouldn't change any time soon. She had just opened her office door when a voice came from the front.

"Hello? Nona?"

Her smile growing, Wynona hurried back out. "Prim! You made it!" She ran forward and grabbed a large vase of flowers from her fairy friend.

Prim blew a chunk of pink hair out of her face and plunked her now empty hands on her hips. "Yeah...sorry...business has been crazy lately and I wasn't sure if I'd get these here today."

"But you did," Wynona added. She took the vase to the side buffet. Smaller ones would go on the individual tables.

"Sure did! Anything for my best friend," Prim said proudly. She rose up on tiptoe, as if to flutter off the ground, except without wings, she never quite left the floor. "I'll go grab the others."

Wynona put up a hand. "Hang on. Let me give it a try." Closing her eyes, she let her magic filter through the air. It still sent a thrill through her every time she used it, though she was grateful she had gotten past the point of dropping with exhaustion with each use.

Honing her senses, she noticed a dozen smaller arrangements and carefully lifted them into the air. She hoped no one would get in her way as she began to pull them inside. She kept her eyes closed as Prim gave a surprised squeak, and Wynona only opened her eyes as she directed the flowers to the individual tables.

Prim was bouncing again. "I'll never get tired of that," she said breathlessly.

Wynona laughed softly. "Me either, I don't think."

*And this time, I didn't even help,* Violet stated proudly.

Wynona reached up to scratch the head of her familiar. *It would appear I'm getting better at this, huh?*

*As long as you don't go crazy, dark witch on us again, I think we can say that, yes.*

Wynona wanted to smile at the teasing compliment. Violet was notoriously stingy with those, but the reminder of the…witch…she'd become when her fiance's life had been threatened was unnerving.

The cold, dark presence hadn't shown itself again and Wynona was very happy to have it stay that way. She'd lost all sense of reason and connection, her only goal to make Lusgu, her brownie janitor, pay for hurting Rascal.

Wynona hadn't been aware enough to be frightened until Violet had bitten her ankle and caused Wynona to snap out of the trance she was in.

*The more you use your magic like this, the more control you have,* Violet soothed, her tail rubbing up and down Wynona's neck. *And the more control you have, the less we have to worry about you going dark.*

Wynona nodded, though she couldn't quite keep the sliver of fear out of her mind completely. She was so thrilled to have her shop back. So excited for the grand opening tomorrow, ecstatic to get back to planning her wedding now that the shop was finished…and yet there were so many things in her life that were a chaotic mess.

Wynona shook her head. She didn't want to go down that path right now. This was a happy occasion. "So…tell me about the flowers," she urged her best friend. Wynona paused and her jaw dropped. "I just now realized they're all white!"

Prim beamed and sauntered over to the table. "Yep. White is symbolic of new beginnings and purity." Her petite fingers brushed alone the petals of a rose and the bloom shivered as if enjoying Prim's touch. "Carnations—" she tapped the edge of the multi-petaled flower "—also represent good fortune." Prim's bright smile flashed over her shoulder as she looked at Wynona. "I figured if anyone needed a new start and a healthy dose of luck, it was you."

Wynona rolled her eyes. "Gee, thanks."

"Anytime."

Wynona huffed a laugh. "Well, they're beautiful. Thank you so much for putting them together."

Prim rubbed her hands together. "Please tell me you've gotten your pastry delivery for the media open house today."

Wynona's laughter grew. "I'm so sorry that you missed Gnox and Kyoz! I'm sure the imps would have loved to see you."

Prim's scowl told Wynona everything she needed to know. Gnox and Kyoz were a brother and sister duo that made some of the best pastries in Hex Haven and Wynona was lucky to have a contract with them for fresh, daily deliveries to go with her tea.

All that had paused, of course, while the shop had been in the various stages of rebuilding, but even Rascal had lamented not having the treats around on a regular basis. The only issue with working with the imps was the fact that they were…imps. Their draw toward the mischievous meant they enjoyed pulling pranks, pinching and knocking pots and pans to the floor whenever the desire hit them.

Before the fire, Wynona had mostly managed to have a handle on their behavior, but when Prim had threatened Kyoz at knifepoint, the imp had developed a terrible crush on the fairy, making his behavior worse than ever.

It was no wonder Prim had asked about the food and not the baker.

Prim's anger turned to enlightenment. "If I missed them, then the food is here! Yes!" She bolted for the kitchen and Wynona shook her head.

*There won't be anything left,* Violet lamented.

"There are two dozen trays in there," Wynona argued. "There'll be plenty left."

Violet grumbled again and Wynona reached up, taking the tiny body and putting her on the floor. "Go on. Grab what you want, but don't make yourself sick!" she said louder as the purple body broke into a frantic run.

A deep chuckle caught Wynona's ears and she spun with a gasp, only to relax a moment later. "Rascal! You scared me."

His golden eyes twinkled with humor as he smirked. "I'm not supposed to be able to sneak up on you," he scolded, though there was no ire in his voice.

Wynona shrugged, twisting her fingers in anticipation as he sauntered closer. "I was distracted," she said, her voice slightly breathy. She couldn't quite help herself. Rascal wasn't just her fiance, he was her soulmate and no matter how much time they spent together, the thrill of his presence never seemed to fade.

He stood directly in front of her, large and looming and oh, so delicious with his dark, messy hair, five o'clock shadow and deep golden eyes that were blazing with his barely restrained wolf.

"That mouse can certainly be distracting," he murmured in his deep tone.

Wynona smiled. "She's a punk, but I love her."

Rascal chuckled and wrapped his arms around her waist, pulling Wynona in for a deep, intimate exchange.

Raising herself up on tiptoe, Wynona wrapped her arms around his neck and hung on. She couldn't wait until she and Rascal were married, but she was so grateful he'd been patient while she got the tea shop back up and running. Now there was nothing to stop them from moving forward with their lives.

A shift of strong magic had Wynona pulling back. She blinked herself to reality and looked around. "What was that?" she asked hoarsely.

Rascal growled, his glowing eyes on the kitchen door. "From the sounds of Prim's annoyance, I'm guessing Lu moved his portal again."

Wynona's eyes widened.

Rascal took her hand. "You don't have to go in there," he told her softly.

She shook her head. "Don't be ridiculous, of course I do. He's my employee."

Rascal's lips pressed into a thin line. "He's also something else and I don't like not knowing what it is."

Wynona nodded and let her forehead drop to his chest. "Me neither," she admitted. After proving Dr. Rayn's innocence in a murder case a few weeks back, Wynona had come to the astonishing realization that Lusgu was cursed. He couldn't talk about who cursed him and he also wasn't actually a brownie.

*What* he was, however, remained to be seen.

The new bit of knowledge had been sitting heavy on Wynona's shoulders, but she didn't have the courage to approach the grumpy creature about it. Lusgu had been difficult, at best, during Dr. Rayn's troubles. There was no telling how belligerent he would get if Wynona brought up the fact that she knew he wasn't actually a brownie.

Violet was the only person who seemed to know the truth behind it and she wasn't speaking, much to Wynona and Rascal's consternation.

"I think we better go."

Rascal nodded and put his hand on Wynona's lower back, guiding her toward the kitchen before pushing open the door for her.

Wynona stepped inside, steeling herself against the feelings of fear and betrayal that she felt whenever she was near Lusgu at the moment. She'd done a pretty good job of avoiding him at the house during the last couple of weeks. The finishing of the tea shop had given her a wonderful excuse to keep a distance between them, but now…she'd see him every day she came into work.

Their suspicions were confirmed when Wynona spotted Lusgu standing with his arms folded over his scrawny chest and a scowl on his face in the same corner his portal had been in before the fire.

His black, beady eyes flickered to her when she entered and

Wynona paused when she could have sworn she saw them soften the slightest amount.

"Nona!" Prim cried. "Tell your janitor that I have permission to eat a few pastries!" She waved at the brownie, glaring her bright pink eyes his way. "He's complaining that I'm dropping crumbs on the floor and that's stupidly ridiculous! I'm not a child!"

Wynona could have argued in Lusgu's favor over the situation, but she wasn't about to be caught in the middle. "Hello, Lusgu," she said carefully.

The brownie's shoulders sagged the slightest amount. "Wynona."

"I see you were able to move back."

His nostrils flared. "Yes."

"Welcome home." Wynona pasted on a smile, gripping Rascal's hand on her back.

*Are you sure I can't eat him?*

*Stop!* Wynona scolded through their mental connection. *I don't know what to do with him, but I don't think he'd hurt us...intentionally anyway.*

Rascal just growled softly in response. He still hadn't forgiven Lusgu for nearly killing Wynona a couple of times during their last investigation.

Lusgu's eyes narrowed. "Wolf," he said by way of greeting.

"Lu," Rascal said curtly. He knew full well the brownie hated the nickname, but it only made Rascal use it all the more.

Wynona sighed and rubbed her forehead. "Okay...well...I have a few more things to get ready before the media arrives in..." She glanced at the wall clock and gasped. "Oh my goodness, I only have an hour!" She turned to Rascal. "Are you staying?"

His frown melted and he smiled, leaning forward to kiss her hairline. "I might have managed to get assigned as a police guard today."

Wynona's jaw dropped. "You think I need a guard?"

Rascal's dark eyebrows rose. "It's a media event," he snorted. "Being thrown by the president's daughter, no less." He smirked. "Everyone's going to need a guard."

## CHAPTER 2

Wynona's smile felt so brittle at this point, she was surprised her face hadn't cracked. It served to remind her, however, how much she hated being in the public's eye. Reporters and gossip rags were terribly good for business...not so much for a person who wanted a quiet, peaceful life.

Whatever had possessed her to try for both?

"Can you tell us more about your custom tea package?" a woman asked, thrusting a microphone into Wynona's face.

Wynona blinked against the bright light of the woman's camera and kept her smile in place. "My grandmother, Saffron Le Doux, taught me how to match teas to each person." Wynona clutched her fingers together, trying to fortify herself from the pain of her grandmother's death, while pretending all was fine and dandy. "When my customer requests that package, I use my gifts to pick herbs that will be of most benefit to them."

"Do they get to request certain attributes?" the reporter continued.

Wynona shrugged. "I'm always willing to listen, but the magic doesn't always work that way. My gift allows me to see what they *need*, not always what they *want*."

The reporter huffed. "Do you use this *gift* when you're helping solve murder cases?"

Wynona stilled. "Excuse me?"

The reporter's smirk said she knew her change in topic would catch Wynona off guard. "You've been awfully busy, Ms. Le Doux. Leaving home. Snagging the Deputy Chief as your fiance." She leaned in. "And dabbling in quite a few cases. Tell me…" Her green eyes sparkled with excitement. "What *other* gifts did the great Saffron Le Doux teach you? I mean…you were raised with no powers, right? Until recently, very few people even knew President Le Doux had a daughter other than Celia." The reporter straightened. "It just seems awfully coincidental that you have your fingers in so many pies for someone who was an outcast only a few months ago."

Wynona's jaw was clenched so tight, she could barely breathe. She felt sparks begin to dance on her fingers and a cold trickle of fear began to drip down her spine. Wynona was fully aware that her emotions made it more difficult to keep her magic in check, but as a person who normally worked extra hard to be forgiving and kind, she didn't have trouble all that often. At least not anymore.

But her magic was powerful…too powerful, some might say. And when it had broken free of the curse, the entirety of Hex Haven had felt it. The fact that this reporter was brave enough to push Wynona on questions she had no desire to answer either meant the woman was ignorant or incredibly brave.

*Or desperate,* Rascal's voice said with a chuckle. *Maybe stupid. I'd go with that.* He slipped up behind her, his large, warm hand on her back. "That's enough questions for now," he stated with absolute authority.

The reporter blinked, the excitement draining from her face.

"If you'll excuse Ms. Le Doux," Rascal said with a short dip of his chin.

"But!"

Rascal kept them moving and the farther they went, the more Wynona relaxed. The shifter's intimidating authority caused those at the party to give them a wide berth and Wynona was grateful for it.

"Thank you," she whispered, pasting another smile on her face and nodding at those they passed.

"She had no right to ask you those questions," Rascal growled in a low tone. He nodded to his boss, Chief Ligurio, who was standing off to the side looking every bit as intimidating as his deputy chief.

Chief Ligurio raised a single black eyebrow and Wynona huffed a quiet laugh. "I don't think he's enjoying being here today." She looked up at Rascal. "In fact, I'm surprised he came."

Rascal's lips were twitching and he responded through their soulmate connection. *I think he was hoping to see Celia.*

"Ah." Wynona nodded sagely. She looked around. "I thought she'd be here as well," she whispered. "After all, this was her design project."

"Ms. Le Doux!" Another reporter, this one much more welcome than the last, waved from across the room.

"Mr. Hesa!" Wynona said with the first genuine smile to grace her face in the last hour. She stepped forward as the small partially see-through body made its way to her. "How nice to see you here."

Mr. Hesa grinned, his small eyes darting around the room. His hands held his camera and he was forever looking for the next big story. His help on a case a while back had been immeasurable and they'd held a tentative relationship ever since. "Deputy Chief," Mr. Hesa said with a respectful nod before going back to watching the crowd. "You got a good turn out today." His ears twitched, reminiscent of his mortal life as a house cat shifter.

Wynona made a point of looking around as well. "It does seem to be going well." She turned back to the ghost reporter. "Heard anything interesting lately?"

Black eyes gleamed. "I hear plenty," he said with a toothy smile. "But I suppose who a person is would depend on whether or not it was interesting."

Rascal growled and Mr. Hesa stepped back.

"Is there something you need to share?" Rascal snapped.

Mr. Hesa shook his head, his eyes darting between Wynona and Rascal. "No. Just rumors, nothing major."

Wynona put a hand on Rascal's chest, then stepped forward. "Mr.

Hesa, how would you like a cup of tea? I'd love to show you how my custom tea gifts can help people."

His eyes rounded. "I…" He chuckled and his ghostly body relaxed. "Thanks anyway, Ms. Le Doux, but I don't think I need it."

Wynona smiled. "I know, but I thought perhaps you could use it in a story. How I use my powers seems to be a hot topic today."

"Oh, well…" Mr. Hesa scrunched up his nose and wiped at his cheek. "Maybe I could take some pictures of you in action? But make the tea for someone else, yeah?"

Wynona nodded and looked around. Her eyes stopped on her brownie janitor, who was slinking through the crowd, grumbling under his breath and keeping the entire area clean. Lusgu looked grumpier than usual…and that was saying something. Still, Wynona knew how much it drove him crazy to have things messy, so she couldn't exactly blame him, since the media were walking and eating at the same time. Crumbs were strewn everywhere, but she knew they wouldn't last long under Lusgu's attention.

"How about him?" Mr. Hesa pointed to someone behind Wynona and she spun, a frown tugging at her lips.

"Do you know who that is?" Rascal murmured.

Wynona shook her head. The creature in question, however, was marching boldly through the crowd as if he owned the tea shop. His eyes were fixated on Wynona and one of his eyebrows was slightly arched, giving him an air of confidence and intrigue.

Rascal growled and Wynona hushed him. "He'll hear you," she whispered.

"I hope he did. Be careful."

Wynona rolled her eyes. *Men.*

*Wolf,* Rascal corrected her. His hand squeezed her side slightly. *And don't pretend you don't like that part of me.*

Wynona looked up and grinned. "Only until it makes you territorial over nothing."

Rascal's eyes began to glow just as the stranger showed up. "Ms. Le Doux," he said, not bothering with any niceties. "It's so good to meet you in person." He held out his hand and Wynona cautiously took it.

She stiffened when the man brought her knuckles up and kissed them. "Uh...thank you," she said, tugging her hand back. The man frowned slightly, marring his perfectly smooth forehead as Wynona put her hands behind her back. She really didn't want this guy touching her again.

Rascal's growling had increased at this point and Wynona was starting to fear she'd have a fight on her hands. "Have you met my fiance? Deputy Chief Strongclaw?"

The men sized each other up, but neither offered their hand. "Deputy Chief," the man said.

Rascal stood stoic, his eyes glowing for a far different reason than only moments before.

"I'm sorry," Wynona interrupted. "I didn't catch your name."

The creature brought his bright blue eyes back to Wynona and put a hand to his chest. "Forgive me. Tororin Braxet, master of The Cursed Circus, at your service." He executed a courtly bow and Wynona glanced at Rascal, unsure how to react.

Upon rising, Mr. Braxet smiled, his teeth nearly glowing in their bright, white intensity.

Again, Wynona felt an odd shiver, but she mentally shook herself and moved on. "Welcome to Saffron's Tea House." She gave him her most polite, but impersonal smile. "Which media outlet are you attached to?"

He scoffed and waved a manicured hand through the air. "No. I'm not a reporter. As I mentioned, I'm the owner of The Cursed Circus." He raised his eyebrows expectantly.

Wynona nodded slowly. "I'm sorry, but I've never heard of it."

"Braxet." Chief Ligurio stepped into their little pow-wow, his face as stern as ever. "I didn't realize the bottom dwellers had been invited today."

Wynona felt her eyes widen and she stepped back slightly. Something was going on here and she had no idea what it was. *Rascal?*

*He owns a circus,* Rascal spat in her mind. *One that exploits the most... interesting of our kind.*

Wynona wrinkled her nose in distaste.

*He named it Cursed Circus because his whole goal is to terrify his patrons.*

*So his acts aren't the Happy Ever After kind, I take it?*

Rascal snorted, but didn't respond.

"Chief Ligurio," Mr. Braxet said with a far from genuine smile. He tugged on the sleeves of his suit coat. "Fancy meeting you here."

"Fancy, indeed," Chief Ligurio murmured. He folded his arms over his chest. "What can I do for you?"

Those eyes snapped back to Wynona. "Nothing that I can think of, Chief Ligurio," Mr. Braxet cooed. "I came to speak to our most gracious host."

Wynona leaned a little of her weight against Rascal. That weird sensation was back. It had something to do with the way Mr. Braxet kept staring at her. His eyes were wide and bright, reminding Wynona a little of when Rascal's wolf came to the forefront. But the look on the man's face said he was expecting something to happen. Wynona had no idea what it was supposed to be. "What did you need to talk about, Mr. Braxet?"

The creature reached out and took her hand, tugging it into his arm, but Rascal snatched her back. "Back off," he ground out, his teeth slightly elongating.

"Rascal," Wynona hissed, looking around to see if anyone else was noticing what was going on. They were surrounded by reporters and cameras. There was no way a brawl would be good for her grand opening. She tugged on Rascal's unrelenting stance. "You need to calm down." The men continued to stare at each other, neither moving an inch. "What's gotten into you?" she whispered, looking to Chief Ligurio for help, but from the scowl on his face, he was going to let Rascal punch the newcomer. "Why are you doing this?"

"He's an incubus."

Wynona's head snapped down to see Lusgu shove his way into their circle. His scowl was deep enough to cause heavy wrinkling on his forehead. "An incubus?" Wynona breathed. She slapped her forehead. "Of course." No wonder she'd felt something funny every time

13

he looked at her. He'd been trying to entrance her! *But why didn't it work?*

*Because you have a soulmate,* Rascal said tightly, his body still between her and her guest.

Wynona blinked and brought her magical sight to the forefront to confirm her suspicions. A blue mist emanated from his person, with a small trail right in front of her face. It made her want to hold her breath, as if sucking in the magic would cause it to work.

She put her sight away and glared at the incubus. "Mr. Braxet," Wynona said in a harsh tone. "You will respect my property and my person by putting away your magic or I will have you bodily removed from the premises."

Those perfectly shaped eyebrows rose high and he smirked. "Well done, Ms. Le Doux. I'm not one to be ignored very often." His eyes flickered to the men still in his way. "This reaction, I expected." His eyes came back to hers and the curiosity in them intensified. "Yours, however…is unusual."

When the tingle hit her skin again, Wynona stepped back. "Rascal."

Rascal grabbed Mr. Braxet's collar and began to shove him backward.

"Wait, wait, wait!" Mr. Braxet put his hands in the air, not fighting Rascal's hold at all.

Rascal hesitated just long enough for the incubus to keep talking.

"Forgive me," he said, his face drooping in a feigned act of sincerity. "But I had to check one more time." He smiled. "I had heard you were magnificent, but to see it in action…"

Rascal's grip tightened. "State your reasons for being here, or I'll tear you apart."

Mr. Braxet's grin only grew. "Why don't we take this to my office?"

"No," Wynona responded before Rascal could.

Mr. Braxet moved his head around, noting the crowd watching them, and came back to Wynona. "Yours then." He chuckled, the sound low and more than likely appealing to most women. "You can even bring your lapdog." His hands shot up in surrender as Rascal began to push him backward.

"Strongclaw," Chief Ligurio shouted.

Rascal paused and looked back.

Chief Ligurio's nostrils flared. "Take him to the office."

Rascal's breathing grew rapid and his eyes glowed brightly.

Wynona rushed up and put her hand on his chest. "Please, Rascal. Not here. Just do as the chief says and we'll work it out from there."

Growling fiercely, Rascal held his grip and practically dragged the creature through the crowd and down the hall.

Wynona turned to Chief Ligurio. "I hope you know what you're doing."

Chief Ligurio grinned, a purely mercenary look. "I've been trying to nail this guy for years. I don't know what he wants with you, but this might be the opportunity of a lifetime."

Wynona closed her eyes and shook her head as the chief walked past her. Why couldn't her life ever be easy? She opened her eyes when she felt a small presence at her side.

Lusgu looked up at her. "You need me," he huffed before walking after the vampire.

Wynona watched them go, then turned to the crowd who were all still staring. "Thank you for coming," she said with a smile. "I'm afraid I have a small business matter to attend to, but please feel free to keep eating and testing the teas. If you have questions, I will be happy to answer them later." She nodded. "Thank you."

With her head high, but her confidence smeared in a puddle on the floor, Wynona walked away, hoping that her second grand opening hadn't just been ruined beyond repair.

# CHAPTER 3

Mr. Braxet was watching Wynona with that same smirk when she walked into the office, despite two police officers staring him down. When Rascal growled, the incubus didn't even flinch, but the edge of his lips twisted, as though Rascal's anger amused him.

Wynona carefully closed the door after Lusgu slipped inside and stood off to the side. She felt a small tingle on her skin and immediately snapped to attention. "I won't say it again," she said through gritted teeth.

Mr. Braxet put up his hands. "Can you blame me for being intrigued?" he asked, both eyebrows high. He narrowed his gaze and tilted his head. "Just what makes you different, Ms. Le Doux?"

Wynona folded her arms over her chest as if she could give herself strength that way, but inside she was quaking. She hated dealing with the privileged and the entitled. She'd spent too many years with her family learning to avoid any and all confrontation for that exact reason. Escaping was supposed to give Wynona the chance at freedom and peace.

*Wishes upon wishes...*she thought sadly.

A scratching sound brought Violet scrambling under the door and up Wynona's leg. *Did you really think you could do this without me?*

Wynona kept her eyes on the incubus, who was staring even harder now.

*I'm not sure I want you around this guy. He's a creep with a capital C.*

Rascal laughed, but tried to cover it with a cough. Mr. Braxet's eyes flashed toward the wolf shifter, far from amused.

"What was it you needed to say, Mr. Braxet?" Wynona asked, proud of how strong her voice sounded.

"Do we really need all this muscle?" Mr. Braxet asked, his eyes moving through every man in the room.

"Another friend of mine, Detective Skymaw, is due to arrive soon," Wynona offered. "Would you like to wait and add another to the mix?"

Mr. Braxet chuckled and waggled a finger at her. "You drive a hard bargain, Ms. Le Doux."

"And you're adept at avoiding questions."

His smile grew and his eyes flashed. "I'm a businessman, Ms. Le Doux."

Chief Ligurio snorted this time, but the incubus ignored him.

"I've come to make you an offer."

Wynona tilted her head. "Oh?"

Casually resting his hands in his pockets, the creature looked completely at ease. "My pet project…The Cursed Circus…is opening a new wing of entertainment."

Wynona held perfectly still. She wasn't quite sure where this was going, but she had a terrible feeling about it.

"I'd like to open a restaurant attached to the attractions," Mr. Braxet continued. One side of his mouth pulled up in a charmingly crooked smile. "And I'd like your tea concoctions to take a starring role." He moved toward Wynona, all grace and strength. "Imagine," he said in a low whisper, getting dangerously close to her personal bubble. "Sipping a blend that helped the patrons feel just a little more fear as they looked upon the most gruesome among us," Mr. Braxet cooed. "Or perhaps, offering drinks that helped those too fearful, but still intrigued, find courage to walk through the very creatures of their nightmares."

Wynona jerked back, nearly stumbling as she tried to get away from the man. "You can't be serious," she gasped.

Mr. Braxet straightened, his voice going back to normal. "Oh, but I am." His smile had gone from charming to malicious. "You won't believe what people will pay to see their nightmares come to life."

Rascal's growling had become a permanent sound in the room.

"And just how legal are these...attractions?" Chief Ligurio drawled from behind Wynona's desk. "Perhaps I need to come take a look at those permits."

Mr. Braxet spun, his voice changing once again. "All above board, Chief," he said back. "You already know that, since you've surprised us multiple times with inspections."

Chief Ligurio's face hardened. "You seem to have an endless supply of creatures that shouldn't be available," he snarled.

"And you don't seem to understand that all my performers are there of their own free will and choice," Mr. Braxet said easily. "I force no one to work for me." His eyes flared. "I give a home to the homeless. I've never needed to coerce."

"You mean you exploit them," Rascal argued.

Mr. Braxet tsked his tongue and shook his head. "Exploit is such a dirty word." He sobered. "They all receive a paycheck, Deputy Chief. They come to me." Slowly, he spun back to Wynona, his demeanor softening. "We would welcome the contribution of a lovely witch such as yourself," he said in a seductive tone.

Wynona shook her head and backed up farther. "I'm afraid I'm not interested, Mr. Braxet." She grabbed the handle behind her. "I'll show you the door."

"You can't be serious."

Wynona paused. "What do you mean?"

Mr. Braxet walked forward, but Rascal lunged and blocked his way to Wynona. Scowling and leaning around the shifter, Mr. Braxet glared. "You can't be serious that you aren't interested."

Wynona shook her head. "I'm not. I have enough to do with my business here. I don't want anything to do with yours."

Mr. Braxet's stare increased. "I'm not used to being turned down, Ms. Le Doux."

Wynona found that her anger was beginning to simmer and with Rascal ready to tear the creature's throat out, she was having a hard time keeping herself from throttling the incubus. "I don't believe that's my problem."

"We'll be rich beyond your imagination."

Wynona stepped to the side of Rascal and stood a little closer. "I have no interest in the money," she said in a low tone. "I spent thirty years of my life being treated like a side show act, Mr. Braxet. The very ones that you display for creatures' amusement. I find it despicable and immoral. I don't care if you claim your creatures are there voluntarily, I want no part of it. My custom teas are meant to help people, not manipulate them." She shook her head, grateful for Violet's soothing rub under her ear as it kept Wynona from completely shouting. "I will *never* support your business."

Mr. Braxet's nostrils flared and his smooth face became mottled.

The tingle that had crept over Wynona's skin several times slammed into her so hard, it knocked the breath out of her. Gasping, she put a hand to her chest and stumbled back. "Rascal," she said breathlessly.

Grabbing Mr. Braxet by his collar, Rascal gave the smaller man a hard shake. "Shut it down, NOW!" he bellowed.

Wynona almost hit her knees when the door behind her burst open. She barely caught herself on the edges of a bookshelf as Lusgu put his hands on her waist to help. "Thank you," she whispered hoarsely, realizing that the pressure of magic against her skin was suddenly gone.

Lusgu's already thin lips had completely disappeared as he muttered under his breath.

"Take him to the station," Chief Ligurio snapped.

"I haven't done anything," Mr. Braxet argued as Rascal began dragging him to the door.

Wynona finally turned to see who had pushed her aside and let out a long breath when she recognized Daemon's large frame in the doorway. He wasn't facing her, but she knew for certain that his eyes would be solid black if she could see, as his black hole magic kept the incubus from trying to enchant her again.

"There are laws about coercion in this town," Chief Ligurio stated as he followed his deputy chief and the incubus out of the room. Pausing in the doorway, Chief Ligurio looked her way. "Ms. Le Doux…are you alright?"

Wynona nodded, her breath still a little rougher than usual. "I'll be fine."

Clenching his jaw and shaking his head, his red eyes glowed. "When you've finished your event, come meet us at the station." The fang filled smile that followed would never be called friendly, making Wynona grateful it wasn't focused on her. "We'll let our little guest cool his heels for awhile until you're ready to press charges."

Wynona straightened from the bookshelf and fixed her blouse. "Are you sure I should do that?" she asked. "I just want him gone."

Chief Ligurio sighed. "Unless you show a bully you can't be manipulated, they'll continue to look for weak spots, Ms. Le Doux. I wouldn't hesitate to hit hard and fast."

Wynona nodded, feeling weak from the little encounter. Oh, how she hated this kind of confrontation. And did it have to hit at her grand opening? Couldn't just one event in her life ever go off without a hitch? "I'll be there this evening."

Chief Ligurio nodded sharply, then turned to his officer. "Well done, Skymaw. We'll put him in your car."

Daemon nodded. Those still-black orbs landed on Wynona. "Prim is supposed to be here soon," he said in a low tone. "Can you tell her what happened?"

Wynona snorted and reached up to scratch Violet, who was still muttering under her breath. "Do you really think I can keep it from her?"

Daemon's lips tugged into a small smile. "I'll see you soon…and congrats, by the way."

Wynona waved him off. "Better get going and let me try to salvage what I can of this party."

Daemon's smile grew and he slipped out the door. For as big as he was, Wynona was always surprised at his agility.

Taking a deep breath, she glanced down at Lusgu.

His beady eyes stared back and if Wynona didn't know any better, she would have sworn they were filled with compassion.

*Lusgu hates everyone,* Wynona thought. *I have to be projecting.*

Violet's tail twitched. *He doesn't hate everyone. Just...most everyone.*

Wynona rolled her eyes and looked down at her shoulder.

*I hate most everyone too,* Violet stated proudly, standing on her back legs. *That's why we're friends.*

Wynona shook her head and went back to her janitor. "Thank you," she said sincerely. "I appreciate you coming in here." Especially after the way Wynona had been avoiding the brownie, she was grateful he was still willing to stick around.

After Dr. Rayn had been cleared from the murder investigation, Wynona had wondered if Lusgu would quit and follow the creature he seemed to have deep feelings for back into the Grove of Secrets. Instead, he'd gone back to work without saying a word. Wynona wasn't even sure if the two kept in touch.

Lusgu grunted. "Incubi are idiots," he snarled before stalking out of the room.

Wynona watched him go and her shoulder drooped. "Yep. He likes a few people," she muttered.

Violet chittered. *He came, didn't he? He likes you.*

Wynona shook her head. "No...I'm pretty sure he just tolerates me because he has some connection to Granny." Tilting her head, Wynona let her mind wander a bit. "Him and Mama Reyna, though I haven't spoken to her in awhile. Their whole job was to make sure I didn't blow up the world."

Violet began cleaning her whiskers. *Think what you want.*

Wynona raised her eyebrows and looked at her familiar again. "What do you know that I don't?" She put her hands on her hips. "Besides, what creature is Lusgu actually supposed to be?"

Violet kept cleaning, completely ignoring the question.

"You do realize that as my familiar, you're supposed to *help* me?" Wynona said in exasperation.

Violet stopped cleaning and looked up. *Sometimes letting you figure things out for yourself is the best way TO help.*

Wynona huffed, but didn't press. She knew there was no point in creating an argument. How she was supposed to figure out what Lusgu was, short of cornering him and demanding answers, Wynona didn't know. But she knew enough to understand that cornering Lusgu would only result in a magic battle. There was no way he was giving up his answers that easily, not to mention Wynona had already learned he couldn't speak about his curse.

Glancing in a mirror on her wall, Wynona straightened her hair and her skirt, threw her shoulders back and walked out of the office with her head held high. The front room was chatty and full of guests and Wynona plastered a smile on her face in preparation.

"Oof." She wasn't quite prepared, however, when Prim nearly bowled her over with a tight hug.

"I ran into Daemon outside," Prim whispered, her arms nearly choking Wynona. Leaning back, Prim's bright pink eyes were wet with tears. "Are you alright?"

Wynona smiled to assure her friend all was well. "I'm fine."

Wiping at her face, Prim put a little more space between them. "Sorry, I just…ugh!" Prim threw her head back. "I just hate that all this stuff seems to happen to you!"

Wynona glanced at the room of reporters, who were trying to look like they weren't listening in on the conversation. She already knew her name would be plastered all over the evening news tonight. "Prim…" Wynona warned. "I love you, but can we talk about this when we don't have an audience?"

Prim's mouth opened and she spun. Huffing, her hands landed on her hips. "What are you staring at?" she demanded loudly. "Can't two besties have a quiet conversation without it showing up in the gossip columns you all call newspapers?"

Wynona closed her eyes and hung her head.

*Well...*Violet huffed. *That's one way to handle it, I guess.* She snickered.

Wynona pinched the bridge of her nose, then looked up. "I apologize for the interruptions," Wynona stated, using her magic to make sure everyone heard her voice. She smiled. "It seems that nothing ever goes according to plan, does it?"

That got her a few chuckles, but most of the guests were still eyeing Prim like she was about to blow like a boiling teapot.

"I'm available for comments or questions at this time," Wynona continued. "And if you'd like to experience your own cup of custom tea, I'd be happy to get through as many of you as I can."

The murmuring rose and the room shifted in Wynona's direction.

Sighing in relief, Wynona helped the group form a somewhat organized line, then took her first guest to a small table to start the process. It was a good thing she'd learned long ago that freebies and schmoozing were key ingredients in keeping a good reputation with the media.

Standing with her hands clasped, Wynona studied the buxom news anchor in front of her. She let her magic swirl around her body in a light purple breeze. It wasn't necessary in order to read her customer, but patrons seemed to love it.

"Hmmm..." Wynona hummed. "Ginkgo biloba and green oats, I think."

"What does that do?" the woman asked in a thick Southern accent.

Wynona smiled at the drawl. It was unusual in this part of the world and probably why she'd been put in front of a camera. "It helps with attention and energy," Wynona explained. Her smile widened. "I have a feeling you need to get a lot of work done today."

"I have a deadline tonight that's kicking my fanny," the reporter responded with a bright, white smile.

Wynona nodded. "Then I think we're on the right track." Turning, she quickly went to the kitchen to gather what she needed. She could have used magic, but the kitchen provided a nice, quiet area for her to gather herself in between patrons.

After building the tray, Wynona picked it up and took another long breath. She could do this. She could turn this afternoon around, offer a few custom blends and get her name in the papers with nothing but good things to say.

Mr. Braxet would soon become only a distant memory, and then Wynona would be able to put her full focus on her wedding.

She smiled. *And then life will be perfect.*

# CHAPTER 4

Wynona turned off her Vespa and tugged her jacket tighter around her body. The temperature this evening was dropping quickly and it made her wish she'd brought a coat to work rather than the slim business suit jacket.

Violet's nose twitched over the edge of her wicker basket. *Are we going in? Or simply freezing out here for the rest of the night?*

Wynona rolled her eyes as she got off the scooter. "It's not that cold," she argued even as a shiver ran through her body.

Violet chittered. *Speak for yourself. My winter fur hasn't come in yet.*

Wynona wiggled her fingers and bent over a little. "Want me to help it along?" She laughed softly at the look on Violet's face before picking up her familiar and setting Violet on her shoulder. "Don't dish it out if you can't take it back," Wynona teased.

Violet sniffed and curled into her favorite sleeping position. *I've never threatened to use magic on you.*

"No...but you've threatened plenty of others," Wynona shot back, but her tone was playful and she knew Violet didn't really believe that Wynona would experiment on her.

*Can I help it if some creatures need a good bite...with sharp teeth...on their face?*

Wynona shook her head and didn't bother responding. It was a fight she'd never win. Violet had a fierce streak and wouldn't hesitate to use it if the situation called for it. The knowledge was equal parts frightening and comforting.

Wynona reached for the handle on the station door just as another hand did the same. "Oh...excuse me," Wynona said with a smile. She held onto the door and pulled it back to allow the small woman beside her to enter.

The creature's short dark hair was all Wynona could see as the figure hunched in on herself and murmured a very quiet bit of gratitude before ducking inside.

Wynona frowned, but didn't comment as she followed the woman inside. Giving a small wave to Amaris, who was busy helping a long line of creatures, Wynona headed straight to the back. Amaris gave her a small glance, but otherwise stayed focused.

*That's probably for the best.* Wynona sighed. The vampire officer had been afraid of Wynona ever since her magic had been released and as much as it hurt Wynona, she was trying desperately to act as if she wasn't hurt by the betrayal.

*I'd suggest killing her with kindness, but...* Violet snickered. *Technically she's already dead.*

Wynona stopped mid-stride and looked at her shoulder. "Please don't tell me you've picked up telling bad jokes."

Violet shrugged. *My tastes are my own.*

"Oh, good grief," Wynona moaned softly. That was all she needed. A purple mouse familiar who told dad jokes. Life would certainly be complete then.

"Are you Ms. Le Doux?"

Wynona spun, being pulled out of her complaints at the soft voice behind her. Blinking, Wynona realized it was the same woman she'd held the door open for. "I am," Wynona said carefully. "Can I help you?"

The woman wrung her hands and looked around nervously. "I...I work for Master Braxet."

"Ah." Wynona nodded slowly, her guard rising even further. She had serious concerns about what type of creature would work with someone like Mr. Braxet.

"I just wanted you to know that I'm a huge fan," the woman gushed, then panted as if the words had taken all her breath.

Wynona frowned and her shoulders relaxed a little. "Really?"

Dark eyebrows rose high and the secretary nodded vigorously. "I came to your tea shop during your very first opening and it was amazing." She brought her clasped hands to her chest. "Your tea was the best I've ever tasted and I've followed your career as a detective as well." Her blue eyes were wide with admiration as she stared at Wynona. "I don't know how you do it all." Pale cheeks blushed and the woman shifted her weight. "I've always wanted to solve a crime myself. I'd like to write a book about it."

Wynona found herself relaxing more and more as the woman spoke. She had never realized there were creatures who actually paid attention to her work with the police, other than Rascal and Chief Ligurio. Several times, they'd actually made sure her name had stayed *out* of the papers, so it was a wonder Mr. Braxet's secretary even knew who Wynona was...outside of being the president's daughter, that is.

*Did you notice she didn't mention my family once?* Wynona sent to Violet.

Violet sniffed. *Yes...who'd have thought you'd ever gather groupies?*

"I'm sorry," Wynona said, ignoring Violet's sarcastic response. "I didn't catch your name?" She held out her hand.

The secretary eyed Wynona's hand before slowly reaching out and lightly grasping it with a quick shake.

The limp grip turned Wynona off a little, but the woman seemed exceptionally shy, so Wynona pushed the worries away.

"Cookie Floura," the woman said, tucking her hair behind her ear. Her eyes darted around and she looked slightly scared, but Wynona wasn't sure why. They were in a police station. Of all the places in Hex Haven, it was one of the safest.

"Nice to meet you, Cookie," Wynona said softly. She had the distinct impression that any loud noises would scare the woman into hiding. She looked over the creature from head to toe. Dark hair, pale skin, blue eyes, slim, petite build...absolutely nothing stood out in the woman's features. She was simply...average.

*Is she a shifter?* Violet asked.

*I'm not sure,* Wynona sent back. Cookie's nose wasn't twitching, nor her ears, which were usually dead giveaways when it came to prey type shifters, and considering how shy the woman seemed, Wynona couldn't imagine her being anything else.

"I came to bail my boss out," Cookie said, her voice getting softer with each word. "Do you know where he is?"

Wynona gave the woman a sad smile. "Not yet, but I was headed back myself to speak to those who *will* know." She touched Cookie's arm lightly. "You can come with me."

Cookie was shaking a little as she tucked her hair in again. "Thank you."

Wynona slowed down her pace to allow Cookie to walk next to her, but it didn't work. The secretary stayed just behind Wynona's shoulder the whole way down the hall.

*How in the paranormal world does someone as scared as her plan to solve a murder?* Violet huffed. *She'd probably faint at her own shadow.*

Wynona had the same question, but she chose to ignore it for now. "Hold on just a moment," she told Cookie when they reached Rascal's door. Poking her head in, Wynona looked around.

"Hey, sweetheart." Rascal stood and walked over to greet her.

Wynona waited for his kiss, but pulled back to keep it short, to Rascal's consternation. Wynona smiled and pointedly glanced out into the hallway. "Rascal, I have Ms. Cookie Floura with me. She's Mr. Braxet's secretary come to bail him out."

Rascal's lips thinned and his nostrils flared, causing Ms. Floura's eyes to widen as she stepped behind Wynona's back.

*Easy, Wolf. She's extremely skittish.*

Rascal raised an eyebrow. "Come on," he growled. "Braxet's in interrogation room five."

Wynona smiled at Cookie, urging her to follow the angry shifter.

Rascal knocked on one more door during their walk. "Chief?" He stuck his head in. "Wy's here, and so is Braxet's secretary."

"His what?"

Rascal huffed. "His secretary." He looked back at the women. "What was your name again?"

"C-Cookie," she stammered.

Wynona put a hand on her shoulder to help bolster the terrified woman.

"Cookie Floura."

Rascal nodded. "Follow me, Ms. Floura."

Chief Ligurio stepped out of his office, laptop under his arm, and he nodded to Wynona before scanning Ms. Floura. "Chief Ligurio," he announced sharply. "You're his secretary? Why did you come?"

Cookie was wringing her hands again and her eyes darted to Wynona as if seeking help.

Wynona felt sorry for the woman. She was obviously far out of her comfort zone, but the level of fear she exuded was nearly choking. Just what was she so afraid of?

"Ms. Floura said she came to bail him out…" Wynona paused to think about what she said. "Cookie…I don't think Mr. Braxet has been formally arrested. How can you bail him out?"

"H-he called," Cookie managed, swallowing hard. "Told me I needed to come get him." She splayed her hands. "I assumed…"

Chief Ligurio growled and Cookie shrank back yet again. The chief's red eyes snapped to her movements and he stopped the noise. "Let's get this over with," he said through clenched teeth. "You're not the first visitor he's had this afternoon and I'm guessing if we don't finish with him soon, he'll keep sending others."

"Who else showed up?" Wynona asked. "I thought we were just planning to press charges for magical coercion?"

"We are," Chief Ligurio said over his shoulder. "But Braxet has always liked to think he's above the law." Chief stopped at the entrance to the interrogation room. "Apparently, he still has his cell because his chauffeur and his bodyguard have both been here, trying to get us to release him."

Wynona looked at Rascal, who snorted. "Are you serious?"

"Deadly," Chief Ligurio said in a low tone. His smile was slow and predatory. "Luckily, your little party lasted longer than we thought." His smile grew and Cookie whimpered. "In fact, Ms. Le Doux…if you find yourself too tired to handle this tonight, I don't mind waiting until tomorrow morning."

Wynona glared at the chief's insinuation. She definitely held no warm feelings for the incubus behind that door, but she wasn't going to go out of her way to hurt him either. "I think pressing charges will be enough," she said wryly.

Rascal huffed again. "It's a start," he grumbled. His eyes went to the cowering Ms. Floura and Rascal cleared his throat. "We'll still need to go through the correct procedures, Ms. Floura…but afterwards, you'll be cleared to take him home."

The woman nodded and Chief Ligurio opened the door, only to halt immediately. Sucking in a deep breath, he roared loud enough to shake the walls.

Wynona gasped and her magic immediately encompassed her, Rascal and Violet. "What happened?" she gasped, grabbing Rascal's arm.

"Take it down, Wy," Rascal snapped, stepping forward.

Wynona forced herself to let go of the protective instincts guiding her magic and the shield slowly dissipated. As soon as it was pliant, Rascal pushed through, rushing into the interrogation room after his boss.

Violet snapped her tail on Wynona's neck. *Get in there!*

Damp sweat coated Wynona's skin as she followed Rascal and Chief Ligurio. She could hear the rushing of voices as others began to run through the building trying to figure out where the bellow had come from. If she didn't move, Wynona knew she'd quickly be trampled. Everything from trolls to dwarves were rushing the space.

Glancing over her shoulder, she was shocked to see that Cookie had disappeared, but Rascal's growling pulled Wynona's attention back to the interrogation room.

"HOW COULD THIS HAPPEN?" Rascal yelled, his voice deep and raspy, a clear sign his wolf was near the surface.

Wynona finally stepped into the room and her heart fell to her stomach.

Mr. Braxet was leaning forward onto the simple, stainless steel table, his back slumped and his head sideways. But the dripping red liquid that pooled around his hair told Wynona the incubus wasn't taking a nap. In fact, he would never take a nap again.

Blood aside, the gaping wound at his temple required no explanation.

Mr. Braxet was dead.

## CHAPTER 5

Wynona once again had a fleeting thought about the whereabouts of the secretary, but she struggled to pull her eyes away from the gruesome scene in front of her. It wasn't until she was bumped from behind that she was able to pull herself together.

*I don't like this,* Violet said with a shudder. *Who kills someone in a police station?*

Wynona could only nod. She'd wondered that herself.

"Wy."

Wynona looked up and realized she was cowering beside the door as officers rushed past her. Rascal's eyes were glowing from clear across the room and were currently pinned on her.

His face softened and he pushed his way through the crowd. "Are you alright?" he asked softly, his hand coming to rest on her waist.

Wynona shook her head. "No. I…" Her eyes went back to the table, but all she saw were the backs of the officers. "I wasn't prepared for that," she whispered.

Rascal nodded. "None of us were." He growled. "I'm ready to string up every officer here."

Wynona gasped. "You don't think one of them did it?" she asked breathlessly.

"Who else?" Rascal snapped, pushing a hand through his hair. "Who else could have come into the room?"

"He had visitors, right?"

Rascal nodded reluctantly. "But none of them would have been alone with him. How could they kill him if they were being watched?"

Wynona let her eyes wander the room. "Are there cameras in here? I don't remember."

Rascal shook his head. "No. Just the observation room." He pointed to a wall with a dark window style area.

Wynona pressed her lips to the side. She couldn't imagine any of the officers here killing the incubus. Unless they had a history with him? Wynona tapped Rascal's chest. "Did anyone here know him?" she whispered. "Could someone have held a grudge?"

Rascal huffed. "I don't know of any off the top of my head. Chief's been chasing Braxet for ages, but as far as I'm aware, it's more of a personal vendetta." He tilted his head, reminiscent of his animal side. "It'll be something to look into, however." He stilled. "Where'd the secretary go?"

Wynona shrugged. "I'm not sure," she admitted. "The chief yelled, then you bellowed and when I went to follow, she was gone."

Rascal scowled. "What do you mean gone?"

"Like…poof!" Wynona emphasized with her fingers. "She was gone."

Rascal walked away from her, glancing out into the hallway before coming back. "Do you know what kind of creature she was?"

Wynona shook her head. "Not a clue. She looked human."

"So she could have been just about anything," he grumbled.

Wynona nodded. "She was extremely shy, so I doubt she was a witch or a predator shifter."

"Right." Rascal looked back toward the table where everyone was still milling around.

"Have you sniffed?"

He frowned and looked down. "What?"

"Have you sniffed around to see if you can smell who all had been in the room?" Wynona pressed.

Rascal rolled his eyes. "Sometimes I'm such an idiot."

Wynona shook her head. "No, you were just caught off guard."

He gave her a playful glare. "So were you and you put up a force field."

Violet chittered and rubbed Wynona's neck. *Tell the pup to get going, then.*

Rascal gave a derisive chuckle. "I'm on it, Vi. I'm on it." He walked toward the center of the room. "EVERYBODY OUT!" he bellowed.

The other officers jerked at the sound and a few left right away, but several turned to the chief.

Rascal held his ground. "I can't smell the area with this many bodies," he said by way of explanation.

Chief Ligurio nodded. "You heard the deputy chief. Get out!"

Wynona hung back, trying to stay out of the way as the officers all filed out. She waved to a couple that she had met during her time working with Rascal, but most completely ignored her.

*Fine by me,* Wynona thought dryly. *I've had enough excitement for the day anyway.*

Violet sniffed and curled her tail around Wynona's neck. Soon there were only four of them left. Wynona hadn't seen Daemon enter, but he was standing by the body.

His black eyes went to Wynona. "You should look," he said in a low tone.

It took a second for Wynona to figure out what he was talking about, but finally she blinked and brought her magical vision into sight. She hesitated and blinked a few more times. "Uh…" She looked back to Daemon. "I think I'm broken."

Daemon shook his head, his eyes going back to normal. "There's nothing here."

"That can't be right," Wynona argued, stepping forward. While the police were very careful to keep those who had been arrested under control, there was bound to be bits of magic everywhere. Even just small skifts of it should be floating around Mr. Braxet's body. But the room was completely clean...too clean.

Rascal growled and Wynona snapped her head to his. "I've got nothing," he snapped through sharp teeth. "Nothing I can pinpoint anyway."

"What do you smell?" Chief Ligurio asked.

Rascal shrugged. "Nearly every officer in the station." He paused. "There are a couple other scents, but they're faint."

"His visitors?" Daemon offered. "He had two."

Wynona nodded. "Ms. Floura was going to be his third, but she's gone."

"Gone?" Chief Ligurio frowned.

"She disappeared when the body was discovered," Rascal added.

Chief Ligurio gave him a look. "And you didn't go after her?"

Rascal's lips thinned. "I was a little preoccupied with the dead body at the table."

Chief Ligurio rolled his eyes and stomped toward the door. Yanking it open, he stuck his head out. "I want that secretary found! The one who was here to see Braxet. NOW!"

Wynona heard more scrambling in the hallway.

*They must've been hanging around,* Violet said with a chuckle.

"It's not every day someone is killed in the police station," Wynona murmured back.

"Chief..." Daemon began, before clearing his throat. "Is it possible this is a suicide?"

Chief Ligurio paused, then rubbed the center of his forehead. "Where would he have gotten the weapon?" His red eyes looked up. "Wasn't he searched before he was put in the room?"

Daemon shrugged. "He should have been. I brought him back the same as always, then stood guard."

"Did you see him with a weapon?"

Daemon shook his head. "No."

Wynona frowned. "Perhaps the coroner can help?" she asked. "Daemon and I noticed that the room is clean of magic."

"Clean of magic?" Rascal pressed.

Wynona nodded. "There's no magic…anywhere."

Rascal frowned. "That seems odd."

Wynona nodded. "I agree." She glanced at Daemon. "Is that a black hole skill? Can you sweep a room like that?"

Daemon's eyes widened. "I've never tried."

Wynona put up her hands and threw a small burst of wind at the wall. Blinking into her magic vision, she could see the remnant through the air as well as splattered to her right. "See what you can do," she encouraged.

Daemon's eyes turned black and he focused on the wall.

"I'm going to call the coroner," Chief Ligurio grumbled and slipped from the room.

Wynona heard voices addressing him in the hall, but she stayed focused on Daemon. His jaw clenched and the muscles in his shoulders tightened, but nothing moved the purple mist.

Finally, he stopped, breathing heavily with sweat dotting his forehead. "I don't think that's a skill I have," he panted.

Wynona nodded. "You can block magic from happening, but can't clean it up once it's there." She ticked her head back and forth. "That makes sense. That's why they call you a black hole. But you can't actually vacuum pre-done magic."

Daemon gave her a look. "Thank you, Captain Obvious."

Wynona put her hands on her hips. "Sometimes it helps to talk things out."

Rascal put a hand on her lower back. "Enough, Skymaw. You should know her well enough by now to not argue with her methods."

Daemon sighed. "Sorry. I guess I'm a tad on edge."

*A tad?* Violet snorted. *He's wound tighter than a banjo string.*

Wynona frowned down at her familiar.

Violet began grooming her whiskers. *What?*

Rolling her eyes, Wynona went back to the problem at hand. "Do you want me to stick around?" she asked Rascal. "Since I can't actually press charges, would it be better if I just got out of the way?"

Rascal shook his head and began to answer, but Chief Ligurio beat him to it.

"Yes," he stated emphatically as he made his way back into the room.

Rascal scowled. "She can help."

Wynona touched his arm. "I'm up to my neck in things with the shop," she argued. "I don't know if I have time to help."

Rascal's golden eyes pleaded with hers.

"Don't give me puppy dog eyes," she said, not being able to help the small twitch of her mouth. "I can't work every case with you for the rest of our lives."

"Why not?" Rascal asked under his breath. He stepped a little closer, but the clearing of a throat cut off their intimate conversation.

"You're already going to be in the news with Braxet having crashed your media party," Chief Ligurio pointed out, one black eyebrow high on his pale forehead. "I would suggest distancing yourself from this case as much as possible."

Wynona nodded. "Agreed." She stood on tiptoe and left a short kiss on Rascal's cheek. "Good luck," she whispered. Walking past the body, she shivered again. Her mind might enjoy puzzling out who the killers were, but she always struggled with the actual bodies that came with the job.

Nodding at the chief, Wynona glanced up at Daemon and gave him a commiserating smile. "It's okay," she told him. "Everyone makes mistakes."

Daemon was standing erect and barely gave her a glance, though he did nod slightly. It was clear he was taking this personally.

Sadness trickled into Wynona's stomach. Daemon was her friend and she didn't like seeing him so upset, or blaming himself for something he couldn't have prevented.

*You don't THINK he could have prevented it,* Violet argued. *He could be guilty for all we know.*

"Violet," Wynona hissed, glaring at the animal.

Violet grunted and curled into a ball.

*He's our friend,* Wynona argued. *There's absolutely no way he had anything to do with this.*

Violet grumbled, but didn't argue again.

Wynona had no idea what had gotten into her familiar, but she was ready for the phase to end. She reached for the door handle, but it jerked open, nearly knocking Wynona on her backside.

"Oh...sorry," the officer said breathlessly, before turning to the chief. "No one even saw her, Chief. She didn't check in at the front desk."

Chief Ligurio growled out a curse. "Put out an APB. And how did she get past the desk without having to sign in?"

Heat flushed Wynona's neck and she slowly raised her hand. "That would be my fault."

The chief's eyes flared. "Explain."

"She stopped and spoke to me in the lobby as I was coming back," Wynona said, feeling guilt added to her already churning stomach. "She told me that she was a fan of my work...both the teas and the murders."

Chief Ligurio grunted.

"Anyway, I didn't know she didn't check in, but when I found out who she was, I told her to follow me and we went to Rascal's office."

Chief Ligurio turned to his second in command.

"I brought them to you, Chief," Rascal said in a sharp tone.

Chief Ligurio grit his teeth. "So, I have a dead creature, who might or might not have managed to smuggle a weapon in here." His eyes flashed to Daemon. "No one was standing guard to hear the shot." His eyes went to Wynona. "And an unauthorized visitor who is now missing. She could be in the hands of the murderer, or could be the murderer herself. We don't know because We. Can't. FIND HER!" he yelled.

Wynona leaned back. Yep. It was time to go home. Several innocent mistakes had been made, only one of which was Wynona's, but it was enough.

*There's been enough blood loss tonight,* Wynona thought quickly as she stepped around the officer still in the doorway. Her relationship with Chief Ligurio was already a little rough. Wynona wasn't going to stick around and see where it was at the moment.

*I don't know...* Violet drawled. *There might be a show if we stick around a little longer.*

"I don't know where you get your blood-thirsty drive from," Wynona whispered. "But I don't like it."

*No one asked you to.*

Shaking her head, Wynona hurried to her scooter. She was about ready to crash. It had already been a long day with the pre-grand opening...add one unpleasant incubus to the mix and then his death? There was no way she wasn't collapsing as soon as she arrived at her comfy little cottage.

The problem was...Wynona knew from experience that sleep would be a long time in coming.

## CHAPTER 6

Wynona yawned and rubbed at her eyes. True to form, she'd been unable to sleep. Currently, she was sitting on the couch in her cabin, trying to read a book that she had no desire to read. The sentences were all blurring together, but every time she tried to close her eyes and rest, the sight of Mr. Braxet's wound and the subsequent gore made her want to throw up.

Groaning, Wynona threw her head back on the couch in dismay. "Get over it," she scolded herself. "You've seen dead bodies before."

*Yeah...but you weren't expecting this one,* Rascal drawled sleepily in her mind.

"Oh my word," Wynona whispered. *Rascal, I'm so sorry. Go back to sleep.*

*I can't...you're thinking too loud.*

Wynona closed her eyes and grit her teeth. *Sorry. I'll put up a wall.*

*It's fine.* He yawned again. *What can I do to help? Need me to come over and kiss it better?*

Wynona laughed softly, despite the seriousness of the situation. *No.*

Rascal sent a playful growl her way.

*Go to sleep. We can talk tomorrow.* Wynona waited, holding her breath until she could tell Rascal had drifted once more. His thoughts became more muddled and none of it translated very well. Taking a deep breath, she put up a wall to keep herself from waking him again. "This soulmate thing is no joke," she said to herself.

A popping noise from the kitchen had Wynona jerking to her feet and she suddenly regretted having just shut out Rascal. Shuffling and grumbling came next and Wynona relaxed. She knew those sounds, though she did wonder why he was here.

Walking to the kitchen, she folded her arms and waited for Lusgu to come out of the utility closet.

"I didn't realize you kept the portal here," she said as the brownie marched out from among her cleaning supplies.

Lusgu glared and brushed himself down. "You don't know everything."

Wynona's shoulders fell. "I'm aware of that, Lusgu." She came farther into the kitchen. "Want some tea?" He huffed and Wynona took it as consent as she set about heating water and pulling out herbs. Finally, she had a full tray at the table, complete with a few tidbits of leftover food from the party. She twirled a finger and poured the water over the diffusers. "What brings you by so late at night?" she asked, wrapping her hands around the warm mug.

Lusgu didn't speak at first. He sat sullenly in his chair, staring at the steaming mug until several heartbeats later, he reached out and took a tentative sip.

Wynona's first instinct was to warn him it was hot, but she bit her tongue. Lusgu was old enough to handle himself…she assumed.

His small, black eyes came up to hers. "You're a lot like her, you know."

Wynona stilled. "Who?" she asked hoarsely, though she wished wholeheartedly for a specific answer.

Lusgu rolled his eyes. "Saffron."

The tension eased from Wynona's shoulders to a degree. "I take that as a compliment, thank you."

"It was a compliment," Lusgu muttered. "Whether you're like the rest of her remains to be seen."

Wynona frowned. "What do you mean?"

"Saffron wasn't the sweet but powerful grandmother you thought you knew," Lusgu snapped.

Wynona set down her cup. "I'm aware. After all, she's the one who cursed me."

Lusgu snorted.

"And she made it all too clear that she wants me to wage the next paranormal war by taking back Hex Haven from my father."

Lusgu grunted again and shifted in his seat. "She had a good heart," he admitted in a softer tone. "But she didn't always go about things the right way."

Folding her hands in her lap, Wynona tilted her head, waiting for him to explain.

Lusgu took another drink. "Thank you," he said, surprising Wynona. "I'm not sure if I ever said that after you cleared Rayn's name."

Wynona nodded. "It was my pleasure," she returned softly. Pinching her lips between her teeth, Wynona leaned onto her elbows. "Lusgu...who cursed you? You and Rayn?"

He gave her a look. "Do you really think I can answer that?"

Wynona held up her hands. "It was worth asking. I'm still confused as to how all this came about. You think my father killed my grandfather in order to take over Hex Haven. Somehow you and Dr. Rayn were involved and have been cursed to not be able to speak about it. Granny set a plan in motion to hide my powers from my parents so that I can do the same thing Dad once did and I'm stuck here with no answers and only grumpy companions who can't tell me anything." She could have sworn that Lusgu's lips twitched at her description of him, but Wynona knew it was wishful thinking.

"As long as Mazey is part of that description, I'll take it," he responded.

Wynona's eyebrows shot up at the reference to the surly wolf shifter. "Did you just make a joke?" she gasped.

Lusgu glared. "I have a sense of humor."

There was no way for Wynona's eyebrows to keep rising, but they wanted to. Lusgu...have a sense of humor? Wynona was more likely to find out she had shifter in her than to believe that.

Lusgu grumbled a few choice words under his breath that Wynona chose to ignore. He cleared his throat, several times, before pinning her with another stare. "I don't want you involved in this case."

Wynona frowned. "Do you mean Mr. Braxet's death?" Wynona leaned in. "How did you even hear about it?"

*From me.* Violet shuffled in and slowly climbed the table leg. Once up on the table, she collapsed in a huff. *Any of that tea have caffeine in it?*

Wynona scratched her familiar's head. "What are you doing up?" she asked. Violet had been slumbering quite heavily when Wynona had ventured into the family room. She hadn't meant to wake anybody up with her restlessness.

*You two are loud enough to wake the dead,* Violet complained.

Lusgu grunted and took another drink, then stuffed a pastry in his mouth.

"Sorry," Wynona continued, but then her mind latched onto something she'd been pondering. "Violet...how can you and Lusgu talk? I've meant to ask you that, but never had much of a chance."

Two sets of black eyes darted to each other, but neither said a word.

Wynona sighed. "How am I ever supposed to learn anything if no one will answer me?"

"Answers come from work," Lusgu snapped.

Violet yawned again and curled into a ball.

Wynona's frustration was mounting. Call it lack of sleep or too many years of unanswered questions, but she had had enough. "I'm sorry," Wynona said curtly. "Was saving Dr. Rayn's reputation not enough for you? Or perhaps building a tea shop from the ground up... twice! Or maybe learning to control a massive amount of magic all at once with absolutely no training... Was that not considered work?" Wynona slapped her hands on the table. "Or saving your life, Violet? Not enough? Hmmm?"

Violet's nose had gone very still and her eyes were widening.

"Keeping Celia from killing you doesn't count?" Wynona turned her head to Lusgu. "Or maybe sticking up for you when no one else would? Or giving you a job when most people would have kicked you out? Forgiving you over and over again when you won't answer my questions or flat out lie to me or even try to hurt me?" Wynona shook her head. "How many times have I invited you or cared for your feelings when no one else did? Rascal has wanted you gone for ages, but I've stuck up for you every time. Every. Time," she ground out, then stood, her eyes full of tears. Whether they were from anger or sadness, Wynona didn't know, since the emotions were both fighting for dominance, but she *did* know she couldn't stand being in this room any longer.

Her nightmares would be a relief after this. "I'm going to bed," she announced unnecessarily. "I'll clean this up in the morning."

The words were utter garbage. She knew that Lusgu would clean up. He never left a mess, but Wynona was done counting on him. She'd hired him as a janitor, then treated him like family…like a crazy, grumpy uncle…but he'd never returned the favor.

He was living in her house, for goodness sake! She didn't complain that he'd left a portal to her residence, though she'd never invited him there.

Sniffling, she shut her bedroom door and wiped angrily at her face. Too bad there wasn't magic that could fix a broken heart. Wynona knew that messing with things like that was what turned witches dark. She shuddered as she thought about what it was like to be cold and heartless. She'd experienced that once and this pain was worth holding onto.

*The trick is to make sure you learn from it,* a little voice said in the back of her head.

Wynona had to pause. So many people had access to her mind that she had to consciously check to see if the voice was hers. She hated confrontation. Hated fighting. Hated hurting people's feelings and she'd expected a wave of guilt to nearly drown her when she got back to her room, but it hadn't. Instead, a very rational side of her was offering a middle ground.

She didn't need to go to extremes like apologize for her feelings and try to hide that they existed. She didn't need to try and get revenge against the people she loved like family. Instead, she could forgive in the future, but keep boundaries now.

Wynona was done being treated like a second class citizen when she worked so hard to help those around her. Her desire to please people and show the mercy her family had lacked had driven her to put her own life on the line many times since escaping the palace and yet there were very few of her own friends who would do the same.

*No more...*Wynona promised herself. *No more.*

She washed her face with cold water to rid her skin of the heated flush associated with tears and climbed into bed. Closing her eyes, she forced her body to relax. Sleep would come. It had to. And since the public grand opening wasn't until next week, Wynona would let herself sleep in.

*Because...why not? I've worked for it.*

The words made her grunt and she rolled over, punching her pillow a little to relieve more of her anger.

She began counting her breaths in an effort to calm down enough for slumber. In for four...out for four...in for four...out for four... surely she could do this. If she could solve unsolvable murders, there was no reason why she couldn't get herself to fall asleep when she was bone tired.

Slowly, the edges of her consciousness began to fray and Wynona's body fully relaxed into her bed.

Her mind, however, never stopped moving and through the dark haze behind her eyelids, Wynona slowly became aware of a figure.

She sat up, squinting to see more. "Who's there?" she asked, the words echoing in her room. The repeated sound made Wynona jump a little and the hairs on the back of her neck stood on end. "I mean it," she said, her voice a little shaky. "Who's there?"

The figure drew closer, seeming to come from a great distance. But the closer they were, the smaller the body appeared, until Wynona realized it was Lusgu.

She huffed and hung her head a moment. "Lusgu, what are you

doing in here?" Flopping back down, Wynona covered her eyes with her arm. "I'm not ready to talk to you yet." When a whistling sound and a pain filled grunt filled her ears, Wynona jerked back up.

Lusgu lay on the floor, light beaming over his huddled body. He writhed, obviously hurting, but Wynona couldn't see what was wrong.

"Lusgu?" She pulled back her covers and stepped onto the cold hardwood. "What's wrong?" Walking toward him, Wynona was surprised to find that with each step, Lusgu got farther away. She picked up her pace, but the distance between them only grew greater. "Lusgu!" she shouted. "I…can't…" Gritting her teeth, Wynona began to run. "STOP!" she screamed as Lusgu began to slip into the shadows.

Wynona's legs came to a halt when she saw something odd in the dark edges of the room. They were…moving. As she recognized the signs of life, two bright yellow eyes blinked open, fixating on Lusgu. "LUSGU!" Wynona screamed, reaching out her hand and trying to run again.

A voice from the darkness cackled and reaching arms moved toward the brownie.

"MOVE!" Wynona shouted, but Lusgu's body remained incapacitated. She could see now what was causing his distress. Wispy chains were wrapped around his entire being. Each movement brought a drop of blood and his body was quickly riddled with holes.

The black fingers reached him and Wynona collapsed to her knees, knowing she could never reach him. *Magic. USE YOUR MAGIC!*

She threw a shaking hand toward the creature, but only a tiny spark of purple left her palm. No matter how hard she cried or pushed, nothing was big enough to stop the black from enveloping Lusgu.

Slowly, it crawled over his legs, up his back, across his shoulders and finally began to cover his head. He looked up, pain and despair written in every wrinkle of his face. "Help," he mouthed just before the dark took him.

"LUSGU!" Wynona screamed. Her voice shook the walls and suddenly she bolted upright in bed as a blast of magic ricocheted through her room, shaking the very foundation of the house.

Panting, Wynona realized it had all been a dream and she waited for the purple remnants in her room and her heart to slowly calm down. Slowly, she lay back down, her back drenched in sweat and her mind replaying every moment of her dream.

Whimpering, Wynona curled into a ball. So much for her rational plan to put down boundaries and stand her ground as a creature that deserved to be treated better. How was she supposed to face Lusgu with this dream hanging around in her head?

*I'm at the door,* Rascal growled. *Let me in.*

Wynona ran out of her room. She didn't know how Rascal had picked up on everything, but she most definitely didn't want to be alone right now. Throwing open the door, she next threw herself into his arms.

His shifter reflexes had never been quite so handy as he caught Wynona and held her tightly to his chest. Reaching down, he swept her legs up and quickly brought them inside, slamming the door with his foot.

Marching to the couch, his chest rumbling with angry noises the entire time, Rascal sat down on the couch, reached for a blanket and wrapped her up tightly. "You don't have to talk," he whispered in her ear, brushing her messy hair away from her face. "Just relax. I'm here. I have you." He kissed her temple. "I love you…you're not alone…and most of all…you're safe."

# CHAPTER 7

Rascal was gone fairly early in the morning, but Wynona hadn't been sleeping anyway. He had work and she had a day of planning ahead. Her grand opening to the public was next week, now that the media event was over and Wynona knew she'd need a little time to recover from…whatever happened last night.

She hadn't had a nightmare in years. As a child, sure, but not since becoming an adult. And not only had this one been frightening, but it had felt *real*. Something about it disturbed Wynona in a way she wasn't prepared for and it was difficult to keep her mind focused on her task.

Lusgu had been gone by the time Wynona began puttering around in the kitchen, and Violet had disappeared as well.

*It's for the best,* Wynona told herself. Deserved or not, Wynona had been harsh with her friends last night and she wasn't surprised that they were both MIA at the moment.

Her hands shook as she poured herself a cup of tea and fired up her laptop. Magic would probably help, but she couldn't bring herself to use it this morning. The inky blackness from her dream wouldn't seem to leave her thoughts. Every time she closed her eyes, she could see it swallowing Lusgu again and it caused her heart to race.

Not to mention that the thick chain choking him was eerily similar to the curse that Wynona could see when she turned her magical vision onto her janitor.

She sipped the tea and hissed as it scalded her tongue. Setting down the mug, Wynona pulled up her vision boards for the opening. She went over the pastry orders, double checking that she had sent all the correct numbers to Kyoz and Gnuq. She checked the appointment schedule. Every custom tea appointment for the first month was already booked out. Customers were starting to get irritated at how far out she was booking, but Wynona knew it was only a sign of good things.

She was so grateful her clientele were so readily coming back after the disastrous event that led to the building burning down. Many creatures would have been turned off by the event, but their draw to her special blends was stronger.

"There's one good thing," Wynona murmured as she went back over her numbers. Next, she checked her supplies and hummed in consternation when she realized she would need to dry and crush some more herbs. "At least you checked it now," she told herself.

Grabbing her cup, Wynona headed out to her greenhouse. It looked like she would be spending the next several hours out there replenishing her supply for the coming week.

Once there, she set down the mug and shook out her hands. Breathing deeply, she let the moist, earthy smell of the room penetrate her senses. This…this was where she was happiest. Growing, brewing, creating…in her greenhouse Wynona felt no judgment, no guilt, no desire for anything more. She just…was.

Humming under her breath, she let the peace work its way into her twitchy muscles until the fear from the night before was gone. It was just Wynona and her plants.

She might not have Prim's gift for growing them, but Wynona did have a gift for combining different herbs to create helpful, healing tinctures. Some of her more popular blends would go fast once she was open again and Wynona let herself get lost in the process. She snipped leaves, creating bundles to dry. Took older bundles and crushed them with her mortar and pestle.

The movements were second nature and the work immensely satisfying. So much so, she completely lost track of time and when Celia burst through the greenhouse door, Wynona almost screamed.

"Oh my word," she gasped, her hand on her chest. "You scared me."

Celia raised one perfectly manicured eyebrow. "You didn't even have any music going. How in the paranormal world would I have surprised you?"

Wynona shrugged. She turned back to her work. "Did you need something?"

Celia huffed and plopped herself at a small bistro table. "I'm bored."

Wynona looked sideways at her sister. "What about work?"

"All my projects are done at the moment."

"Is that why you didn't come to the media event yesterday?" Had it really only been yesterday that Wynona had been schmoozing the newspapers and meeting a man who would end up dead only hours later? It seemed like such a long time ago.

Celia rolled her eyes. "I do have a life, you know."

Wynona scrunched her eyebrows and turned toward her sister. "Yet you're here complaining that you're bored." She wiggled a finger from side to side. "Somehow those two statements don't seem to work together."

Celia studied her nails. "Maybe I was busy yesterday, but I'm bored today."

"Were you?"

Celia shrugged again.

Sighing, Wynona set down her equipment. "What's going on?"

Celia pretended as if she didn't hear.

"Celia…" Wynona pressed. "You wouldn't be here if you didn't want to talk, so you might as well spill it or I won't offer you any of the leftover pastries."

The flash in Celia's eyes let Wynona know she'd pushed a button. Celia sniffed again. "Fine. I…was avoiding certain company."

"Who?" Wynona asked.

Celia gave her sister an unimpressed look. "Do I really have to answer that?"

"Chief Ligurio?"

Celia didn't respond.

Wynona rubbed her forehead and walked over to the opposite chair. "I don't really understand why you're so harsh with him." She sat down. "If you like him, then talk to him. If you aren't interested, then quit teasing him."

"Teasing him?" Celia shrieked.

"Don't give me that," Wynona snapped, then immediately pulled herself back. Apparently, a lack of sleep made it hard for her to stay calm. "You swing those hips for all their worth every time you walk away. You flaunt your motorcycle like you're daring him to give you a speeding ticket. And the way you throw your hair is like a lure for any fish swimming in the sea."

Celia stared with wide eyes before snorting. The snorting eventually turned into laughter and she slapped the metal table. "Wynona... you're really something else."

Wynona huffed and folded her arms over her chest, waiting.

"I do that for anyone," Celia finally got out. "It's called being confident in myself as a woman."

"I call that centaur droppings," Wynona argued. "You absolutely *do not* do that for anyone else." Wynona raised her own eyebrow. "Unless you're simply trying to make the chief jealous."

Celia's lips pressed into a thin frown.

Releasing her arms, Wynona tapped her fingers on her knee. "Why is it so hard to admit you actually like him?"

Celia's nails once again became interesting. "Because it makes me look weak."

Wynona threw up her hands. "How? Does loving Rascal make me weak?"

"What would you do if someone used him to threaten you?"

Wynona stilled. "What do you mean?"

Celia leaned forward. "If some crazed murderer that you were chasing captured Rascal and held his life in his hands, what would you do to get him back?"

"Anything," Wynona breathed without hesitation.

Celia nodded. "Then yes…it makes you weak."

Wynona shook herself. "Why are you asking that?"

All pretense of arrogance dropped from Celia's face. "Because we both know there are people in our lives who would use any weakness against us."

The words sat between the two sisters like an explosive hex.

"So you're protecting him," Wynona said, thinking as she spoke. "Then why throw lures?"

Celia shrugged one delicate shoulder. "Maybe I can't help myself." Her dark brown eyes glanced up from under heavily mascaraed lashes. "Sometimes life is lonely."

Wynona hung her head for a moment before leaning forward. "Don't you think Chief Ligurio deserves the chance to choose?" she asked softly.

Celia didn't respond.

"Do you really think that Rascal would have taken 'no' for an answer if I said we couldn't be together because I wanted to protect him from my power crazy parents?"

Celia snort-laughed. "Like you could get that wolf to do anything."

"Exactly," Wynona agreed. "If Rascal didn't want to be around, he wouldn't be here." Wynona leaned in. "And I know he loves me enough that if anything were to happen, he'd be the first in line to try and help. He'd protect me with his life, if necessary."

"And that doesn't frighten you?" Celia whispered thickly, disdain heavy in her tear-filled tone. "Would you really want him to give his life for you?"

Wynona shook her head, unable to keep her own eyes from filling as well. "No. It would break me if he died." She hesitated. "It did break me…twice."

Celia frowned. "Rascal hasn't died. Or is there something I'm missing?"

"He's come close to dying…twice," Wynona clarified. "The first time was when I broke the curse."

Celia's eyebrows shot up. "And the second time?"

Wynona chewed her bottom lip. She wasn't sure she wanted to share what had happened with Lusgu. "I…became someone I don't want to ever become again." When Celia continued to wait expectantly, Wynona gave her a bit more. "If Rascal was to be taken from me, I'm pretty sure I'd destroy the world."

Celia's jaw dropped. "You can't be serious."

Wynona nodded. The fear she'd kept hidden from that unfeeling, dark version of herself came rushing back full force. Seeing exactly what her grandmother had been afraid of, in the flesh, had given Wynona a healthy dose of understanding for her grandmother's actions. She'd already forgiven Saffron for cursing her at that point, but that experience had solidified Saffron's reasons. Wynona's powers, unchecked, were deadly…to everyone.

Celia huffed. "I'm not sure I buy it, but…" She eyed her sister. "I'm still not sure I can try again." Her shoulders drooped. "I hurt him, Wynona. Badly."

Wynona nodded. "I know. But if I can forgive Granny, why can't he forgive you?"

"Because you make a point of forgiving everyone," Celia pointed out. "It's one of the reasons I chose to risk leaving home."

"And you don't think Deverell will be the same way?" Wynona used Chief Ligurio's first name, trying to help break down the barriers between Celia and the man she loved.

Celia shook her head. "Vampires have really long memories."

"That should also mean they have the capacity to love for long times as well."

Celia shook her head. "I don't know why I'm talking about it. It's hopeless."

Wynona stood and stretched her back. "Nothing's hopeless, Celia. You haven't even tried yet, for goodness sake."

"I don't see you…" Celia cut off when Wynona spun. "Sorry," Celia stated in a rare show of humility. "I suppose that of the two of us, you've sacrificed yourself more times than I have." She sighed and slunk. "In fact, I think I've spent more of my life doing everything *but* being brave."

"You were brave when you delivered Dad's messages," Wynona pointed out.

"No. That was stupidity. Obedience derived from fear."

"Okay…you were brave when you left," Wynona tried again.

"I knew you'd catch me."

"You were brave when you started your own business."

"I knew you wouldn't let me starve."

Wynona rolled her eyes. "Come on, Celia. Knock it off. *This* argument is the real stupidity."

Celia grumbled. "I don't know what to do. I love him. But I'm afraid."

"You only have two choices. Either witch up and tell him, willing to take whatever he says. Or hide it and be miserable." Wynona shrugged as she picked up on her work where she'd left off. "Either way, there are consequences to live with. If you tell him, he might say he loves you and together you'll live happily ever after. Or maybe you'll get together and spend your lives running from Dad. Or maybe he'll say he never loved you and you'll have to let him go. Or—"

"Got it!" Celia shouted, glaring at her sister. "I can't predict the future. No need to explain more." She pouted. "If only Granny's gift of foresight had been passed down to me."

Wynona slowed. "Are you talking about her tea reading?"

Celia ticked her head back and forth. "Sort of. She could read the future in the tea leaves, but she also had visions, or dreams, sometimes."

The pestle in Wynona's hand dropped to the counter, making a loud clanging noise.

Celia jerked back. "What?"

Wynona blinked several times and shook her head. "N-nothing… Lost my grip." She wrapped her fingers around the counter edge, trying to stop the trembling in her hands. "Do you want me to read your tea leaves? I'm not as good as Granny, but maybe I can offer you a little something." Wynona had no desire to use her skills for something like this, but if it distracted Celia from her reaction, it would be well worth it.

Celia stared for a moment, then stood and dusted off her pants. "I'm starved. Want something?"

Wynona stared.

Celia smirked, looking much more like herself. "I'll bring lunch. You bring the tea." She winked. "I never thought I'd have my sister do a love reading on me, but hey...I'm sure stranger things have happened."

Wynona felt as if her smile would break from being so brittle, but she held it in place. "There's a first time for everything, I suppose."

Celia nodded. "Be back in a half hour." Without warning, the witch disappeared and Wynona crumpled to her knees.

She pressed her forehead against one of the stainless steel shelves, wishing the cool metal could bring down the fever raging through her brain. If Granny had had the gift of foresight, why had she never told Wynona? And was that what last night's dream was? How was Wynona supposed to know the difference between visions and regular dreams? *Was* there a difference?

Wynona realized that she was about to hyperventilate and she forced her breathing to slow down. Questions still ran rampant through her head, but the most important one of all hadn't been spoken yet.

"What's coming for Lusgu...and how do I save him?"

## CHAPTER 8

Wynona's hands were shaking as she took the teacup from Celia.

Her sister made a face. "Is it really that scary to read my fortune?"

"No," Wynona assured her. "Sorry. Got something on my mind." She looked in the cup, but nothing was coming to her. Sighing, Wynona closed her eyes. She needed to relax and use her magic or Celia was going to be ticked and this would all be for naught.

Blowing out a slow breath, Wynona did her best to take control of her body. Slowly, the trembling ebbed and she found a soothing calm coming over her. Her skin buzzed slightly and Wynona recognized the sensation of magic moving along her limbs.

When her hair began to blow in a breeze that hadn't been in the room a moment before, Wynona knew she was on the right track.

"Whoa…" Celia breathed, but Wynona ignored her.

Wynona opened her palm and let the cup lift into the air. For some reason, Wynona's magic liked to add a fancy flair when she did things like read teacups, though Wynona had never quite figured out why. Apparently, Granny's work had been much more subtle.

The fluttering papers and spinning porcelain of Wynona's experience was far from subtle, but she couldn't argue with the results.

When the cup landed again in her outstretched hand, Wynona opened her eyes and stared at Celia's shocked face. It almost made Wynona want to smirk, but she held back the urge. It would serve her cocky sister right, however, if Wynona rubbed it in her face a little. Glancing down at the cup, Wynona tilted it toward her when the front door of the cottage burst open.

"NONA!"

Wynona jumped, having been too deep in her magic work to hear Prim arrive at the house, and the teacup fell from her palm, landing on the floor with a crash.

"NO!" Celia shouted, jumping to her feet.

Wynona sighed. "In here, Prim." She looked down at the shattered cup. *Shoot. That was one of my favorites.* Sighing, Wynona wiggled her fingers and lifted the shards to the garbage.

Celia cursed and stayed upright, glaring at Prim as she rushed in, still in her small fairy form. "Nona," she gasped. "They have him. They're going to fire him!" she wailed.

Wynona jerked back a little. "Whoa, whoa, whoa. Hold on a second." She stood and walked over to Prim, whose face was red and tear-streaked. Against her bright pink hair, it wasn't Prim's finest look. "You have to calm down a little," Wynona told her. "I don't understand what you're talking about."

Prim lost control of a sob and put a fist against her mouth. "It's Daemon," she managed to squeak out. "Ligurio has put him on leave."

"What?" Wynona gasped. "Why?"

"Because they think he had something to do with that guy's death," Prim said in a hoarse whisper. "He was supposed to be in charge and he left for a few minutes."

Wynona frowned and fell back in her seat. "But...Daemon wouldn't kill someone in cold blood like that. Chief Ligurio knows that."

Prim shook her head, unable to speak further.

Celia huffed. "This is stupid." She also plopped back into her seat and folded her arms over her chest. "So, he's on leave. Who cares? They'll find the real murderer and it'll be all over."

Prim's hands dropped to her sides in tight fists and she poofed into her larger form. "You wouldn't understand!" she shouted at the witch. "All you care about is yourself! Well, get over it! When you love someone, you don't want to see them hurt and this has hurt him deeply!"

Celia's cheeks flushed a deep red and Wynona put up her hands. She knew she was about to have World War III on her hands if she didn't do something quickly. "Okay, ladies. Enough."

Celia opened her mouth, but Wynona cut her off.

"Prim. Celia was just stating her opinion. She's allowed to have it, even if she expresses it in…unkind ways.." She raised her eyebrows when Prim shot her a glare. "Just like you're allowed to yours. We both know Daemon is innocent. That man would never hurt a creature, no matter how annoying he was." Wynona let her hands fall to her lap. "My guess is that Chief Ligurio is just following the book. Has he formally charged Daemon with anything?"

Prim's face fell again and she sniffled, wiping her nose on her sleeve. "Not yet. But they said they'd be investigating him."

Wynona sighed and rubbed her forehead. "What is it about me that always seems to draw murder accusations?"

"You do seem to have a high number of friends involved in such escapades," Celia said in a snarky tone. She grinned unrepentantly when Wynona looked her way. "Perhaps, if you'd finish doing tea readings once in a while, you wouldn't have this problem because you'd always know what was coming."

Wynona pinched her lips. "Celia. I'm sorry we didn't finish, but a man's life and career is a little more important at the moment."

"You mean your *friend* is more important than your sister," Celia snarled.

"No," Wynona said firmly, her own temper trying to match her sister's. "That's not what I said at all. But Daemon has helped me numerous times and I wouldn't be a friend in return if I didn't try to help him. Truth is…most of my friends are just as much family to me as you are."

There. The words had been said and while Wynona felt bad about them, she couldn't take them back. Something was stirring in her at the moment and it had first come out when she'd called out Lusgu and Violet on their multitude of secrets. Now Wynona had managed to put Celia in her place, despite the olive branch Wynona had been holding out for ages.

How many times would she be expected to forgive and forget while those around her refused to do the same? It was exhausting to try keeping the peace when no one else seemed to care.

Celia shifted her jaw back and forth. "I see." She stood slowly. "Well, I can see I'm not getting anywhere here." Her fingers started to sparkle with silver glitter, but paused momentarily. "Before I go... maybe I'll offer just a bit of sisterly advice."

Wynona waited and braced herself for whatever harsh critique Celia was aiming to shoot her with.

"Word on the street is that Mom is on the hunt," Celia sneered. She gave Wynona a humorless smile. "She wants something that's been taken from her." She stopped, as if waiting for Wynona to catch on.

*The grimoires!* Her realization must have been seen on her face because Celia chuckled darkly.

"Keep one eye open, dear *sister*. You're going to need it." With one last glare at Prim, Celia's silver magic burst and the witch was gone.

Wynona wasn't sure how to handle the warning that sounded more like a threat. If her mother was coming after the grimoires, then Wynona needed to do two things. One, find out why they were so valuable. And two, find a better hiding spot. Her closet wouldn't even come close to keeping them safe if her mom went on a rampage.

Prim huffed and took Celia's vacated seat. "Is it still hot?" she asked through her sniffles, pointing to the teapot.

Wynona shook her head, then touched the pot, causing the water to boil within seconds.

"Thanks." Prim poured herself a cup and dunked in a waiting diffuser.

"You don't even know what type of tea it is," Wynona said with a soft smile.

"It's yours," Prim said with a shrug, as if that was good enough.

The trust of her fairy friend helped soothe over some of the anger left from Celia's departing words. "Thank you," Wynona whispered.

"Sorry about Celia," Prim continued, shifting in her seat and poofing back into her fairy size. "I didn't mean to cut in on whatever you were doing, but I need your help."

Wynona sighed. "I know. I'm sorry she didn't understand and got upset."

"Not your fault." Prim wrapped her hands around the mug, her eyes on the steam from the water. "But your little chat with her made me realize how much I have to apologize for as well."

Wynona frowned.

Prim's pink eyes were brimming with tears when she looked up. "Nona...I've been so selfish. I've argued and stomped my foot, demanding your time and making life harder for you as you've tried so hard to help us all get along. Instead, your business got burned down. Your mom is on a witch hunt."

Wynona snorted at that one.

"You saved me from prison. You've saved yourself multiple times. You've broken a curse. Discovered your family has lied to you. The ones you thought you knew betrayed you. Nothing about you is normal and yet no matter how difficult the rest of us make things, you offer to help without batting an eye."

Wynona slumped slightly in her seat. "Uh...I don't even know what to say to that. You're my friends...my family. Why wouldn't I?"

"Other than Rascal, I'm not sure any of us have actually done anything to deserve your loyalty." Prim swallowed hard. "Thank you," she whispered. "Thank you so much and I'm sorry. I'm sorry I made things hard with Daemon. I'm sorry I made things hard with Violet. And I'm sorry I made things hard with Celia just now. I'll understand if you want to handle her situation first."

Wynona shook her head and reached across the table, grabbing Prim's hand. "Celia's situation isn't urgent. I'll get to her as soon as I can. Daemon's situation needs to be dealt with before any more damage is done."

Prim sniffled and nodded, giving Wynona a grateful smile. Letting go of their hands, Prim took a sip of tea. "Whoa. What's that?"

Wynona laughed lightly. "It's got ginger in it. I think Celia was fighting a small cold. It gives it quite a kick, huh?"

Prim made a face. "Or something."

Wynona shook her head. "How long ago did you find out about Daemon?"

Prim set down the cup. "I came straight here from his house."

"So he's at home?" Wynona asked. "How come he didn't come with you? Is he on house arrest?"

Prim shook her head. "No…but he said it was better if he just stayed out of things. That way no one could accuse him of a conflict of interest."

Wynona pursed her lips. "Okay…give me a minute." She closed her eyes for better concentration. *Rascal?*

*I knew you'd be calling.* He sounded tired and Wynona's frown deepened. *There's nothing I can do about it, Wy.*

*I don't blame you two,* Wynona assured him. *I'm just wondering if Chief Ligurio would let me help. I don't think I can sit out with a friend's life on the line.*

Rascal's presence disappeared for a few minutes and Wynona assumed he was talking with someone else.

*Chief says come in in the morning and we'll discuss it. But if you get involved, he's not sure he can hold back the media fallout.*

*Understood. Are you coming by to eat?*

*Are you sure you want to wait up that late? I figured I might grab a bite and slip in later.*

Wynona's lips twitched. *I'll wait up for you. And we can put you in the guest room, you know. You don't have to sleep on the couch.*

*My wolf doesn't mind. It's better than the forest floor.*

Wynona rolled her eyes behind her lids. *Love you.*

*You too. See you later.*

"Well?"

Wynona opened her eyes to Prim's eager expression. "I'll go meet with Chief Ligurio in the morning. We'll see what he's got and if I can help." She left out the media issue. That wasn't important. Wynona had survived media storms before. She could do it again.

"What about your grand opening?"

*The grand opening, the murder, my mom coming after me, Lusgu and Violet being MIA... The opening might be the least of my worries.* "I'm sure it'll all work out."

Prim sniffed again, then launched out of her seat and came around to hug Wynona tightly. "You're the best."

Wynona hugged her friend back. "I'm just me," she whispered, her own emotions catching up with her. "But I'm so grateful to have the chance to help."

Prim stepped back, wiping at her eyes. "I know you don't like to talk about it, but I can see why your grandma thought you'd be a good leader."

Wynona's smile was weaker, but she mostly ignored it. She had enough on her plate. There was no way she was taking the time to consider anything more than she was already juggling.

Maybe, however, she could take a few minutes to study those grimoires while she waited for Rascal. It would help her make progress in at least one aspect of her life. Tiny steps might be all she could manage at the moment, but it would be better than nothing.

## CHAPTER 9

Wynona tightened her ponytail as she pulled up in front of the police station the next morning. A pause at the front of her scooter allowed the time for regret to pool in her belly as she wished to see a purple nose twitching over the top of the wicker basket.

She missed Violet. The familiar hadn't been back since their fight, but Wynona wasn't quite ready to back down. She didn't feel like she was in the wrong and was growing tired of being the only one willing to bend.

The trouble was, Violet wasn't really the problem either. Lusgu held a lot of secrets. Wynona knew they were probably not meant for her, but his cryptic words and difficult behavior made it hard not to take it all personally. Violet, however, had been on the brownie's side and that hurt.

She was Wynona's familiar. Shouldn't her loyalty be to Wynona?

Sighing, Wynona flipped the ponytail over her shoulder and marched inside. She really should apologize, but it was so hard when she still felt just as frustrated as she did before.

*Come on back*, Rascal's voice said softly.

Wynona hesitated. He wasn't usually quite so demure. Was something going on?

*Too many things from the sounds of your thoughts,* Rascal answered her unspoken question.

"Stay out of my head," she whispered, forgetting to answer him back mentally.

*You were broadcasting loud and clear, sweetheart,* Rascal said with a deep chuckle. *Come on back and we can talk things out.*

Another deep sigh left her and she pulled open the front door, slipping inside and heading straight past the front desk.

"Hi, Wynona," Amaris called out softly.

Wynona almost fell on her face. "H-hello," she said, too shocked to say anything else. She tried to smile, but Wynona was positive she looked more confused than anything. Which she was.

Amaris gave a tight lipped smile back, then clicked away on her computer.

Shaking her head to clear it of the weird emotions, Wynona went straight for Rascal's office and knocked, but didn't wait to go in.

"Morning, beautiful." Rascal stood and walked around his desk, giving her a sweet kiss. His hands looped around her back and he held tight. "Did you sleep well?"

Wynona patted his chest, smiling genuinely for the first time all morning. "I did. I have this amazing wolf who keeps guard every night. It helps me sleep better."

He kissed her forehead. "Good to know." Letting go, he walked back to his seat, pulling up a chair for her to sit close to him. "Sorry I had to leave before you got up, but I needed to get some paperwork filled out this morning."

Wynona shrugged. "It's fine, but I felt bad not getting you breakfast." She sat down and put her elbow on the armrest, then her chin in her hand. "Have you eaten at all?"

Rascal shook his head. "Not yet, but I'll have someone grab me something." He continued to shuffle through a large pile of paperwork. "I'm trying to go over the contracts Braxet had with outside companies." Growling, Rascal's golden eyes came up to hers. "There

NO MATCHA FOR MURDER

are almost too many to count. And the few I've called have nothing good to say about the man."

"Huh." Wynona frowned. "From what I've been looking up, he's certainly successful. That makes it odd that so many people would dislike him."

"We've seen before that money speaks louder than personality," Rascal replied with a grunt.

"True enough." She reached over and ran her fingers through his wild hair. Just once, she wondered what it would look like if it were actually combed.

"Get us a wedding date and I'll comb it however you want," he said absentmindedly.

"Stay out of my head."

"Close your mind," he teased with a smirk.

Wynona closed her eyes and built a wall, relaxing as she felt her projections stop.

Rascal leaned back. "I always miss your chatter."

Wynona laughed. "That can't be true. At least half of my thoughts are nonsense."

"But they're your nonsense," Rascal said with a grin. "What man wouldn't kill to know what his woman was thinking all the time?"

"Your woman?" Wynona pressed. "What are we? Cavemen?"

Rascal leaned over, crowding her in her seat. "I'm what the cavemen were afraid of, sweetheart," he said in a low tone. "Preda-tor...remember?"

Wynona felt her cheeks flush, but she absolutely didn't want him to move back. "I think I just figured out a date," she whispered.

"Today?"

"Well, I was thinking tomorrow, but..."

Rascal growled and pulled back. "I suppose I can make it one more day."

"Prim would kill us, you know."

Rascal shrugged, his eyes back on his work. "Let her. It's not her wedding."

Wynona laughed softly. "So...the case."

"Yes...the case." Rascal copied her tone of voice. He glanced up without moving his head. "I thought you weren't getting involved."

"I didn't realize one of my good friends would be considered a suspect."

Rascal huffed and leaned back. "Skymaw is fine. It's a formality."

"Did anyone tell Prim that?" Wynona asked, leaning forward. "She was devastated when she came by last night," Wynona said in a softer tone. "She's sure this is the end of his career."

Rascal rolled his eyes. "A black hole is far too valuable for this to be the end."

"Do you think he killed Braxet?"

Rascal hesitated and it made Wynona gasp.

"How can you?" she asked. "You *know* him. You work together. He's kept me safe countless times."

Rascal put up a hand. "Sweetheart, I'm a cop. A jaded one at that. You forget that I've seen an underbelly to our society that you can't even imagine."

She raised an eyebrow and Rascal had the good conscience to clear his throat in discomfort.

"I don't know who killed Braxet," he said finally. "But it very well could have come from within our station, and we have to take precautions."

"Why would he kill him?" Wynona asked. "Other than the fact that you all seem to think he's involved in the black market, why would Daemon personally have the need to kill him?"

Rascal scratched the edge of his chin. "I don't know," he admitted.

"Then what's your motive?"

"We don't have one."

Wynona threw up her hands. "Then why was he let go?"

Rascal growled again. "Wy...he wasn't let go. Stop and realize for a second that Prim gets a little dramatic when she tells a story." He made a sign with his fingers to indicate something very small. "I know she's your friend, but she's a drama queen. Isn't it possible that everything she told you isn't one-hundred-percent accurate?"

Wynona slumped in her chair. "Fine. Why don't you tell me the facts?"

"Gladly." Rascal leaned, twirling a pencil as he sat sideways in his chair. "A man was murdered in an interrogation room that only a few creatures had access to. One of them was Officer Daemon Skymaw. He was on magic duty, and since Braxet hadn't been officially arrested, he didn't have a hag's thread on."

Wynona nodded. This was all stuff she already knew.

"The man in question had two visitors through his time. His chauffeur, Mr. Nasille. And his bodyguard, Echoe." Rascal smirked. "Both came, thinking they could spring their boss, but because you hadn't been in to formally press charges, we were able to keep him here a little longer."

Wynona pinched her lips together. She had a good reason for waiting, since she was finishing her reception, but she didn't exactly like that Rascal and Chief Ligurio had used her time this way on purpose. It seemed a little cruel.

"Both visits were supervised and neither employee made any comments that sounded threatening or like hidden messages."

Wynona nodded again.

"Skymaw stood guard most all day, just outside the room, so he could keep magic from being available. An incubus will enchant anyone if they think it'll get them what they want."

Wynona tried to hide a small shiver at the thought of the creature's magic hitting her at her own shop, but knew Rascal saw it anyway when he reached out and took her hand, rubbing his thumb over her knuckles.

"Just before you arrived, Skymaw took a bathroom break. Since he had only planned to be gone a few minutes, he didn't ask someone to cover and simply slipped away." Grunting, Rascal pushed his free hand through his hair, bringing it back to attention after Wynona had calmed it down. "He claims he was only gone a couple of minutes before he came back to the hubbub of the chief, you and I shouting about the murder."

"See? Someone else could have gone in during that time," Wynona argued.

"That hallway has a dozen offices in it," Rascal said gently. "No one saw another creature come and go. Not to mention he had been dead less than two minutes when we found the body."

Wynona swallowed hard. "Less than two minutes?"

Rascal nodded. "The coroner said the body temperature hadn't even changed yet."

Wynona closed her eyes. "Still…there was time."

"Someone very fast could have done it," Rascal agreed. "But we have no evidence anyone else was there."

Wynona took a few calming breaths before sitting up straighter. "I understand your position, but he didn't do it."

Rascal nodded wearily. "I knew you wouldn't believe him capable." He looked sympathetic as he continued. "But even good cops make bad choices sometimes, Wy."

"I'm going to prove it."

Rascal nodded. "I figured that as well." He squeezed her hand and leaned in, leaving a feather light kiss on her cheek. "I have to be as unbiased as possible, but I'll do my best to help. I might believe it's possible for an officer to break, but I don't want it to be him."

Wynona softened. "Thank you."

"Believe it or not, he's not just my officer, he's my friend. And if I didn't have so many brothers, I'd have asked him to be best man at the wedding."

Wynona's smile widened. "I know."

Rascal gave her a half smile. "Except there isn't going to be one, right? We're just going to get married tomorrow?"

Wynona laughed, but didn't respond and Rascal gave her a put-out look.

"Okay, before we go barging down the doors of the Cursed Circus this morning, why don't you tell me what's going on with Lusgu and Violet?"

Wynona scrunched up her nose. "Where would I start?"

"The beginning?"

Wynona shook her head. "You already know all that."

"Then what happened that I missed? There's something you haven't told me."

Wynona tapped her fingers against the armrest. "I got mad at both of them and yelled."

Rascal's eyes widened. "Wow. I wasn't sure that day would come."

She made a face and Rascal chuckled.

"Hon, Lusgu's been asking for your anger for a long time. And Violet is...well...Violet. She's loyal, but a pain in the rear."

"She's my familiar," Wynona said, her voice growing softer as emotions began to creep up. She blinked to stop the tears, but her vision grew watery anyway.

"And that cranky little mouse adores you," Rascal assured her, wiping at her face. "But she also seems to know some things we don't. Her tendency to lord that kind of stuff over you isn't going to win her friends."

"Isn't she supposed to be loyal to me over Lusgu?"

Rascal thought about it for a minute. "Yes...but have you thought that maybe her loyalty to Lusgu really is loyalty to you?"

Wynona's black eyebrows pulled together. "I don't follow."

He shrugged. "Maybe she's protecting you?"

"By keeping secrets?"

He pushed a hand through his hair. "Secrets tend to seem good at the time," he said softly. "Keeping them often feels noble and protective." His golden eyes met hers. "But in the end, they have a tendency toward betrayal."

The tears spilled over and Rascal groaned.

Tugging on her hand, he pulled Wynona into his lap and wrapped his arms around her. "I've got you," he whispered against her hair. "Take the time you need."

"I love you," Wynona whispered back, letting her forehead rest in the crook of his neck.

"When we get married tomorrow, I'll show you just how much I love you back."

Laughing softly, Wynona took a few minutes to calm down and

relax. She wasn't sure where she stood with most of her friends right now, but at least she had Rascal. The other half of her soul would always be one she could count on and nothing about that was to be taken lightly.

## CHAPTER 10

Wynona let Rascal wrap his hands around her waist and lift her down from the truck. It was a good thing too, since her eyes couldn't leave the spectacle in front of her. "Oh my goodness," she whispered.

Rascal grunted and stepped to the side. "Yeah…it's something."

The words "Cursed Circus" were in lights so bright that Wynona was positive they would have lit up the whole of Hex Haven if the business had been inside city limits. Bright neon borders and flashing signs were enough to make a creature nauseous or trigger some kind of mental madness.

"Is it still running?" she asked Rascal as they began walking toward the entrance. "Who's keeping it up?"

"The producer," Rascal said in a low growl. His eyes were starting to glow as he looked around. "As soon as I find a violation, however, it's gone."

"Mr. Braxet made it sound like he was helping creatures, that they wanted to be here." Wynona knew she was gawking like a wide-eyed newt as they walked up, but she couldn't help it. She'd never seen anything like this place. Despite the bright lights and the music that shook her to her bones, she had the unnerving feeling that the massive black building wasn't a fun adventure at all…but a prison.

*The question is, is it keeping creatures in…or out?*

"I suppose you can see for yourself," Rascal said wryly. He held open the door. "Though I'll warn you…you're not going to like what you find."

Wynona stepped inside and felt something slide off her skin. She rubbed the goosebumps on her arms. "What was that?" she whispered.

Rascal shook his head. "Not sure. Can you see it?"

Wynona blinked a few times, her vision turning purple as she brought her magic sight to the forefront. Red slime covered everything. "It's red," she murmured, her eyes following the spell. "I think it's Mr. Braxet's magic, or at least something similar to his." She reached out and poked at the spell, shivering slightly when the coldness brushed her skin. "It's not affecting me," she said to Rascal. "Just like at the shop. I'm immune."

"Immune? No one's immune," a voice said with a loud scoff.

Wynona jumped, but had the wherewithal to shut down her vision before turning to see who had joined them.

Rascal stepped forward, blocking Wynona ever so slightly. She glanced around his broad shoulder and her eyes widened at the human-looking man approaching them.

Sharp, orange eyes were trained on her and Wynona could practically hear the wheels turning in his head. His face was all sharp lines and angles, though rather handsome as far as men went. But it was the three bushy tails that matched his eyes that caught her attention the most.

"Kitsune…" she breathed. Wynona had never seen the elusive creature before, though she had read about it in several legend books. How in the world did one work just outside her city and she never knew it?

The man paused, one eyebrow raising and a look of intrigue replacing the initial disdain. "Deputy Chief Strongclaw…" the creature drawled. "Do introduce me to your companion."

Rascal's jaw clenched and his growling grew louder. "My fiance," he said tightly. "Ms. Wynona Le Doux."

Orange eyes flared and he stepped forward again, but Rascal's warning cut off the movement. Finally, the stranger looked at Rascal, one side of his mouth twitching in amusement as he looked back at Wynona. "Since your escort doesn't seem to want to share knowledge both ways…" He tilted his head and Wynona couldn't decide if it was condescending or not. "Budayo Fumoio." That lip twitched again. "I'm the executive producer around here, but most everyone simply calls me Bud."

Wynona blinked. "Bud?"

That nod came again.

Wynona was having a hard time wrapping her head around the casual nickname. Nothing about the man was casual. Not his hair, or the way his slacks were pressed or the air he held himself with. Even his address was on the formal side, so to be called something so… mundane seemed ridiculous.

Bud put his hands in his pockets and looked at her expectantly. "What brings you to our establishment?"

*Are you going to keep gawking? Or should I punch him in the nose?*

Wynona gave herself an internal shaking. *I wasn't gawking,* she defended herself. *I've never seen a kitsune before and there's something off about him. I can't decide if he's creepy or just odd.*

Rascal huffed slightly and his demeanor relaxed. "Ms. Le Doux is often hired as an independent consultant when we're working on murder cases."

"Ah…" Bud nodded slowly "A woman with a keen eye for the unusual, huh?" He smiled. "Then I have just the thing for you." He held an arm out, inviting them to walk. "Please…join me."

Wynona looked at Rascal, who furrowed his brows, but nodded. He put his hand on Wynona's back, shifting so he was between Wynona and the kitsune. Bud, for his part, looked amused once again at the wolf's behavior.

Wynona normally would have rolled her eyes, but she refrained. She wasn't the least bit drawn in by the creature's demeanor, but she also wasn't sure what she thought of him. That made her wary and she tried hard to follow her gut instincts. They rarely led her wrong.

"Tell me, Mr. Fumoio," Wynona began, breaking into the odd silence. "What exactly do you do as Executive Producer for the Cursed Circus?"

His orange eyes came over his shoulder. "The easiest explanation would be to say I'm the creature in charge of financing. We have a team who does the actual numbers, but I approve...or disapprove... as the case may be, where the money goes." He paused at a set of double doors. "And it's simply Bud," he said with a smile at Wynona, his hand reaching out for the handle. "And I warn you to prepare yourself, Ms Le Doux." His eyes flared. "What you're about to see will most likely frighten you, but to the right soul..." his voice dropped. "It will delight and entice you in ways you didn't know existed."

Wynona pinched her lips together, already hating where this was going. Nothing about the thought of exploiting creatures, no matter how odd they were, was enticing to her. But she held her tongue. She needed to see where Mr. Braxet worked. And then she needed to speak to his employees. Obviously, they weren't hurting much since the business was still running and Bud had yet to even mention his former boss.

With a flourish, Bud opened the doors and all the noise that had been absent from before, flooded Wynona's senses, nearly knocking her to her knees. She grabbed Rascal's hand, clutching it tightly and locking her knees.

*I can feel...their pain...*she thought through her clenched jaw.

Rascal's head snapped her direction. *What?*

Wynona kept her eyes closed. *I can feel them. Why can I feel them?* Images, similar to those she had experienced in her dream, flew through her mind in an avalanche of screenshots. Darkness, grotesque shapes, mouths swallowing screaming creatures, fear deep enough to drown in and hurting...anguish...despair... "So much pain," Wynona wheezed, her lungs tight. She bent over, Rascal's arm her only hold on reality.

"Shut your mind, Wy," Rascal demanded. "Put up your wall!" he bellowed.

The boldness of his demand broke through Wynona's haze and she fought to obey. Brick by brick, she laid the foundation, but it was moving too slow. Her will grew weaker with each passing second as she felt the weight of the creatures in the circus begin to crush her.

*DON'T YOU DARE!* a squeaky voice screamed. *FIGHT, WYNONA! FIGHT! I'M COMING!*

Relief knocked at the edge of Wynona's mind when she heard Violet's screaming, and she felt a small burst of energy, just enough to lay a couple more bricks before a sharp sensation tugged at her leg. It moved upward and settled at her neck, rubbing in a soothing motion.

Violet's touch caused a split in the emotions and Wynona sucked in a deep breath. With a renewed sense of purpose, she used the strength of her familiar's power to finish closing off her mind, then stood, panting to catch her breath.

"Well, well…" Bud's voice said in an intrigued whisper. "What have we here?"

Wynona glared up at him from under her lashes. "What. Is. This. Place?" She stood, her head spinning for a moment before Rascal's arm steadied her. "What have you done to these poor creatures?"

Bud spread his hands. "I assure you, madam, everything here is above board. I have all the necessary paperwork for our line of work." He tilted his head to the side. "Tell me…where did you find this…mouse?"

Wynona started to reach up to cover Violet, but she quickly realized it was too late. She had a unique creature inside a circus. Of course, the kitsune would be interested. "I didn't find her," Wynona said. "She found me." She narrowed her gaze. "And she's where she belongs."

Bud smirked and nodded. "If you say so." He leaned in, his eyes on Violet. "Tell me, little one…would you enjoy being a star?"

A sound Wynona had never heard before, something that sounded suspiciously like a hiss or light growl, came from a very tiny set of lungs, but the meaning was more than clear.

Bud chuckled deeply and straightened. "I see. Well..." He sighed. "Onward then." He paused after taking a step. "That is...if you're up for it, Ms. Le Doux? You seem to have a weak constitution for someone who works on murder cases."

Wynona straightened her shoulders. "I'm afraid the noise caught me off guard," she lied. Nothing could make her tell this man what had really happened. Wynona wasn't completely positive herself. "I'm sensitive to sound and the spell you have on the outer part of the building is surprisingly good."

The compliment seemed to distract him just enough for Wynona to relax. "We only employ the best," he said. "Which was why Brax was interested in your tea." His smile never moved. "I never did hear if he offered you the position?"

"He did." Wynona ignored Rascal's grunt.

Bud looked her up and down. "Pity." He pursed his lips, obviously having read her answer without asking. "We could have been good together."

"I think I'd like that tour now," Wynona pressed as Rascal's growling grew again. If she didn't get this done with, there would be two murders and two police suspects. *One is enough, thank you very much*, Wynona sent to her soulmate.

*If he doesn't stop with the innuendoes...*Rascal threatened.

Wynona let herself reach up to Violet finally, brushing the mouse's fur, ever so grateful her familiar was back, even if Wynona wasn't quite sure how it had all happened. They would talk later. "Onward, please Bud."

He nodded again and began walking. "Our show isn't running right this second, but you can meet the performers and some of them might be willing to grace you with a trick or two." He led them down into a large stadium, the stairs seemingly endless.

With each step down, Wynona couldn't help but feel that they were descending into the underworld. She could feel the pressure building against her skull and only Violet and Rascal's help kept her from crumbling.

*Who'd have thought you'd become an empath?* Violet sent to Wynona.

*No kidding,* Wynona sent back. *And why now? How am I still developing new powers?*

Violet chittered and shifted on Wynona's shoulder. *I think we'll keep seeing more emerge the better you get with what you already have. I don't think you're the strongest witch in the paranormal world simply because of your power, but perhaps because of how many powers you have. As you master one, more may continue to appear.*

Wynona groaned in her head. This wasn't what she signed up for.

*Can you imagine what it would have been like to deal with this as a child?* Violet snapped. *I'm starting to understand why Saffron was so scared of you.*

Guilt almost made Wynona's wall break and she stumbled slightly.

*Sorry,* Violet grumbled, nuzzling into Wynona's ear. *I didn't mean that how it sounded. I guess I'm still a little on edge from what's happening, but I'm also starting to understand Saffron's position. I don't like it, necessarily, but I can see why she went to such drastic measures to save you. All of this would have been too much for any child to handle...and with parents like yours...Saffron's fear that the world might not survive was probably realistic.*

The guilt eased, but didn't fully go away and Wynona chose not to answer. She couldn't completely disagree with her familiar, though that didn't make it all hurt less. But why did no one care about how *she* felt? They all talked about her powers, but Wynona was the one having to deal with the weight, the pain, the fear, the new problems and sensations that arose at every corner and no one seemed to want to see it from her point of view.

Violet's touch soothed her less and less with each step they took into what Wynona was now thinking of as a dungeon, until Rascal's hand grabbed hers, squeezing tight.

She looked at him, seeing the concern in his golden eyes, and immediately retracted her thought. With her wall up, she had noticed that her link with Rascal was dulled. It didn't seem quite right that Rascal, who was the only one who never seemed to ask anything of Wynona, was harder to communicate with, while Violet couldn't be pushed out.

Violet sighed, having heard Wynona's thoughts. *You're right. I'm sorry.*

Wynona's eyes widened and she glanced at her shoulder. "I beg your pardon?" she whispered.

Violet huffed. *Don't make me say it again or I might scream.*

"Are you ready?" Bud asked as they finally reached the bottom. He began walking across a sawdust covered ring, Wynona and Rascal following.

*I don't like the smell of this,* Violet muttered.

Rascal looked over. "What did she say?" he asked softly. "I didn't quite catch it."

Wynona leaned in. "She said she doesn't like how it smells."

*It's more than that,* Violet corrected. *I smell magic here. Strong magic. And none of it good.*

Wynona gave her familiar a look. *Should I take a look?*

Violet clenched her jaw. *Yes. But be careful. I don't like foxy dude. He's creepy.*

Wynona nodded. "Cover me," she said in an almost inaudible tone to Rascal. Letting herself fall slightly behind to hide her eyes, Wynona blinked on her magic vision and almost passed out. Violet was right. Wynona wasn't sure how she'd missed it, usually she felt it when she passed through spells, but this place was so covered in layers of enchantments and hexes that it was amazing it didn't implode.

*Your mental wall,* Violet offered. *It's shutting down some of your senses.*

Wynona's jaw hung open as she tried to pick apart all the layers in the building. Some of the spells made her want to recoil and others made her want to touch, though she didn't dare. This place was absolutely a horror house, not the fun, interesting circus that Mr. Braxet had painted it to be.

They reached a set of large curtains and Bud brushed them aside, slipping into a dark area.

Wynona gripped Rascal's hand and let go of her vision. She had a feeling she was about to see everything she needed to know about the kind of men Mr. Braxet, Bud and anyone else who ran this circus were. And none of it was going to be good.

## CHAPTER 11

It took a moment for Wynona's eyesight to adjust to the low lighting behind the curtain, but when it did, she wished she was anywhere but there. Cages upon cages lined the cavernous space on the right hand side. Doors, presumably dressing rooms or offices, lined the left hand side.

Bud was waiting for them, a proud smile on his face. "As you can see, we take the safety of our personnel seriously."

"You've got creatures locked up in cages," Wynona said tightly. "How is that safe for them?"

His eyebrows twitched. "Have you ever seen a Bluecap, Ms. Le Doux?"

Wynona frowned. "Those don't exist."

Bud smirked and walked away from her, toward the line of cages. He waved to one of them. "This is Breezy."

Wynona bent down slightly to get a better look. She couldn't see anything inside.

"Careful," Bud warned in a low, slightly excited tone.

A paralyzing scream burst into the air only a split second before a blue flame launched at Wynona's face. She gasped and nearly fell on her backside into the sawdust. Her chest was heaving as she stared at the small, fire creature as he ran into the wall of the cage over and over again, all while yelping in the most uncomfortable pitch Wynona had ever experienced. His teeth were too long for his body, though calling anything a body for a Bluecap was a stretch.

They had once been known as fairy ghosts who haunted mines and when they appeared, seemed to be a small, blue ball of flame. Hundreds of years before, the history books claimed that if a miner caught the attention of a Bluecap, it meant the miner would be safe for the rest of their lives.

*There's nothing safe about this guy,* Violet muttered with a shudder.

"What did you do to him?" Wynona asked, her throat closing up at the insanity she was watching.

Bud tsked his tongue. "Come now, Ms. Le Doux."

She straightened and turned to glare at the producer.

"Do you really believe we hurt our creatures?" Bud leaned over and ran his finger up and down the walls of the cage in a slow, methodical motion.

Wynona's jaw nearly hit the ground as she watched the flame's frantic movements slow to match the pace of Bud's finger. The ghost fairy began to float lazily and look less deranged as it stopped trying to attack everything in sight, until it disappeared in a small puff of smoke. Wynona's gasp caused Bud to chuckle.

"Breezy was brought to us by a witch who'd found him attacking creatures in a mine from Cauldron Cove." The look Bud gave the empty-looking cage was almost…fatherly. "He'd been injured and would never truly be sane again. Rather than having him put down, our informant brought him here." Bud grinned. "We're able to take care of him and provide a home instead of death." He stepped toward Wynona, who backed up on instinct. "What do you think now, Ms. Le Doux?"

Rascal stepped up close to her back, but didn't speak.

"I think you traded one prison for another," she said honestly.

The kitsune's eyes narrowed, but his amused grin never faltered. "I can see you'll be a hard sell." He waved a hand through the air. "But no matter. With Brax gone, I doubt we'll be pursuing the offer, even if you were amenable."

"About that..." Wynona hesitated. "Tell us your relationship with your boss."

For the first time since they arrived, there was a flash of anger in the kitsune's eyes, breaking his nonchalant facade. Bud schooled it so quickly, however, that Wynona found herself impressed, despite herself. "Brax was *not* my boss."

"Oh?" Wynona feigned ignorance. "I thought he owned the circus?"

The darkening of Bud's ears was the only sign of his emotions. "While he may have been the majority shareholder," Bud said in a carefully controlled voice, "he and I were board directors together."

"Ah..." Wynona nodded. "You were one of the men who came by to try and release him on the day he was at the police station, correct?"

One eyebrow slowly rose. "Why, Ms. Le Doux..."

Bud stepped forward and Wynona forced her feet to stay still, though she wanted to be as far from this man as possible. The weight of the magic and emotions on this cursed place was pulsing against her skull like a dwarf swinging his axe, but she also had the distinct impression that a show of weakness would hurt her ability to obtain information.

"Don't tell me that you believe that *I* might have had something to do with Tor's death?"

Wynona shrugged. "I don't know what I believe yet, Bud. I'm simply here to gain information."

"And will that information include your conflict of interest?"

Wynona stiffened.

"Did you really think I wasn't aware that you were pressing charges against Brax when he was *killed* in the interrogation room?" Bud's deep chuckle echoed through the space and several of the animals stopped making noises as if they recognized the sound.

*Or maybe they hear the sound of a predator worse than themselves,* Violet offered, her tiny body shivering.

Wynona kept her eyes on her host. "There's no conflict of interest,

Bud. While Mr. Braxet tried to use magic on me without my consent, I would never have wished him ill. The charges were to keep him from trying again to influence my ability to make decisions." She gave Bud back a challenging stare of her own. "Or do you agree with his tactics to use his powers as an incubus to win me over to his way of thinking?"

Bud put his hands in the air. "I had no idea that Brax would go to such extremes." His hands came down slowly and his eyes darted to Rascal before coming back to Wynona. "Though, I also never see a creature turn down the opportunity to make money, so I suppose there's a first time for everything."

"Money doesn't interest me," Wynona stated firmly.

"Hmm…" Bud turned and began walking again. "If you look up two rows, you'll see our manticore."

"What?" Wynona's head jerked up and she stopped in her tracks. Manticores were normally large, bull sized creatures, but this one could have fit in the palm of Wynona's hand. "I don't understand." She watched the resting creature, his scorpion tail twitching in its sleep. How it slept through all the noise was anyone's guess, but its size was Wynona's biggest confusion.

"Not all creatures are meant to breed," Bud said airily. "At times we receive creatures from cursed unions that create odd or… unstable…results."

Wynona locked her limbs to keep from shivering at the unattached tone of his voice. Bud didn't seem to view these paranormals as living, breathing entities. They were props; tools he used in his work. It made Wynona wonder if the kitsune was capable of emotionally attaching to anything or anyone.

Kitsune were known for their intelligence and sneaking abilities. The more tails one had, the more they'd progressed as their shifting animal. With three tails, Bud was anything but a novice in his work.

Rascal's hand on her lower back brought Wynona's mind back to the present. A door opened on their left and Wynona's eyes widened. A tall, muscular man with twisting horns rising from either side of his head glared at them as they walked by.

Rascal gave the creature a nod, but kept them moving.

Wynona could feel the demon's eyes against her back as they continued to follow Bud.

"Mr. Bud!" A thin man walked hurriedly in their direction and Bud sighed as he stopped walking.

"Ms. Le Doux, meet Paphila Nasille," Bud said in a bored tone. "He's our resident chauffeur."

Wynona glanced at the kitsune, trying to figure out why he chose that exact wording, but the approach of the new creature forced her to set it aside. "Mr. Nasille," she said politely.

The creature gave her a quick glance, but otherwise ignored her for Bud. "Mr. Bud," he said breathlessly. "Someone's been in the garage. My tools are all messed up and there were cigarette butts around the garbage can."

Bud held up his hands. "You know that the imps like to blow steam," he said like a parent talking to a child for the thousandth time. "I'm sure it's nothing to worry about."

Wynona's eyes darted back and forth between the two. It wasn't clear what type of creature Mr. Nasille was and that made Wynona curious. In a place where everyone seemed to be some kind of legend or something entirely new, Wynona couldn't begin to imagine what this small, thin man was.

"I've told them to leave my things alone," Mr. Nasille said in a low tone. "I can't keep the cars driving safely if the imps are constantly breaking my stuff."

"Perhaps we could talk about this another time?" Bud's leading tone brought Mr. Nasille's attention back to the visitors.

"D-deputy Chief," Mr. Nasille whispered, swallowing hard. He stepped back slightly, his eyes rounding.

"Nasille," Rascal stated coolly. "This is Ms. Wynona Le Doux, my fiance and an independent consultant on the case of Braxet's death." Rascal looked at Wynona. "This is Braxet's chauffeur. He was also at the station that day."

Wynona nodded. "Oh yes." Clasping her hands in front of her, Wynona smiled at the nervous man. "I'd like to ask you a few questions, if you don't mind, Mr. Nasille."

He tugged at his collar, backing up another step. "I...think I might have a job to do..."

"I think you can spare some time," Rascal said, though the words were far from a suggestion.

Mr. Nasille swallowed hard again, then nodded jerkily. "I need to put my tools back," he explained. "You'll have to come to the garage."

Rascal nodded when Wynona gave him a questioning look.

"Are you coming?" Wynona asked Bud, who held still while the rest began to walk.

"You're welcome to find me after," he said with a smile. "But I'll say upfront that I had nothing to do with Brax's death." His orange eyes flashed. "There was no love lost between us. In fact, you'd be hard pressed to find anyone in this circus who felt anything but disdain for the creature that was Tororin Braxet, but this circus is a family, Ms. Le Doux." His smile looked slightly unhinged. "Most creatures don't go around killing family."

Without another word, the kitsune turned, his tails whipping as he walked toward the long line of doors and disappeared inside one.

Wynona held back a shiver, but barely. There was something a little off about the rare shifter.

"Nasille," Rascal warned.

Wynona's head jerked around and she realized that their chauffeur was trying to sneak away, but he wasn't as good at it as Bud. "I'm coming, Mr. Nasille. Thank you for waiting."

The man's cheeks turned bright red and his legs picked up their speed as Wynona and Rascal caught up to follow him to the garage.

The large concrete garage was attached to the underground backstage through a series of tunnels and once again, Wynona was shocked at the sheer size of the production. There were several floors of cars, trucks, buses and other vehicles that were obviously custom made to carry specific creatures and keep them safe and contained.

*I don't even want to know,* Violet muttered.

Wynona reached up and scratched her familiar's ears in agreement. The less they knew about certain aspects of the circus, the better it would be. Wynona wanted to go home and take a shower after walking through this place. She felt, somehow, tainted from the aura of it.

"Mr. Nasille," she said as the man began picking up tools that had been scattered on the floor. "Can you tell me what you do for the Cursed Circus?"

The man snorted. "Such a stupid name." He stood and paused. "Though I suppose there's some unholy truth in it," he muttered and shook his head. "I'm the head *chauffeur*. Or didn't you hear?"

Rascal's teeth snapped. "Careful, Nasille. Ms. Le Doux is under my protection."

Mr. Nasille pressed his lips together. He seemed much more bold now that they were out of the main building. His eyes were a muddy brown in the bright light of the vehicle showroom when they turned to Wynona. "I'm a driver, a mechanic and in charge of scheduling any and all drives from those other than myself." He straightened his shoulders. "I was Mr. Braxet's personal driver and rarely drove for anyone else."

"Were you there at the shop the other day?" Wynona asked.

His cheeks turned red again and he rubbed the back of his neck. "No. Mr. Braxet chose to take Methuselon. Said he needed some muscle on this trip." His eyes went to Rascal and back.

Wynona tilted her head and tried to look unassuming. "Would you mind telling me what your powers are, Mr. Nasille?"

He glared. "You're asking what I am."

She nodded. "I suppose I am."

"Because you want to know if I killed Mr. Braxet? Is that it?"

Wynona held her hands to the side. "Right now I'm asking everyone questions, Mr. Nasille," Wynona assured him. "You're no more a suspect than Bud is. But the fact that you were at the station means I most particularly wanted to talk to you." She clasped her hands again and waited.

The man fidgeted, but finally sighed. "I'm a nymph."

Wynona blinked a couple of times. "Excuse me?"

He rolled his eyes. "A nymph," he sneered. "No, they're not all women, but the men are rare." He huffed. "Rare enough that we tend to stay out of the public eye."

"So you have an affinity with trees?" Wynona asked, trying to place him in her mind. She'd never heard of a male nymph. Even in the vast library at the castle, she'd never run across a mention of them.

He shook his head. "No. We males tend to be wild cards. There are less than five of us alive at any given time."

Wynona's eyebrows shot up and Violet chittered. "That is rare."

He nodded. "I have an affinity with sound."

"Sound."

Mr. Nassile nodded and looked over at the cars. "It's actually why I'm so good at cars. I can hear the running parts and pinpoint when something isn't working correctly."

Wynona gasped. "Are you the one who put the spell up to keep the noise of the creatures out of the stadium area?"

Mr. Nasille slowly turned, his eyes narrowed and curious. "Yes. How did you know?"

Wynona shook her head. "I, uh..."

Rascal's hand landed on her back. "She's sensitive to noises and walking through the barrier caused a harsh reaction."

*Thank you,* Wynona sent his way, though she wasn't sure if he could hear her at the moment. She wasn't bringing down her wall until they were far away from this place.

*Smart witch.*

Mr. Nasille studied her a moment more before nodding. "It's my spell."

"You must be very powerful," Wynona added.

His eyes narrowed ever so slightly more. "And just what are you, Ms. Le Doux? I shared my story."

She gave him a small smile. "I'm a witch."

"Ah...that explains it." Mr. Nasille began to put a wrench away before pausing. "As in...President Le Doux?" He gasped and nearly tripped in his haste to get away. "You're the president's daughter! The witch everyone's talking about! You were cursed!"

Wynona held up her hands. "Please," she said soothingly. "Please calm down."

Mr. Nasille held up the wrench like a sword. "You need to leave. I won't be taken in by someone like President Le Doux. I won't. He can't have me."

Wynona felt the blood drain from her head and held onto Rascal when his arm cinched around her waist. "I…I would never do that," she whispered hoarsely.

The wrench only dropped minutely before going back up. "I didn't kill Mr. Braxet. I have witnesses that I came here after the station and he was alive when I was there." Mr. Nasille took another couple of steps back. "But if you want to look somewhere, you might try his ex. I hear she's getting a hefty payout."

"Ex?" Rascal growled. "What ex?"

"His ex-wife," Mr. Nasille clarified. "The ink on the paper is probably still wet enough that the life insurance policy will still go to her."

The next few minutes were a blur as Rascal spoke a few more words then led them outside without going back through the main building. Wynona's head was swimming as they stepped out into the sunshine. Why would someone be afraid she would turn them into her father? What would her father do with someone like Mr. Nasille?

"We need to finish this quickly," Wynona said softly to Rascal as they climbed into the truck. "And we need to see if we can help those poor creatures."

Rascal sighed and pushed a hand through his hair. "I don't know if there's anything I can do, Wy. Most of them are seriously dangerous and as long as the circus has the right paperwork, they have the right to handle them."

She nodded, her eyes straight forward. "I eventually need to figure out what my father has to do with this as well, but right now…I have one creature I *can* try to free." She turned her head. "Please take me home, Rascal. We need to talk to Lusgu."

## CHAPTER 12

Wynona's heart was going to give out before she could utter a word. She'd been holding back this chat for a long time and she was just as scared now as when she first discovered that Lusgu was cursed. But after seeing all those poor animals in cages, Wynona knew she had to do something. Lusgu's cage might not be quite as literal, but it was there nonetheless. Wynona, of anyone, ought to know.

"Lusgu?" she called out as she and Rascal came through the front door. "Are you here?"

Violet climbed down and raced toward the kitchen, disappearing into the pantry where Lusgu's portal had been.

Wynona paused. "Actually, I'm not sure why his door is still here," she said with a droop of her shoulders. "Not now that the tea shop is getting ready to open and especially after our fight."

Rascal snorted. "Oh, he kept them both. Despite trying to kill you, he doesn't seem to let you out of his sight."

"He wasn't himself," Wynona reminded her fiance.

Rascal grunted and shook his head. It seemed he wasn't going to be forgiving Lusgu anytime soon.

A shuffling sound caught Wynona's attention and she turned to see Lusgu and Violet coming out of the closet.

"You wanted me?" the brownie muttered, glaring at Wynona.

Wynona straightened her shoulders and stuck her chin in the air slightly. "I have a few questions for you."

Lusgu didn't move.

"Why do you want my grandmother's grimoire?" Wynona had a suspicion it was about his curse, but she needed to know for certain. Their last conversation had been anything but forthcoming and as much as she wanted to help Lusgu, she also needed to put some boundaries in place. She was at her wit's end and she didn't like it.

Lusgu sighed and his eyes dropped to the ground. "I'm…looking for a spell."

"Is it to counteract your curse?"

His head snapped up so fast and his eyes flashed so brightly, Wynona almost stumbled backward from the smack of power. "How do you know about that?" Lusgu paused and tilted his head, his ears perked.

Wynona frowned as she realized Violet was chittering, but Wynona couldn't hear her in her mind. "How do you do that?"

Lusgu glanced her way, but didn't answer.

Wynona threw up her hands. "Lusgu. I want to help. I saw your curse when you were walking Dr. Rayn back home. But we've already been through this. Unless you're willing to talk to me, I can't do anything and I'm tired of fighting."

"Do you really think I won't share information simply out of spite?" he spat, stepping in her direction. The small creature held still when Rascal growled in warning. "Not everything is as it seems," Lusgu continued, his teeth clenched. "Has it ever occurred to you that I *can't* answer your questions? That my life hasn't been easy either? I lost *everything* that was important to me!" he said, his voice growing in fever and pitch. "Everything! Following Saffron's plan was the only chance I had at getting it back and instead of making progress, I'm stuck with a witch too scared of her own powers to do anything but make tea and get upset when someone offends her!"

Wynona hadn't realized she was crying until a tear dripped off her chin. Her shaking hand moved to wipe them away, but they never seemed to stop. "I'm sorry you lost so much," she stammered, leaning back into Rascal's chest as he slipped up behind her. "My life hasn't been easy either."

Lusgu huffed and pinched the bridge of his nose. "I know," he conceded, his tone much less angry than before. He looked up. "But you're not the only one."

Wynona nodded. "I'm not scared of my powers," she clarified. Lusgu's brows pulled together. "But I also refuse to be someone's weapon."

He nodded slowly. "As it should be."

"I feel like Granny set me up to be just that."

Lusgu grumbled and shifted his weight. "That wasn't her intent."

"Binding my powers, knowing they would hit me at full strength, then revealing that she wanted me to start a war to take over Hex Haven isn't using me as a weapon?" Wynona asked. She folded her arms over her chest. "Could have fooled me."

"I'm not saying she went about everything the right way," Lusgu snapped. "But you aren't a weapon and we…she never thought you were."

Wynona pinched her lips. She was already done with this conversation, but she hadn't gotten to the heart of it yet. "Are you, or are you not, looking for a cure in the grimoire?"

Lusgu's jaw clenched and he nodded once.

"Are you allowed to talk about the curse at all?" Wynona felt Rascal stiffen behind her. His chest had been rumbling constantly with growling, but she was grateful he hadn't given too much into his wolf yet. She needed to have this conversation whether she wanted to or not.

Lusgu hesitated, but managed a short shake of his head before wincing.

"If I talk about it, does it hurt you?" Wynona asked, her tone inadvertently soft. She wanted answers, but not at the expense of his life.

Lusgu shrugged.

Wynona blew out a breath. "I'm going to get the grimoire." She started to walk, then paused. "Can you give me any clue as to what I should be looking for?"

Lusgu tapped his lips.

"Can you look through the book with me?"

He thought about it then nodded.

"Violet?"

The mouse stood on her hind legs, nose twitching.

"Can you do anything to help communicate between us?" Wynona had a sudden thought. "Can you create a mental link between us three?"

Violet sat down. *I'm not sure. I've never thought about trying.*

Rascal's hands tightened on Wynona's waist. "Are you sure that's a good idea?"

"What choice do we have?" Wynona asked, twisting to look at him. "Plus, it might mean some kind of loophole. If he can't talk out loud, maybe he can send mental information."

Lusgu pursed his lips and nodded. "It's a good thought." He glanced at Violet. "Give it a try."

Violet gave a curt nod, then closed her beady eyes.

Wynona held very still. At the edge of her brain, she could feel a slight buzzing and she concentrated on it. The feel of magic skittered over her skin, raising her hair on end. Instead of fighting it, however, Wynona welcomed the sensation. She tried to mentally open a door to the entity working its way closer, until the snap of what could only be described as a rubberband ricocheted through her brain, sending a sharp pain from the crown of her head through the bridge of her nose.

"Ow," Wynona gasped, automatically bringing a hand to her forehead. A thud caused her to look up and her eyes widened when she saw Violet lying on the floor. "No." Rushing over, Wynona scooped up her familiar, putting a finger to the creature's tiny chest. A slower than normal, but steady heartbeat met her touch and Wynona let out a harsh breath.

"It was too much," Lusgu said sadly. The droop of his lips let

Wynona know he'd gotten his hopes up just like she had. "She's not strong enough to break through."

Wynona cradled the mouse. "Violet. I'm so sorry. I shouldn't have asked that of you."

Lusgu reached out, his knobby finger shaking slightly as he touched Violet's forehead. A tiny jolt went through her body before Violet pulled in a long breath and she relaxed.

Opening her black eyes, she glanced from Wynona to Lusgu and chittered for a moment before rolling over and curling into a ball. *I think I need a nap.*

"Hold on," Wynona said, rubbing Violet against her cheek. "Let me get you some tea and a sandwich first." She put the small body on her shoulder, waiting until Violet was stable and had her tail stretched across the back of Wynona's neck, then walked into the kitchen and began to grab supplies. *I'm so sorry, Violet.*

Violet yawned loudly. *Not your fault. I think I can try again soon.*

"Not a chance," Wynona muttered. She jumped when Rascal came up beside her.

"Let me," he whispered, taking Violet down and holding her carefully in his palms.

*Oooh...warm...*

Wynona chuckled, the sound slightly shaky since her nerves were still on edge, but she couldn't help but smile at Violet's response to Rascal's wolf heat. It only took her a few minutes to have Violet eating voraciously in the middle of the kitchen table and by the time Wynona sat down, she wasn't sure she wanted to get up again. Her heart was done for the day.

Lusgu cleared his throat and shifted his feet, giving her a look.

"Right." Wynona stood, ignoring the protests in her mind to keep Violet in her sights at all times, and walked to her room. She braced herself before opening her closet, preparing for the onslaught of dark magic that permeated the space.

*Careful,* Rascal sent her way.

Wynona nodded, then gripped the handle and opened the door. The spell keeping the magic contained worked well, but the unintended backlash was how strong the feeling was when finally released.

Wynona gasped, feeling as if the very air had been sucked from her lungs, and she gripped the sides of the opening. *I need to keep Granny's grimoire somewhere separate. This is terrible.*

*Agreed,* Violet chirped.

Gritting her teeth, Wynona grabbed the book she wanted and slammed the door, throwing the magical lock and barrier back in place. Breathing a long sigh of relief, Wynona walked on shaky legs back to the kitchen area.

Lusgu nearly jumped out of his seat, but sat back down at Rascal's snarl.

Wynona chose a seat across the table. She wanted to help, but she was struggling to trust her janitor. There had been too many lies between them. "Why don't you men eat and if I find a spell that sounds promising, I'll bring it up?"

Rascal stared at Lusgu until the brownie grudgingly agreed.

Ignoring the angry men, Wynona began to flip through the book. Smells and sounds floated through the air the longer Wynona sat, but her mind grew further and further away from the present.

Spells and incantations, one after another, were recorded in the grimoire and Wynona was fascinated with them all. Some of the pages were...heavier...than others, she noticed. Not every spell Granny Saffron was privy to seemed to be completely legal, but they were nothing like the ones that had to be contained in the grimoires still in the closet.

It was the family history, however, that kept Wynona's attention the most. She had learned very little of her family's magical background, only what she had picked up from her parents' conversations and her sister's smug bragging.

Wynona's mother's library was full of books on magic's history, but not necessarily her family's. Wynona knew a lot about creatures, but she was quickly realizing she knew very little about herself.

She gasped.

"Are you okay?" Rascal asked quickly.

"Did you find something?" Lusgu jumped in.

Wynona's eyes were wide when she looked up. "Did you know Granny had a brother?"

Lusgu slumped and Rascal frowned. "A brother? Where is he?"

Wynona shook her head, flipping the page back and forth. "I'm guessing he must be dead. He's only mentioned twice." Wynona grumbled. "I wish I just had a book about the entire family line. It would clear up so many questions."

"And the spells?" Lusgu asked, his voice tight. "What spells have you found?"

Wynona gave him a sympathetic look. She was going slower than she should, but it was all just so interesting! "I haven't read anything that I thought might be helpful yet, I'm sorry. I'll keep looking. But right now, most of what I'm seeing is tea concoctions, family history stories and sickness cures."

Lusgu nodded his understanding, but the pain in his expression tugged at Wynona's heartstrings. She hated disappointing people and she knew what it was like to be trapped in her own body. "Lusgu..."

His eyebrows went up.

"You're technically cursed twice, right?"

He pursed his lips and nodded.

"One not to speak and the other for..." Wynona waited, but he didn't speak. "Something else?"

He nodded.

"I'm guessing you can't tell me what that is?"

Lusgu's head shake was short and his brows furrowed. They were beginning to tread in dangerous territory.

"If we cure one, will we cure the other?" Wynona asked. "Or will we need separate spells?"

Lusgu didn't move, but he rested a hand on the table, tapping a finger.

Wynona watched, noting that he tapped it three times over and over again. "Is your name Lusgu?"

One side of his mouth pulled up and he tapped three times.

Wynona nodded. "If we cure one, can we cure the other?"

One tap.

Wynona exchanged looks with Rascal. "So we need two spells?"

Three taps.

Wynona sighed and slumped. "Should we cure the speaking one first?"

Lusgu's fingers were still.

Wynona frowned and tried to figure out what he was saying. "Does it matter which one we cure first?"

Two taps.

"Okay, then." Sighing, Wynona sat up straight and went back to the book. "I guess I'll worry about Great Uncle Arune later." *Dang it.*

Rascal chuckled, then cleared his throat. "I'll make dinner," he said, rubbing her back.

Wynona gave him a grateful smile. "You sure you have the time?"

"We can pick the case back up tomorrow," he assured her. "You let me worry about you for a change."

Those words were like music to her ears. Wynona so rarely had someone else worry about her needs and for once, she wasn't going to argue. "I think I'll read on the couch." Taking the book, grabbing her favorite blanket and settling into the cozy cushions, she prepared for a long night.

Something told her this wasn't going to be an easy process, but Lusgu deserved to be free and whether it came tonight or six months from now, Wynona was determined to help it along.

## CHAPTER 13

Wynona frowned as she glanced over her shoulder again. A long, black SUV was behind her. That in and of itself shouldn't be a problem, but that exact vehicle had been on Wynona's tail since she'd pulled out of her driveway.

*Why don't you use a bit of magic to get rid of them?* Violet asked, glaring over the basket she rode in on the scooter.

Wynona pinched her lips. *I'm tempted. But I don't want to accidentally hurt someone when this all might be an innocent situation. I'm probably just paranoid after the way Bud looked at you.*

Violet laughed darkly. *If someone's here for me...well...let them come.*

Wynona shook her head. *Sometimes you frighten me.*

*I'll frighten them more.*

Sighing, Wynona stopped at a stop sign. She was eager to get through this crossroads, because the edges of town were only two minutes away and hopefully the vehicle would leave her alone at that point.

Before she could take off, however, her engine died. Wynona frowned and stared at the Vespa. "What just happened?" she wondered.

"Ms. Le Doux...if you'll please come with me."

Wynona jerked around. She'd been so caught up in her dead engine, she hadn't heard anyone get out of the SUV. "Mr. Nasille!" she cried.

The chauffeur's returning smile was anything but genuine. "Ms. Le Doux?"

Wynona jumped off the scooter and put her hands on her hips. "What did you do to my Vespa?" Mr. Nasille didn't move. Wynona glanced sideways at Violet, feeling decidedly uncomfortable.

*We can take him,* Violet snarled.

*Take who? Wy? What's going on?*

Wynona closed her eyes. With Rascal in her head, it was now a very crowded place. *Mr. Nasille is here. He did something to my—*

When Wynona came to, she felt as if a jackhammer were trying to dig into the back of her brain. "Ow…"

*It's about time you woke up,* Violet grumbled. *Now fix your head and let's get out of here. Rascal's gonna kill that nymph…if I don't do it first.*

*WY!*

"Ow," Wynona whined again, her hand rising to her forehead. "Hang on," she said out loud, even though Rascal was speaking in her head.

A litany of curses and growling rang through her mind as Rascal vented his frustration. Doing her best to push them aside, she focused on sending a small strain of magic up her neck and to the damaged spot. It only took moments to sigh in relief that the pain and injury were gone, but she wondered why Mr. Nasille would hurt her in the first place.

Sitting up, she looked around.

*Wy. Where are you? Nevermind. I'll just follow our link.*

"Hold on," Wynona rasped, then cleared her throat. *Hold on, Rascal. Let me see what's going on before you break in and eat something you shouldn't.*

He growled in response, but Wynona felt like he was holding still "Violet?"

The mouse rose on her hind legs, nose twitching. *Want me to eat someone instead?*

Wynona smiled. "Not yet. Do you know where we are?"

Violet rolled her eyes. *The Cursed Circus garage.*

"What?"

The door creaked open. "Oh, good. You're awake."

Wynona rose, grateful her magic had healed her injuries. "You've got two minutes before the police blow down your door, so I would answer very carefully." She tilted her head, hoping she looked confident and intimidating. "Why did you bring me here? And why kidnap me to accomplish it?" She let her magic travel down her arms and spark between her fingers. The most powerful witch in Hex Haven and she'd been caught off guard enough to be knocked out and dragged to a car garage of all places.

Mr. Nasille looked less frightened than he should have, considering not only what he'd just done, but how intimidated he'd been at Rascal's presence only yesterday. "No harm meant, Ms. Le Doux. But I knew you wouldn't come willingly. And president's daughter or no, we need to speak to you."

Wynona frowned. "We?"

Mr. Nasille nodded. "We." He stepped back and waved an arm out the door. "Shall we?"

*What's going on, Wy?*

*Hang on,* Wynona responded. *I'd like to see this through. There's someone else involved.*

*If you feel the slightest bit of unease, I want you to shoot to kill, do you understand?*

Wynona nodded, then picked up Violet and put her on her shoulder. "Lead the way, Mr. Nasille. I'll listen, but I don't promise anything more than that."

"Fair enough." He walked through the door and Wynona followed behind.

She wasn't comfortable with him at her back. Sure enough, just like Violet had said, Wynona found herself walking out of a bedroom and into the main part of the garage. *He must live here,* Wynona mused.

*Not much of a home.*

Wynona raised her eyebrows at Violet. *Better than nothing, I suppose.*

Violet snorted.

Wynona stopped short when they arrived at a sitting area in the corner. A beautiful woman sat on the edge of a couch, her make up, dress and demeanor screaming that she was a siren. It immediately put Wynona's magical radar on edge. She'd dealt with a siren before, and it hadn't been pretty.

"Please..." the woman said in a soothing tone. "Have a seat."

The prickle of magic caressed lovingly over Wynona's skin and she scrunched her nose, shaking it off.

The woman raised her eyebrows, looking amused. "Interesting..." she murmured.

Wynona was more grateful than ever that she had a soulmate and was immune to magic such as this. "I'd rather stand, thank you," she said curtly. "I'm Wynona Le Doux. And you are?"

Perfectly shaped lips curled just right at the sides. "The soon to be *ex*-Mrs. Braxet."

Realization slammed into Wynona and she had to lock her knees. "You're the ex wife."

Mrs. Braxet tilted her head back and forth consideringly. "Almost anyway. The papers had yet to be finalized at the time Tororin was killed."

Wynona folded her arms over her chest. "So you don't believe in the possibility of a suicide?"

Mrs. Braxet rolled her eyes. "Come now. We don't need to stand on pretext here. I'm aware there's an officer who's been put on leave, and I'm not unaware of you asking around at the circus." She patted the couch again. "Please, relax...I'm here as a friend."

"There's nothing friendly about kidnapping." Wynona's eyes darted to Mr. Nasille, who was practically salivating as he stood off to the side of Mrs. Braxet. It was clear he was entranced. The question was...was it real? Or magic-induced? And was it returned?

*Hmmm...*Violet murmured. *So many questions...so little time.*

Wynona ignored the sarcasm.

"Would you have come to speak to me otherwise?" Mrs. Braxet asked.

"I don't know," Wynona replied. "I had plans to talk to everyone about the case, so probably. But taking me by force certainly changes how I'll approach the situation."

Mrs. Braxet chuckled in a sultry tone and leaned back against the couch. "I like you, Ms. Le Doux. We'll get along just fine."

"Why am I here?" Wynona asked firmly. She was getting tired of this. And Rascal was pacing in the back of her mind. She wouldn't be able to hold him off much longer.

"Like I said, I wanted to talk to you."

"About?"

"About my husband."

"Which one?" The words were out of Wynona's mouth before she could think better of it. She'd seen women like this and odds were that Mr. Braxet wasn't this woman's first husband, but Wynona hadn't really meant to be so blunt about it.

Mrs. Braxet's smile lost a little of its luster. "You've been reading up on me."

Wynona shrugged, neither confirming or denying the accusation.

Sniffing, Mrs. Braxet tossed her deep auburn hair over her shoulder. "Would you believe it if I told you that out of all my husbands, Tororin was the one I loved the most?"

Wynona raised her own eyebrow. "No."

Mrs. Braxet huffed a laugh. "Nice to know you won't easily be fooled."

"You were in the process of divorcing him," Wynona said wryly. "It hardly takes a genius."

Mrs. Braxet leaned forward. "Tororin was...ambitious. Which meant he was more willing to use me than to appreciate me."

"Are you saying you're a woman who demands attention?" Wynona pressed.

Those lips curled again. "Come now, Ms. Le Doux. Don't tell me you don't enjoy the attentions of a certain man...or wolf...as the case may be."

Wynona scowled.

"I'm fully aware of my powers, Ms. Le Doux," Mrs. Braxet continued. "Which means I understand their capabilities as well as their limitations."

Wynona gave a firm nod. She didn't like to spread around that she had a soulmate, but in this case, there was nothing to do about it. "Please cut to the chase, Mrs. Braxet. As I'm sure you can imagine, Deputy Chief Strongclaw is ready and willing to take you and Mr. Nasille in. All I have to do is give him the go-ahead."

"It'll be your word against ours," Mr. Nasille butted in, but Mrs. Braxet waved him off.

"Circumstances are a bit different than we thought, dear." Mrs. Braxet smiled at the nymph, then turned back to Wynona. "I thank you for your discretion. I had you brought over because I wanted to make sure that you're truly taking this case as murder, and not a suicide."

*I think someone needs to rearrange that pretty face of hers,* Violet grumbled.

Wynona reached up and scratched Violet behind the ears. "You already made it clear you were aware of my actions. Why push it?"

*Oh, ho!* Violet crowed. *It's the money.*

Wynona's eyebrows shot up. "I see."

"Do you?" Mrs. Braxet asked.

"I'm guessing that his life insurance policy won't be paid out if it was a suicide," Wynona said, her hands going to her hips.

Mrs. Braxet winked and leaned back again. "I knew we'd be on the same page."

"What I don't understand is why?" Wynona tilted her head. "I've already been pursuing this as a murder. Why risk the public exposure by taking me?"

"Call it added insurance," Mrs. Braxet said. She snapped her fingers and Mr. Nasille rushed to hand her a checkbook. "I'm prepared to offer you a hundred thousand dollars in order to make sure this is classified as a murder."

"I neither need nor want your money," Wynona said through gritted teeth. "And somehow I don't think the police would appreciate your bribe offering either."

Mrs. Braxet stared Wynona down and handed the check to Mr. Nasille, who walked over and waved it in Wynona's face.

She grabbed it to stop it from annoying her, but the look on Mr. Nasille's face was enough to have Wynona tearing it into little pieces.

"You can give it to your favorite charity then," Mrs. Braxet said, rising from the couch so gracefully it almost hurt to watch. "Come, darling. Our work here is done."

Wynona huffed. "So, what? I'm supposed to just walk out of here now? Did you bring my Vespa along when you kidnapped me?"

"I do wish you'd stop saying that nasty word," Mrs. Braxet said with a long-suffering sigh.

"I'm afraid I prefer the truth," Wynona stated. She walked over to Mrs. Braxet, raised the check and dropped it to the ground. "If it's a murder, then we'll find the killer. If it's a suicide, then I'm afraid you'll just have to make due with whatever assets your multiple husbands have left you over the years." She ignored Mr. Nasille's angry grunt. "I'm not afraid of you, Mrs. Braxet, or anyone else at this circus."

Thoughts of the animals and the heavy despair clawed at her brain, but Wynona pushed them aside. This case was starting to get on her nerves and Wynona had enough on her own plate to last a lifetime. It was time to focus and put a killer behind bars, or call the case closed. Whichever ending came first.

"I suppose you wouldn't be," Mrs. Braxet said coolly, not the least bit intimidated by Wyonna's rant. "But you just might be a bit afraid of your father."

Wynona jerked back. "What does he have to do with this?"

"Oh my dear..." Mrs. Braxet cackled and walked away with her head high. "He has to do with absolutely everything," she whispered right before disappearing through a door Wynona hadn't noticed before.

Wynona stood in silence for a few moments before her brain caught up to what had been said. She looked down at Violet, her hands starting to shake with excess adrenaline now that the confrontation was over. "Did you catch that?"

*You should have let me eat her.*

Wynona closed her eyes and shook her head. "She would have tasted terrible." *Rascal?*

*It's about time. Be there in five.*

Wynona walked toward the large, overhead doors, not knowing how else to get outside, then planted herself at the edge of the building. Mr. Nasille hadn't brought them to the top level yesterday and she found herself at the edge of a forest of unknown origin.

Eyeing the dark interior, Wynona huffed and turned her back on the woods. The last thing she needed was to wander off and get lost. Police sirens quickly caught her attention and she called mentally to Rascal so he knew where to come.

His massive truck skidded around the corner, followed by two more cars, and Wynona found herself struggling to breathe as he leapt from the truck and engulfed her. "I'm going to kill them," Rascal ground out as he held her tightly.

Wiggling so she could breathe, Wynona leaned back just enough to look into his eyes. Rascal's golden eyes were glowing, his hair standing on end and his incisors larger than normal. His wolf was ready to protect what was his. "Let them go," she said softly.

"They broke the law," Rascal snarled.

"I know. But I'm fine and I believe their antics will catch up to them sooner or later." She frowned. "Mrs. Braxet is familiar with my dad. But I don't know how."

Rascal shook his head. "Doesn't matter. We can still arrest them."

Wynona put her hands on his cheeks. "We need to keep my dad out of this for now. Let's solve the case, then if we want to dig further into whatever he's up to, we can. Alright?"

"I don't like it."

Wynona nodded slowly. "Me neither. But having the president breathing down our necks and trying to pull me back to the castle isn't going to help either."

Rascal's growl seemed neverending, but Wynona wrapped her arms around his neck and waited until his breathing had calmed down. Her feet were dangling as he carried her to the truck.

"Back to the station, boys!" Rascal shouted, waving off the other officers. "I'll take Ms. Le Doux with me."

He hoisted her inside, then gave a gentle nudge. "Scoot over. I'm not letting you out of reach for a while."

Wynona smiled. "You'll hear no complaints from me."

# CHAPTER 14

"Stop hovering," Wynona said in exasperation as she looked over her shoulder.

Rascal flashed his teeth and went back to pacing behind her chair. "Every time I leave you alone, something happens," he growled.

Chief Ligurio snorted and Wynona gave him a glare. The vampire rolled his red eyes. "He's not exactly wrong. You have a penchant for finding trouble, Ms. Le Doux."

She rubbed her forehead. "Chief haven't we known each other long enough to say our first names? I really would like to be Wynona, or Wy, or Nona, even, instead of Ms. Le Doux." She stared him down, watching the flash of emotions cross his face.

When they'd first met, Chief Ligurio had been anything but pleased to be dealing with a Le Doux, but Wynona had been patient. She was fully aware that her family was only liked in certain circles and those circles were not the type that were friendly with the police department.

Ever since breaking free of the castle, she had spent her time trying to be the exact opposite of her family, and for the most part, she'd succeeded. But here, now, with those she counted as loved ones and friends, she wanted to break down the barrier the vampire chief of police had established back when she was an unknown entity.

Slowly, he nodded. "I think you've earned that…Wynona." His eyes flashed up to Rascal. "I think I'll leave the nicknames to others though."

"Fair enough." Wynona smiled at him in gratitude, but she really wanted to grin wide enough to split her face. One small victory among so many failures felt huge.

"You can call me 'Chief,' like everyone else."

*Or…not…*Violet snickered. *I don't think he wants you to forget who's in charge.*

Wynona nodded in return. "Thanks, Chief. I appreciate it."

Rascal's snort wasn't as quiet as he was probably hoping for.

Chief Ligurio cleared his throat pointedly and leaned forward onto his desk. "So tell me again what happened."

Wynona slumped and went through the whole tale for the third or fourth time. She'd lost count at this point.

"That was pretty bold," Chief Ligurio said, pursing his lips. He looked at Rascal. "I know you want to bring her in. But can you do it without personal bias?"

Rascal growled. "No."

Chief Ligurio shook his head. "I need to know that nothing would happen to her or the chauffeur if I sent you after them."

"I don't think you'll find them," Wynona offered.

Red eyes pinned her in place. "Oh?"

"Do you know who Mrs. Braxet is?" Wynona pressed.

"The widow of a man who may or may not have killed himself," Rascal snarled.

His pacing was driving Wynona crazy, but she tried to push her emotions to the side. "Yes, but this isn't her first seance. I made a guess that she had been married before and I'm guessing if we looked up her name, we'd find out that she's a bit of a black widow. And that she's *very* good at hiding."

Chief Ligurio narrowed his gaze and pulled out his computer. "What was her first name?"

Wynona shook her head. "I don't know. She didn't say." Wynona folded her arms over her chest. "I'm guessing she didn't want me to know. But…there can't be that many women who are known for marrying rich creatures and then running away with their fortunes."

Chief snorted and grabbed the receiver of his phone. "Nightshade? I want you to look up a Mrs. Braxet. See if there are newspaper articles or any other gossip on social media that might allow us to find her background. Bring it to my office ASAP." He slammed the phone down. "We'll see what that brings in. Meantime, the chauffeur should be easier to pick up. Strongclaw, send a team to bring him in for questioning."

Rascal pinched his lips, but nodded. Walking toward the door, he pulled his phone from his back pocket and punched a couple of buttons as the door slammed behind him.

"We'll be lucky if Mr. Nasille makes it here in one piece," Wynona murmured.

Violet chittered a laugh while Chief grumbled in annoyance.

"I believe a little more faith is in order, Ms…Wynona."

Wynona gave him a sheepish look. "You're right. Sorry."

The chief waved her concerns away. "Tell me what else you discovered at the circus. I don't think you ever came back to report after visiting there yesterday."

Wynona felt heat travel up her neck. "Uh…no. I needed a break and went home to do some research."

"Case related?'

She shook her head, wringing her fingers in her lap. Her search for a cure for Lusgu's curse had come up empty, but somehow she didn't think Lusgu would want her discussing the particulars of his predicament with anyone and everyone.

Chief Ligurio stared, then grunted. "Okay…did you discover anything while at the circus?"

Relaxing slightly that he wasn't going to push, Wynona nodded, then paused. "Not much related to whether or not it was a murder, but we spoke to the other owner of the circus, a man who goes by

Bud, and he basically told us any creature under that tent would be willing to take out Mr. Braxet if given half a chance."

Rascal walked back in. "Somehow I don't think our ambitious circus leader had many friends."

Wynona looked over her shoulder at him and nodded before going back to the chief. "Bud was a kitsune."

Chief's eyebrows shot up. "Really?"

"Yep."

"Don't see one of those every day," the vampire muttered.

"The whole circus is full of legendary creatures," Wynona gushed. "Though most of them are not quite…"

"Sane?" Rascal offered.

Wynona had to give him that. "Many of the creatures were in cages and from what I could see, it was for good reason. There was a bluecap, a manticore, a demon, though he wasn't in a cage," Wynona added.

"I also saw a genie," Rascal continued. "And there were a few creatures that looked human, so who knows what powers they held."

"And none of them were right in the head?" Chief asked.

"I don't know what the demon did for an act," Wynona said. "He was frightening to look at, but didn't appear unstable. However, the creatures in the cages weren't rational." She shivered. "I also discovered a new power."

"Not another one," Chief groaned, falling back in his seat. "Ms… Wynona…I can't keep up at this point."

"Good thing she's on our side then," Rascal said pointedly.

Chief Ligurio gave a grudging nod. "I suppose that's correct." He steepled his fingers and gave her an expectant look.

"When we walked through the curtain to the back of the circus, I could *feel* not only the immense amount of dark magic, but the emotions of the animals."

Violet huffed. *You could use that skill with me once in a while, you know.*

Wynona paused, then looked at her shoulder. "I hadn't thought of that. Can I really feel your emotions?"

Violet sniffed.

"Give it a try," Chief Ligurio snapped. "We'll never figure this all out otherwise, though the underworld only knows how this will help solve cases in the future."

"The onslaught nearly knocked her out," Rascal said through gritted teeth. "I'm not sure this is a power we actually want to keep using."

"Violet is only one mouse," Chief Ligurio argued with an amused smirk. "An entire circus worth of animals would be hard to handle, but a single mouse?" He tsked his tongue.

Wynona swallowed hard. "Okay…I think this would be a good thing to try. I'm not sure why it didn't occur to me before, or why I haven't felt you before, but now's as good a time as any, I suppose." She closed her eyes and reimagined what had happened when she'd walked into the circus.

Her muscles stiffened and she gasped when a phantom ache of the pain hit the back of her skull.

*Follow it*, Violet suggested.

Wynona's fingers gripped the arm rests of her chair and she was sure her knuckles were white and bloodless. Slowly, she pushed her consciousness toward the mass of writhing pain and despair, but she refused to be swallowed. Instead, she did her best to stay just on the outside and observe.

In her mind's eyes, it was a black, gaseous ball, constantly shifting and terrifyingly strong.

*Come on, Wynona,* Violet urged. *Find the link and follow it.*

Voices were speaking in muted tones and Wynona almost lost her concentration when she realized it was Rascal and Chief. Rascal sounded angry and it pulled at her, making her want to respond.

*He's always angry,* Violet snapped. *Now focus. Find the connecting cord. Move around the ball.*

A ball was a simple way to describe it, but Wynona followed her familiar's instructions. Shifting her view point, she moved around and around until she spotted what the mouse had been referring to. There at the bottom of the mass was a tiny, connecting string. It trailed away from the emotions and the further it went, the more it lightened.

Wynona imagined herself as a spirit, floating along the cord until it was a bright, white light that was difficult to look at. Deeper into her own brain than she had ever been consciously, she found the point where the string attached to its own core. Multiple strings, each a different color, were stemming from the heart of this power.

The two most prominent ones were gold and purple. *That's you, isn't it?* Wynona asked Violet, as she followed the purple string. It wasn't nearly as long of a cord as the black one was and Wynona quickly found the end, a small purple ball bursting with radiance.

Reaching out her mental fingers, Wynona brushed it and gasped, her body jerking at the punch of sensations. Arrogance, contentment, determination and love all intermingled together in a fast paced dance that Wynona could barely keep up with.

*Violet, I don't know how you handle all that in such a tiny body.*

Violet chittered. *I might look all cutesy and amazing, but inside I'm a roaring lion.*

Wynona chuckled. *The heart of a warrior. This is amazing.* She mentally looked back at the white center of power. *But what about that gold one?* Floating back, Wynona found the connection again and followed it.

The gold was blinding and before her fingers ever touched the heart, she knew she'd found her soulmate. His frustration, worry, love, and anger were awe-inspiring and Wynona pulled back quickly. She had the distinct impression that if she allowed herself to sit, she'd be completely consumed by him and would be happy to die there without ever coming back to reality.

Still feeling the connections on her fingertips, Wynona surfaced, blinking against the bright yellow lights of the chief's office. "Oh my word…" she gasped, putting a tingling hand to her chest. "I found you." She looked at Violet, then Rascal. "I found you both." She paused and her eyes widened. "I can still feel you!" Her breathing was heavy and her chest barely keeping up. "I can feel both your emotions… because you're animals!" The realization slapped her in the face. "I can feel the emotions of *animals* and that includes you, Rascal, because you have a wolf side!"

Chief Ligurio cleared his throat. "Fascinating as this is," he said in an ominous tone, "I'm afraid we discovered something while you were…researching."

Wynona stiffened. "What happened?" Rascal's hand landed on her shoulder and she reached up to hold onto his warmth and strength.

Chief sighed and pushed a hand through his hair, messing up his slick style. "Mr. Nasille was found dead inside one of his cars."

Wynona jerked back against the chair. "That can't be."

Chief Ligurio scowled. "Gather your things, Wynona. I think we just solved the question of suicide versus murder, but this development opens up a whole new can of sprites."

## CHAPTER 15

For the third time in two days, Wynona found herself at a place she was beginning to hate as much as her childhood home. She was, however, grateful that she was prepared to protect herself against the magic to be found here. That barrier was up in her mind as she and Rascal crossed the edge of the grounds. With Mr. Nasille dead, Wynona had a sneaking suspicion that she'd be able to feel everything no matter where she was.

"Doing okay?" Rascal grunted, his eyes focused on the winding road that led around to the backside of the compound. When he'd followed their connection earlier that morning, he'd discovered the hidden road. Most patrons wouldn't have looked twice, but Wynona was sure that the workers of the circus knew exactly how to get around without having to walk through the main tent.

"Fine," Wynona said, though her nerves were on edge. "But I can't figure out why someone would kill Mr. Nasille."

Rascal grumbled. "Maybe he was involved in Braxet's murder and a partner was shutting him up."

Wynona considered the idea, but discarded it. "I don't think so. If Mr. Nasille was involved, why would he put himself in the spotlight by kidnapping me?" She waited for Rascal's growling to calm down.

"It would seem to me that Mr. Nasille would want to be as far from the police eye as possible, not breaking laws left and right. That just seems stupid, and I don't think he was a stupid man. Angry, maybe... but not stupid."

Rascal threw the truck into park and paused before getting out. "Anger can make a man do stupid things," he offered. "Plus...if Mrs. Braxet was the killer, and his infatuation with her was as strong as you seemed to think, then I can see him doing some utterly dumb stuff to keep her attention."

"Again, I ask why?" Wynona opened her door and slid down just as Rascal came around the front of the truck. "Why draw attention to themselves? Why try to bribe me if she murdered her husband? Why murder him after already getting divorce papers ready?"

Rascal ground his teeth. "I don't know, but I don't like any of this. Multiple dead bodies always means trouble."

"Agreed." She took Rascal's hand as they walked up the open garage doors. All of them were open and from the sickly scent coming from inside, Wynona guessed it was to allow the toxic gas to filter out. "Are you going to be okay?" she asked Rascal. His wolfy sense of smell was probably going crazy right now.

Realizing she could probably sense his feelings, Wynona tried to open up that line she'd discovered earlier. Immediately, she was assaulted with pain and paralyzing depression and fear. She gasped and doubled over.

"Close it off, Wy," Rascal pleaded, wrapping his arms around her. "Close it off."

Squeezing her eyes tight, Wynona followed his orders, but it still took several moments for her to be able to stand upright without swaying. "Sorry," she rasped. "I was trying to sense your emotions and forgot I had that barrier in place for a reason."

"I guess we know you can feel things from a distance now," he grumbled. Shaking his head, he kept his arm wrapped around her shoulders. "Come on. Let's get this over with and then get you out of here. If you weren't already so involved, I'd cut you out, but you're the only link we've got to the ex right now."

"Widow," Wynona corrected. "And I wouldn't let you cut me off."

He gave her a sideways glare, but Wynona ignored him.

She knew his wolf instincts made him ultra protective, but she wasn't going to let their life together be her sitting at home twiddling her thumbs while he risked his life every time he walked out the door. She could help, and she would. He didn't have to like it, but she knew that ultimately he would understand. Despite his grumblings, she knew he wanted her happy more than anything else. He really was the perfect soulmate.

"Deputy Chief," an officer said as they walked in.

"Where's the body?" Rascal asked, his "in-charge" voice full and vibrant.

The officer pointed toward a group of creatures surrounding a large, black SUV. Wynona tugged on Rascal's arm. "That's the car he chased me down with."

Rascal growled and began walking. "Come on."

"Ms. Le Doux," Bud drawled as she and Rascal approached. The kitsune was standing just outside the officers and coroner. "What a surprise."

She raised her eyebrows. "Is it?"

Bud chuckled and dropped his arms from his hips. "Not really. But still…it seemed like the thing to say."

Wynona couldn't figure this guy out.

"Who found him?" Rascal demanded of the officers.

Bud raised his hand. "That would be me."

Rascal turned his glowing gaze on the kitsune. "Tell me what happened."

Bud shrugged, looking completely at ease. "I already went through this."

"Go through it again."

Giving Rascal a patient look, Bud turned to Wynona. "Phil wasn't answering his phone, and I needed a vehicle transfer set up. So I came to find him and…" He trailed off.

"What was the transfer for?" Rascal demanded.

Bud only gave the officer a passing glance. "I have a creature that needs to be taken to the hospital."

"What's wrong with it?" Wynona immediately asked, then regretted it. Bud's eyes seemed to see too much, even if she wasn't trying to hide anything. She was grateful Violet had decided to go home rather than take a joyride. Even the tiny, bloodthirsty creature wasn't a huge fan of murder scenes.

"Nothing to concern yourself over," Bud assured her. "It's a shifter who's due for some medication. The kind we can't administer in person."

Wynona frowned. She had no idea what that was supposed to mean.

*Later,* Rascal sent her way.

Wynona gave him a subtle nod. "Where was the body?"

Bud waved at the SUV. "Inside. It appears he closed the door and turned on the engine." The kitsune tsked his tongue. "Nasty business that. Either we have another suicide on our hands, or there's a creature loose."

"Is it possible you have someone loose?" Rascal asked, stepping in front of Wynona. It hadn't missed his notice that Bud seemed particularly interested in her.

Wynona didn't bother trying to maneuver around, she didn't like Bud focusing on her any more than Rascal did.

"There are security measures in place that would alert me if that were the case," Bud said, finally looking Rascal in the eye.

"And who put together that spell?" Wynona asked. "I'm assuming your backstage has become much louder now that the noise spell is no longer in effect. What else did Mr. Nasille help with?"

The kitsune gave her a toothy, utterly fake smile. "Sound was his specialty, so that was the only thing he did." He tilted his head consideringly. "Besides, if any of the creatures that have to be kept under lock and key were out and about, they certainly wouldn't have thought to plan out a killing such as this. It would have been much more…" His eyes flashed. "Messy."

Wynona swallowed back the bile in her throat. The owner was just as insane as the inhabitants. She could not, for the life of her, figure out why creatures were drawn to this kind of entertainment. It was sick.

"So you believe he was killed?" Rascal jumped back in. "This wasn't a suicide?"

Bud pursed his lips as if thinking. "Phil was…easily frightened and depressed, but I wouldn't have said he was suicidal."

"Any ideas who would want to kill him?" Rascal pressed.

Bud shook his head. "Unlike Brax, Phil was generally well liked among the staff. Those he knew anyway. He often kept to himself… not as social as some of the other workers…you understand."

"How long had he been with Mrs. Braxet?" Wynona knew she was jumping the gun a little, but she also was positive she wouldn't get the chance to talk to Mrs. Braxet anytime soon, dead lover or not.

Bud's eyebrows went up and an amused smirk crossed his face. "Well, well, well…you've been busy, Ms. Le Doux."

Wynona waited. His arrogance would demand he answer in a moment, not wanting to lose her attention. Rascal growled low and she put a hand on his back to calm him down. She needed these answers.

The amused grin grew. "I don't know when the affair began," Bud said carefully. "But I will say it wasn't new…nor was it the first." He gave a dramatic nod and turned to walk away.

"I hate that man," Rascal said in a low tone.

"I'm not fond of him myself," Wynona assured her fiance. "But he hasn't done anything you can take him in for."

"Maybe I need to take off the uniform—"

Wynona gasped. "Rascal!" she hissed, stepping up close. "Don't you dare say things like that." She searched his eyes for the playful hint that often accompanied his sarcastic comments, but there wasn't any.

One eyebrow twitched. "I'm trying here, Wy. But every time I turn around you're either in danger or someone is trying to take you away from me." His lip curled. "I don't know how much longer I can keep the wolf from striking out."

She stepped up even closer, ignoring all the milling officers, and cupped Rascal's face. *Rascal, listen to me very closely. I am YOURS. No one else's. I know we deal with a lot of junk in these cases and the creatures we run into are far from upstanding, but they are NOT competition. Most of them, Bud included, are scumbags and even if we weren't engaged I wouldn't give them the time of day.* She gave him a soft smile and left a too-short kiss on his lips. *I love you. Please trust in that.*

His shoulders slumped and his hands went to her waist, flexing several times. "I'm sorry," he said softly. "I just get so…"

Wynona nodded when his words trailed off. "I know. Me too."

"I think we should elope," he said with a grin as he stepped back. "You did promise we could get married today."

Wynona laughed and shook her head. "That would just solve everything, wouldn't it?"

"It would, actually." Looking a lot less like he wanted to kill someone, Rascal led her over to where the body lay. "Report!" he barked.

Azirad looked up, adjusting his red hat. "I don't see any sign of foul play, Deputy Chief. As far as I can tell, he died of carbon monoxide poisoning." His gnarled finger pointed to Mr. Nasille's chest. "You can see that he threw up at one point, which is a common symptom. But the fact that he didn't leave when that happened tells me he wanted to be there."

Wynona was feeling nauseous herself and she backed away a little.

*Do you see any magical foul play?* Rascal asked.

"Dang it," Wynona muttered. Without Daemon there, she was the only one they had who could see magical residue. *Hang on,* she replied. Blinking her vision on, she began to search the area. Grabbing Rascal's arm, she kept herself upright at the infusion of color permeating the space.

"What is it?" Rascal asked quickly, his arm going around her waist.

*There's way too much magic in this place to separate any of it,* Wynona replied, her eyes wide. Slowly, she turned a circle. Every square inch of the garage was covered in a film of multiple layers of colors. *Green is dominant, and I'm guessing that was Mr. Nasille's color, he was a nymph after all. Plus the color is all over the vehicles. It hasn't worn off yet since his death is so recent.*

Rascal waited patiently as she tried to work her way through it all.

*But nothing looks out of place. The mix of colors is almost like a painter's palette. In fact, some areas almost appear brown or black because there's so much mixed together. But it's like that everywhere.* She turned toward the body and tried to see if anything looked wrong. *His fingertips are green,* she added, giving credence to her thought that it was Mr. Nasille's magic. *But otherwise, he's clean.*

*In a place with so much magic, does that seem odd?* Rascal asked.

Wynona frowned, thinking about it for a moment. *I don't think so. I'm guessing the layers of color have to do with the sound spells and the safety spells and anything else they've needed in this crazy place. But Mr. Nasille himself wouldn't have needed a layer of spells. I don't think so anyway.*

Rascal huffed and Wynona blinked back into her normal vision.

"So there are no signs of foul play?" Rascal reiterated.

Wynona gave a subtle shake of her head just as the coroner answered the same.

Scrubbing a hand over his face, Rascal nodded. "Bag him and do whatever tests you need to to find out for sure. Be sure and let me know if anything else looks suspicious."

The redcap rolled his eyes. "Like I haven't done this for fifty years," he muttered before giving instructions to the workers he brought with him.

Rascal led Wynona away from the body, ignoring the disgruntled worker. "And nothing else looked out of place?"

Wynona pinched her lips and shrugged. "I don't know what each spell was for, so I can't exactly answer that. But the layers of magic were consistent through the space. That's all I can offer."

Rascal nodded. "Got it." He sighed. "Two dead people. The same company. Both look like suicides." He snorted. "I don't buy it."

"It does seem odd." Wynona put her hands on her hips. "But I wish we had a bit more to go on than simply intuition."

He chuckled. "Says the queen of following her gut." He kissed her temple. "Come on. Let's ask a few more questions, then report back to the chief. He'll want to hear about this."

"He won't be happy we're coming back with more questions than answers."

"He's never happy anyway," Rascal said cheerfully. "So I doubt our report will cause much pain."

Wynona smiled and laughed lightly. "Careful. He's got vampire hearing."

"And I've got wolf smell. It's why we make such a good team."

Still smiling, Wynona followed Rascal as they questioned a few more officers before going back to the station.

## CHAPTER 16

*You need to come back to the house.*

Wynona frowned and put a hand on Rascal's arm. "Hang on," she told him. "Violet's talking."

Rascal put on his lights, then jerked the wheel and parked half on, half off of the sidewalk.

Wynona gave him a look.

"Perks," he reminded her with a wolfish grin.

Rolling her eyes, Wynona put her concentration back on her familiar. *Violet? What's going on? Are you okay?*

*I'm fine, but there's someone here you need to see.*

*Can you tell me who?* Wynona pressed. *I've had enough nasty surprises in this case, I'd rather not have another one.*

*I don't know her name,* Violet said. *But Lusgu let her in and she was the stupid incubus's secretary.* She snickered, but Wynona gasped.

"Cookie?" Wynona said out loud, looking at Rascal with wide eyes.

Glancing over his shoulder, he roared the truck into action, causing a few screeches from angry drivers and headed out toward Wynona's house.

*Keep her there,* Wynona instructed Violet. *We need to talk to her.*

*I thought as much,* Violet said smugly. *Lusgu has her occupied, but she's shaking like a leaf and her image keeps flickering in and out. I'm not sure what kind of magic she has, but she's barely holding on.*

"Right." Wynona took a long, cleansing breath, but it did nothing to calm her racing heart. *We'll be there as soon as we can,* she assured her familiar.

*Sounds good.*

Wynona held onto the bar above her seat with all she was worth as Rascal navigated the city streets, then hit the gas once they were outside the limits. Living so close to the Grove of Secrets let her enjoy peace, quiet and a little extra magic. But it also meant that in times like this, when they were in a hurry, it seemed to take forever to reach her cabin.

With dust billowing behind them, Rascal finally slammed on the breaks in her gravel driveway. "Hang on," he said in a harsh tone, jumping from his seat. He ran around to her side and whipped open the passenger door. "Sorry about how rough it was," he said, helping her down with a gentleness that was at odds with the tone in his voice. After closing the door, he grabbed his stun gun and made sure Wynona was behind him.

"Do you really think that's necessary?" Wynona asked, her jaw dropping.

Rascal nodded. "She ran out of a crime scene and has been missing ever since. Innocent people don't just disappear for days on end."

Wynona nodded, understanding his logic, but she didn't believe that petite creature could have anything to do with Mr. Braxet's death. Nonetheless, she followed Rascal up to the front door, where he walked in carefully.

Soft, murmured voices were coming from the kitchen area and she and Rascal headed that way. The clinking of a teacup let Wynona know that Lusgu had taken care of her guest in every way possible and she felt a soft lurch of affection for the brownie who obviously had a soft heart, despite his grumpy behavior.

Cookie's back was to them when Rascal crossed the threshold of the kitchen. "Stand up slowly, Ms. Floura," he said in a steady, commanding tone.

Violet had been right. Cookie was shaking like a leaf and her image flickered as if she were almost incorporeal.

Wynona stared, fascinated. Ms. Floura was *not* a ghost. So what was going on with her?

"Turn around with your hands where I can see them," Rascal continued.

Wynona blinked a couple of times and turned on her sight. She needed to see the magic behind this flickering. It was like nothing she'd ever seen before. "Oh!" Wynona cried when Cookie gasped at Rascal's gun and disappeared completely.

Well...almost completely. With her sight on, Wynona could see a very tiny fleck of pink, like a fleck of glitter, floating just above where Ms. Floura's head had been.

"Where'd she go?" Rascal growled.

"Hold on," Wynona said softly, her focus transfixed. She touched Rascal's arm and slowly walked forward. "Cookie? Can you hear me?"

The fleck bounced up and down a few times.

A disbelieving laugh bubbled up from Wynona's throat. "Rascal..." she said breathlessly. "She's still here. But she's really, really small."

"A portune," Lusgu offered.

Wynona's eyes widened. "Just how many creatures of legend does that circus have a hold of?" she asked, her temper flaring. Shaking her head, Wynona waved behind her at Rascal. "Put away the gun. It's going to be alright."

"No."

"Rascal..." Wynona warned. "Please."

Huffing and growling, he did as she asked. "Come out, Ms. Floura. We need to talk."

It took a few moments, but finally the glitter speck flashed and turned back into the fairy.

Wynona blinked away her magical sight and smiled kindly down at the woman. "You didn't tell me you were a portune."

Cookie wrung her hands, her knuckles white and tightly stretched. "It's not something I share all the time."

"Please...sit," Wynona said, indicating the chair Cookie had occupied before. "No one here will hurt you, but we do need some answers."

Cookie eyed Rascal fearfully, then nodded her trembling chin and sat down.

Wynona sat across from her and waited for Rascal to stand behind her chair. She knew he'd be too worked up to sit down.

"Before we get started on anything else," Rascal snapped, "I need to know what a portune is."

Wynona smiled up at him, then looked back at Cookie, who still looked ready to bolt. "They're a special, rare type of fairy," she explained.

Lusgu snorted. "They hate attention and are easily spooked," he added.

Cookie hung her head.

"It's okay, Cookie," Wynona said softly. "I promised you were safe here, and you are. These two are all bark and no bite."

*Haha,* Rascal sent to her.

*Good one,* Violet said with a laugh. She climbed the table leg and Wynona put her on her shoulder. *I'll have to remember that, eh, Wolfy?*

He flashed his teeth at the purple mouse, which only made Violet laugh harder.

Cookie's eyes darted around from creature to creature, but she nodded at Wynona again.

"When portunes get frightened," Wynona continued, offering her remarks mostly to Rascal, "their defense mechanism is to transform into a speck. One too small for most creatures to see with the naked eye."

Cookie narrowed her wide eyes and studied Wynona. "How did you see me? Witches shouldn't be able to do that."

Wynona hesitated, but finally decided it didn't hurt to tell Cookie the truth. She didn't often share the magnitude of her powers, it tended to scare creatures off. "I can see magic," Wynona explained. "So when you disappeared, I was able to still see a tiny, flittering piece of color, letting me know you were there."

"Ah." Cookie nodded slowly. "I see." She chewed her lip. "But you couldn't do that at the police station?"

"I wasn't using that power at the time," Wynona explained. She folded her hands on the table and leaned forward. "Speaking of, why don't you tell us what happened at the station and where you've been for the last few days? Have you heard that Mr. Nasille was killed?"

Tears filled the fairy's extra-large eyes and she bit her bottom lip again while shaking her head. "No. I didn't know." A tiny fist slammed onto the table. "I *knew* he needed to stay away from Mrs. Braxet. She's nothing but an evil seductress."

"I don't think she can help some of it," Wynona offered. "It comes with being a siren."

"Hmph."

"But…at the station?"

Cookie closed her eyes and slumped in her seat with a sigh. "I was already upset about being at the station," she explained. "I hate crowds. Even though I work…worked…for Mr. Braxet, I never went into the main arena. I had a small office that had an outside entrance, so I very rarely dealt with more than two or three creatures at a time."

Wynona nodded her encouragement.

Cookie's bottom lip trembled. "Earlier that day, Mr. Braxet and I had had a fight." Tears trickled down her soft cheeks. "I hate fighting, but…" Pink eyes came up to Wynona, then back down to Cookie's lap. "But I knew he was going to confront you about building a cafe in the circus…and I didn't agree with it."

"What part didn't you agree with?" Wynona pressed.

"The part where he was trying to create a relationship with a witch who was clearly stronger than he was and had connections to the president," Cookie said in a rush. "Mr. Braxet might give me an office to stay away from people, but he doesn't honor his commitments… ever." She leaned forward, her eyes pleading with Wynona to understand. "He'd have used and abused your contract," Cookie said in a raspy whisper. "And if even half the rumors are true about your powers, then I knew he was in way over his head, even if you're one of the nicest people I've met."

Wynona could feel heat climbing up her neck and into her face. She really wasn't quite sure what to take from this conversation. "So, you thought that if things went sour in our contract that I'd use my powers to hurt Mr. Braxet?"

Cookie nodded jerkily. "Something like that. Or hurt the circus. I might not agree with everything that goes on there, but there are dozens of creatures, like me, who have found a refuge there. We don't like Mr. Braxet necessarily, but...it's our home. And without it..." She shrugged as if that was enough of an answer.

*Don't let it bother you*, Rascal said, squeezing Wynona's shoulder. *We both know you'd never retaliate like that.*

*Clearly, they were thinking of me*, Violet said with a sniff, her tail curling around Wynona's neck. *My ferocity precedes me, it seems.*

A broken laugh almost made it out of Wynona before she swallowed it back down. She tried so hard to be the opposite of her family and at times felt like she was succeeding at changing the public's opinion of her and witches in general, only to have moments like this hit her in the gut like a lead cauldron.

"I can see now that you would never have done that," Cookie continued, "but I didn't know that at the time and I didn't want to risk myself and everyone else who might get caught in the crossfire."

Wynona nodded. "Okay," she said carefully. "So when you saw his body?"

Cookie splayed her hands to the side. "My instincts took over and I disappeared, then left as quickly as I could."

"Why not come back immediately? Why stay away so long?" Rascal asked.

Cookie made a face and shrunk in her seat. "Because even for a portune, I'm...defective."

"Explain," Rascal snapped.

"I get stuck in my small form if I can't get my fear under control."

The room was silent as the group processed the words.

"So you've been stuck all this time?" Wynona clarified.

Cookie wouldn't look her in the eye, but nodded.

"And you just today were able to break out and back into your regular size?"

Again the fairy nodded.

Wynona blinked a few times. "Wow…I'm sorry. That must have been terribly frustrating."

The fairy pointed at her. "There. That right there. That's why I came here. You're much nicer than I expected and I knew I'd be able to be in control if you were here."

Rascal huffed. "Well, I hate to break it to you, but I'm afraid you're going to have to come down to the station and make a statement." He put his hands in the air when her image flickered. "I'm not arresting you, Ms. Floura, but you need to make a formal statement about everything you just told us. Plus, I'm sure Chief Ligurio will have a few questions for you."

Cookie looked to Wynona. "Can you come with me? Do I have to go alone?"

Wynon gave the fairy a sympathetic smile. "It will be better for the statement if I'm not there, so as not to look like I'm playing favorites or guiding your answers. I'm sorry."

Cookie nodded in understanding, but she was clearly not happy about it.

Rascal leaned down and kissed Wynona's cheek. "I'll run her in and then be back."

*I'm going to call Daemon and Prim and have them come over,* Wynona said through their mental link, not wanting Cookie to know everything that was going on. *I think we four should sit and talk. Daemon always has a good head on his shoulders and I think we should take his story and what we've gathered and try to put it all together. Maybe there's something we've missed.*

Rascal nodded and guided Ms. Floura away. The fairy was shaking with every step, but her image appeared steady and Wynona hoped it would stay that way.

As the front door closed, she turned to Lusgu. "I'm going to have a few guests over. Do you want to stay?"

He made a face. "No."

Wynona nodded. "Thank you for taking care of Cookie until we could get here."

He huffed and slipped out of his seat. "Someone had to keep her from disappearing. If you can get rid of this case, maybe we can get back to the grimoires."

Wynona smiled slightly as Lusgu disappeared through the closet. He was a difficult creature to understand. He was mean, rude and contentious. But underneath it all, Wynona had seen a few instances where his heart was definitely in the right place. Today had been one of those moments and Wynona tucked it away for later consideration. She needed to remember these times when she was angry with him. Sometimes they were the only thing that kept her going when everything appeared as bleak as it did right now.

## CHAPTER 17

"Can't...breathe..." Wynona gasped as Prim squeezed her tight.

Prim relaxed and backed off a little. "Sorry," she gushed. "It's just been too long and I'm so glad you're clearing Daemon's name." She looked over her shoulder at the tall, silent man behind her.

Daemon gave Prim a small smile, but Wynona could see how strained it was. "We'll get this cleared up," she told her friend. "No one really suspects you anyway, you were just in the wrong place at the wrong time."

Daemon shrugged. "I understand." The dark circles under his eyes and pale sheen to his skin said he was struggling more than he was willing to let on.

Knowing the best thing she could do would be to get down to business, Wynona ushered them inside. "Come into the kitchen. I've got tea and some cookies."

*About time they arrived,* Violet complained. *If I had to wait any longer, I was going to hide the cookies all together.*

Wynona rolled her eyes. *We're sharing,* she told her mouse. *I made them for the guests.*

*I'm a guest.*

*You live here.*

Violet grumbled.

Once at the table, Wynona handed a cookie over to Violet, then passed the plate to Daemon and Prim, before reading each of them for a custom blend. "Fenugreek and turmeric," she muttered to herself while working her magic through the kitchen. It only took minutes to have cups in front of everyone. "Rascal had to run an errand to the station, and then he'll be back," Wynona informed everyone. She sat and clasped her hands around a mug. The heat penetrated her cool fingers and she felt herself relax slightly. "How are you holding up?" she asked Daemon.

Daemon shrugged. "I'm fine."

"Are you keeping busy or taking the opportunity to sit in front of the television with junk food?" Wynona teased, trying to get him to open up a little.

One side of Daemon's side quirked up, but the sadness in his eyes didn't budge. "I've been helping Prim at the greenhouse."

Wynona smiled at her friend, who beamed up at the black hole. *I think he's her boyfriend,* she thought.

*They're holding hands under the table,* Violet offered. *I think that's a fair assessment.*

Wynona hid her smile behind her cup. "Okay...so can you tell me exactly what happened on the afternoon Mr. Braxet was killed? I know you told a quick version at the station, but I'd like to hear the longer story."

Daemon shook his head. "There wasn't much more to tell. I stepped away for a bathroom break. The door had to have been unmanned for less than five minutes."

"Which is plenty long enough for someone to slip inside and off the guy," Prim said through a clenched jaw.

Wynona frowned. "Get inside, yes, but is it enough time for someone to get away? Mr. Braxet was sitting in his seat. It didn't look like there had been a struggle."

"So you think it was a suicide," Daemon said flatly.

Wynona tilted her head. "No, I don't. It doesn't make sense that he would kill himself just hours after asking me to join in on his business."

Daemon nodded firmly. "I've seen depressed and despairing men. Braxet wasn't one of them."

"I do find it interesting, however, that he wasn't killed with magic," Wynona said. "Especially since the person involved waited until you were gone. It seems that magic would have been quicker."

"But it's also easier to trace," Prim said.

Wynona paused. "You realize that that just implicates that this was someone in the station. They all know that Daemon can see magic. If an officer killed Mr. Braxet, they would have known that Daemon could see the residue."

Daemon slumped, his fingers toying with the tiny teacup. "I can't believe we have a mole. It just doesn't seem possible."

"A grudge makes people do things they wouldn't normally do," Wynona said softly.

"So you think this was premeditated?"

Wynona shook her head as she swallowed some tea and set the cup down. "I don't see how it could have been. No one would have known that Mr. Braxet was coming to the station that day."

"True," Prim responded. She leaned onto her elbows. "What can you tell us about what's going on?"

Wynona pinched her lips together. *Rascal...can I share what we know?*

He sighed in her mind. *Yeah, but keep it on the down-low. Technically, Skymaw's an officer, but he's on leave. He has to promise not to do anything with the information.*

Wynona nodded. *Got it.*

*I'll be there in about ten.*

"Rascal's almost here," Wynona announced. "And he said it's okay to tell you as long as Daemon promises not to use the information to go after anyone."

Daemon's eyes flashed a deep, fathomless black, but he nodded. His clenched jaw, however, said he didn't like it.

Wynona gave him a pleading look. "Please, Daemon. Let us handle it, okay? We know you aren't guilty and Chief has said that it was the best way he could protect you."

"I know."

The words were deep and dark, but Wynona took him at his word.

"Okay…I'm just gonna lay it all out, including stuff you probably already know."

Prim nodded eagerly.

"Mr. Braxet was killed in an interrogation room. One shot to the temple. No magic was involved and by all standards it looked like a suicide, but he didn't have a gun on him when he was taken in. He was visited by his chauffeur, his bodyguard and I was walking with his secretary when we discovered his body." She paused. "I just now realized that I haven't spoken to the bodyguard yet."

Daemon tapped his long fingers on the table. "He didn't have much to say. His conversation with Braxet was short. There was some shouting and Braxet accused the man of wanting to save his own skin. Then the creature stormed out, leaving Braxet behind."

Wynona pursed her lips, then jolted when the front door opened.

"Honey! I'm home!" Rascal called as he came into the kitchen. He grinned and kissed the top of Wynona's head.

She smiled up at him. "Have a seat. I've got cookies."

"Ah…" He slipped into the chair beside her. "If I wasn't already in love with you, I would be now."

Wynona scoffed and shoved against his shoulder, but the wolf only chuckled.

Rascal nodded with his mouth full. "Prim. Skymaw."

"Deputy Chief," Daemon said, more formally than he had been a minute ago.

"Well, if it isn't wolfy-boy," Prim teased.

Rascal flashed her a sharp-toothed smile. "What were you talking about?" he asked around another cookie.

"Going through all the facts," Wynona stated, pouring him some tea. "I just realized we didn't talk to the bodyguard. Do you know his name?"

Rascal nodded. "Yeah. He goes by Echoe."

Wynona waited. "That's it? Echoe?"

"Yep." Rascal put another cookie in his mouth.

"What is he exactly?" Prim asked. "That's kind of an odd name, unless he was, like, a wrestler or something."

"He's a nightmare shifter."

Wynona gasped. "I don't know why I keep finding myself surprised at all these creatures," she said with a shake of her head. "That circus might truly be cursed in some ways, but their luck in finding creatures only heard of in storybooks is unbelievable."

"Or...it's like Ms. Floura said," Rascal pointed out. "These creatures come to them because they're looking for somewhere to belong. When you're the only one of your kind, it's hard not to feel like a sore thumb in public. Especially if other creatures are scared of your powers."

Wynona nodded slowly. "I suppose being able to turn into people's worst fears would make a creature quite the topic of gossip."

Rascal nodded.

Prim whistled under her breath. "That's crazy." She leaned back when Daemon gently massaged her neck. "So you need to talk to the nightmare. What else?"

Wynona splayed her hands at the table. "We met the co-owner of the circus. He goes by Bud. He told us Braxet was generally hated among the crew. He was a little too ambitious to care about anyone else's wellbeing but his own."

"Nice," Prim said sarcastically.

"Braxet's chauffeur, Mr. Nasille, popped up dead this morning," Rascal added. "After he and the ex-wife kidnapped Wynona."

Prim's pink eyes widened to the size of dinner plates. "Wait, wait, wait...back up the circus train. Kidnapped?"

Wynona rolled her eyes. "It wasn't quite that bad."

Rascal growled. "He followed you in his car, knocked you out, and took you back to the garage where they kept you hostage until the ex-wife had a chance to bribe you to declare the case a murder so she could get the life insurance payout." He leaned in nose to nose with Wynona. "It was kidnapping, plain and simple."

"Why do all the exciting things happen without me!" Prim shouted, throwing her arms in the air.

*It wasn't that exciting,* Violet grumbled. *Those two were plum loco and I wasn't allowed to eat anyone.*

Wynona threw back her head with a groan. "For the last time, Violet. You can't eat anyone."

A moment of stunned silence was followed by snickering and heavy laughter.

Violet stood on her back legs and glared at the group. *Let me at 'em,* she ground out, stalking toward Prim, who was laughing the hardest. *I wonder if fairies taste like glitter.*

"Oh for goodness sake," Wynona said, scooping the irate mouse into her hands. "Can we get back to the topic at hand?"

Violet wiggled violently until Wynona finally handed her off to Rascal, who cooed softly in her ear until the mouse huffed and calmed down. With a smirk, Rascal put the creature in his front pocket and leaned back in his chair, pumping his eyebrows at Wynona.

*Charmer.*

His eyebrows went on another up and down adventure.

"Okay," Prim said on a sigh, wiping at her eyes. "Kidnapped, bribed and finally released. When was this Nasille guy killed?"

"After I left," Wynona said, the topic drawing the humor out of the situation. "It was another situation where it was meant to look like a suicide and no magic was involved."

"And you don't believe the crime scene," Daemon stated.

Wynona shook her head. "No. Again, the man had plans. Why kidnap me and then kill himself? He and Mrs. Braxet were awfully chummy. With the husband out of the way, this was his chance. Why throw it away?"

Rascal pursed his lips and nodded as he nibbled another cookie.

"You're not going to want dinner," Wynona pointed out.

"I don't think I've ever actually reached my limit," Rascal stated proudly.

Wynona laughed softly.

"So two murders, no magic and no real clues," Prim summed up.

"That's about it," Wynona said.

"And the ex? Would she be willing to kill?" Daemon asked.

"I don't think so, but she's gone into hiding and we can't ask her more questions," Wynona grumbled.

Daemon pinched his lips and tapped the table more rapidly. "Isn't there anything to help?"

"I think the first order of business is to prove that they're murders," Rascal said firmly. "It's hard to arrest people if we don't have evidence the victims were actually killed by another creature."

"True," Wynona murmured, deep in thought.

"I'm assuming the ex and the bodyguard are suspects?" Prim poured herself more tea.

"And the secretary," Wynona added. "Though I don't think she's guilty."

"And your gut is always right," Prim said with a smirk.

"Yes it is," Wynona said with a playful sniff.

Rascal chuckled. "Witchy intuition," he grumbled good-naturedly.

"So now what?" Daemon asked. "It doesn't sound like you have anything to go on."

Wynona took a deep breath and she and Rascal exchanged looks. "I think maybe the bodyguard?" she asked. "It's a long shot, but maybe we can get something from him?"

"It's as good an idea as any," Rascal conceded. "After that, if we still have nothing, then we can circle back."

"Maybe we should look closer at the crime scene," Wynona declared. "I never did get to study the interrogation room much."

"We'll plan on it." Rascal dusted the cookie crumbs from his fingers and leaned in close. "Now…what should we have for dinner?"

Wynona gave him an extra sweet smile. "I need to do a little research," she cooed. "Maybe tonight it's your night to cook."

"I see how this is going be." Rascal gave her a glare.

"Yes…you do."

"I'll cook!" Prim hopped to her feet. "What kind of greens do you have?"

"Nope!" Rascal rushed after her. "I got it!"

Wynona laughed and was grateful to see Daemon smiling as well. Prim's vegetable-driven diet had always been a source of contention with Rascal's desire for meat. It was nice to see the old rivalry was helping pull Daemon out of his doldrums.

*We need to get this figured out*, Wynona sent to Rascal. *I don't like seeing Daemon so sad. Not when I can do something about it.*

*Agreed*, Rascal replied. *Put a bad guy behind bars and save a cop's life. Nothing better.*

Wynona's smile dropped. *You realize there's a possibility an officer was involved?*

Rascal growled low. *A bad cop is a bad cop. He, more than anyone, deserves to be taken out.*

Wynona sighed. She knew this would be a personal thing for the men. Knowing there was a mole among their ranks would be a hard thing to handle. Rising, she headed to her bedroom. If Rascal and Prim were taking over dinner, then Wynona was going to read the grimoire. Maybe a fresh set of eyes would help her find what she was looking for. After all…Lusgu needed her just as much as Daemon did.

## CHAPTER 18

"This is where he lives?" Wynona asked as she and Rascal pulled up to a dilapidated apartment building.

Rascal checked his phone. "Yep."

"I'm surprised he doesn't live at the circus," Wynona mused. "Everyone else seemed to."

"Maybe he likes having a little more privacy than that."

Wynona frowned. "And maybe he killed his boss because he didn't make enough to live on." She waved at the frightening looking place. "Who would choose to live here?"

"The type of creature who frightens small children without even looking at them," Rascal said with a grunt. He opened his door. "Hang on. I'll come get you."

Wynona sat still, smiling softly to herself. She loved that Rascal was so intent on being a gentleman with her. She wasn't sure how many men there were still like that in the world, but here was one… and this one was all hers. "Thank you," she said softly as he helped her down.

Stepping back, she looked up at the apartment building again. "I'm a little afraid to go inside."

"Can you pull your magic up?" Rascal asked, his hand on his stun gun. "I've been to places like this before and I don't want us going in unprepared." His golden eyes gave her a sideways glance. "In fact, if you want to wait this one out, I'll take you back right now."

Wynona shook her head. "If you think I'm letting you go in there alone, you better think again."

"I've done this before."

"But I have magic that can protect us," Wynona argued back.

Rascal rolled his eyes. "No one gets past the wolf."

"Let's make sure it doesn't come to that, Mr. Ego," Wynona teased. She started walking. "Are you coming?"

Giving her a playful growl, Rascal caught up and walked beside her.

She bit back a small laugh, knowing he desperately wanted to step in front so he could protect her, but was being too much of a gentleman. It was just another reason that she loved him.

Rascal pulled open the front door, dutifully ignoring the broken glass at the bottom of the frame and looking inside before allowing Wynona over the threshold.

As soon as she was inside, Rascal stepped up, his stun gun in his hand. Rotting wood and wet carpets made Wynona wrinkle her nose. Who knew what kind of mold was growing in a place like this. It seemed such an odd choice for a creature who had a full time job.

"We need to go up three flights," Rascal muttered. "Somehow I'm doubting we'll find elevators."

"I'm not sure I'd trust them even if we did," Wynona said.

"Do you feel okay?" Rascal asked. "No weird emotions or anything?"

Wynona paused. "You know, I've been so careful to have my shield up that I'm not feeling anything at the moment." She pinched her lips. "Hold still a second while I give it a try."

"Careful," Rascal warned right before she gasped, grabbing her chest.

Wynona had her shields up immediately and she closed her eyes to get her equilibrium back. "There's a lot of anger here," she wheezed.

"I could have guessed," Rascal grumbled, his arm around her waist. "Anything in particular we should note?"

Wynona shook her head, then stilled. "Hold me for a moment, please. I want to try again."

Rascal's arm tightened and she could see by the set of his jaw that he wasn't happy about her desire, but he let her go.

Instead of bringing the shield down, Wynona decided to try simply thinning it. She didn't want to let everything in, but she wanted to try and understand what was there. Instead of imagining an impenetrable steel wall in her mind, she slowly worked to make the walls transparent. Her walls, which had been opaque, became first glass...then something infinitely more limber.

She imagined she could see the emotions floating in a fog around the cover and reached out, letting her fingers brush the soft shield. Her hand jerked back when a hateful emotion shot up her arm like a lightning shot. *Black is hate,* she muttered. Moving on, she tried the green fog next to the black. Jealousy made her stomach churn. The red of anger caused her skin to flush and her heart to race.

"Wynona," Rascal said firmly, giving her a slight shake. "Wynona, come out of it."

Wynona shook her head, rebuilding her shield and coming back to the present. "Whoa..." She put a hand to her forehead until the world stopped spinning. "That was different."

"Please don't tell me you found another power," Rascal groaned. "I love you, sweetheart, but I can't keep up."

Wynona shook her head. "No, I just found some ways to use this one, I guess." She cleared her throat. "I discovered I can touch the individual emotions." She scowled. "But I can't tell where they're coming from, so it's not that helpful." She huffed. "But I did manage to give them useful colors."

"Great. Let's take that rainbow and get this over with." He took her hand and began dragging her toward the stairs.

Wynona stumbled a moment before catching her feet. "Why are we in such a hurry?" she whispered, eyeing the peeling wallpaper and smears of black in every corner.

"Because there are lots of eyes on us right now," Rascal whispered back. *And I don't want them to get any ideas.*

Wynona swallowed and nodded, picking up her pace. They worked their way through the small staircase and finally landed on the third floor. Wynona almost gasped for breath once they came out of the stairwell. She had never been one to get claustrophobic, but something was pushing on her shield with ferocity while they were closed in and Wynona was glad to be out.

"Three-oh-four," Rascal announced as they reached the door. Making a fist, he banged hard on the wood, rattling the walls with every hit.

Wynona warily watched the other doors, positive someone was going to come out and scream at them for making such noise.

Letting go of Wynona's hand, Rascal shifted his weight and pulled out his stun gun.

Unsure how else to help, Wynona allowed her magic to spark between her fingertips. She didn't want to come across as threatening, but she also didn't want to be caught off guard.

"Who's there?" a thick voice bellowed.

"Hex Haven Police," Rascal shouted back. "Open up, Echoe."

Wynona didn't miss the sound of several doors slamming and she was positive Rascal didn't either. Curious neighbors must have decided they didn't want to be involved with a police raid.

The door in front of them, however, suddenly swung wide, startling Wynona and causing her to jump. "Deputy Chief?" Echoe said, his heavy accent making his words difficult to understand. "Why are you here?"

Rascal straightened slightly, acknowledging that Echoe wasn't being threatening. "Can we come in?" He waved toward Wynona.

Echoe's eyes widened. "Yah, yah. Come in." He backed up, waving them inside.

Wynona followed Rascal inside, then stood awkwardly in the middle of the sitting room as she waited for Echoe to shut the door.

"Why are you here?" Echoe asked again. He stood with his back to the door, legs apart and arms folded over his chest.

When Wynona looked up, Echoe's dark eyes darted away, as if he was afraid to be caught looking at her. She frowned when she noticed a bead of sweat trickling down his temple. Was he nervous? Wynona glanced at Rascal, who was mimicking Echoe's stance.

"Ms. Le Doux would like to ask you some questions about Braxet's death."

Echoe glanced at Wynona again, then at the ground. "I told police everything," he said, his voice softer than expected.

Wynona gave him a tentative smile, though the creature wasn't looking at her. He was impressively large and it was interesting to think that he could shift into a person's greatest nightmare. Did it hurt when he shifted? Did he retain his mental faculties?

"Wy?" Rascal pressed.

"Oh, yes, sorry." Wynona clasped her hands at her waist. "Mr...Echoe," she said, mentally smacking herself for being so awkward. "How long did you work for Mr. Braxet?"

"Since I was young," came the answer. Echoe shifted his weight.

"What did you do for him?"

Echoe jerked slightly, looking away from her and Rascal. "Whatever he ask."

Wynona gave Rascal an exasperated look, but he shrugged. Apparently, he wasn't sure how to get the creature to open up either. "Did you enjoy working for the circus?"

"I work for Mr. Braxet," Echoe clarified.

Wynona hesitated. "So you weren't involved with anyone else? You worked strictly for Mr. Braxet?"

Echoe nodded curtly. "I have appointment. Will this take long?" He wiped at his forehead and Wynona noticed he was still sweating.

*What is going on?* she asked Rascal.

*No idea, but I don't like it. He's a little too eager to be rid of us, but then again...he's probably spent his entire life skirting the line of legal versus illegal. He's probably not very comfortable around the cops.*

*Maybe.* "Can you tell me what you and Mr. Braxet fought about before he was killed?" Wynona asked.

Echoe's head snapped in her direction, looking fierce for the first time since they'd arrived. After a moment of staring, he dropped his gaze again.

Wynona huffed. "Mr. Echoe?"

"Echoe," he corrected. "My name is Echoe."

"Alright...Echoe. What did you fight about?"

Echoe shifted his weight again, his eyes darting to the door, then back to the floor. "We fight about money."

Wynona's shoulder fell slightly. "Did he pay you enough?" she asked gently. "I'm surprised you live here instead of the circus. I've noticed most of the workers live on the property."

Echoe shrugged. "I can live there, but do not like being so close. Mr. Braxet not want to pay enough for me to have rent money. He say he provide house, and I don't need more."

It took a moment for Wynona to translate what he said. "So he paid you less because he offered you housing at the circus?" she clarified.

The shifter nodded.

"And you wanted him to pay you enough to live on your own."

Another nod.

"Echoe...did you kill Mr. Braxet?"

Echoe tensed and his lip curled. Wynona saw Rascal step in her direction and put his hand on his gun. "I not kill *anyone*," Echoe shouted. "I protect him!"

Wynona put her hands in the air, hoping Echoe couldn't see how they were trembling. She was getting the feeling that the creature wasn't completely stable, but also that he truly didn't want to hurt anyone. In fact, a sneaking suspicion in the back of her mind told her that if she knew his childhood story, she'd cry for whatever he went through. There had to be a reason someone as strong as Echoe would be loyal to a man who didn't pay him enough to live on.

*Like Ms. Floura said,* Rascal ground out. *It's the only place creatures like them find belonging.*

Wynona gave a subtle nod. "Thank you for your time, Echoe," she said carefully. "We'll leave now."

Echoe's shoulders stopped heaving and he wiped at his forehead again, swallowing hard. Without saying a word, he grabbed the door and swung it open.

Wynona worked hard to keep herself calm as they walked past the giant and into the hallway. "Thank you for your time," she said right before the door closed in their faces.

Rascal snorted. "Please tell me you got what you need."

Wynona gave Rascal a look and nodded toward the stairwell. She found herself holding her breath until they were outside, but the darkening sky didn't help loosen the heavy blanket that was trying to settle over them. "Something wasn't right," Wynona said softly as they got in the truck.

"Hang on," Rascal said tightly. He lifted her into her side of the truck, then hurried around to his. Without another word, he drove down a couple of blocks, pulled into an alley, then parked the truck.

"What are we doing?" Wynona asked.

"He's going to run," Rascal said as he prepared to jump out of his seat again. "He's got all the classic signs."

"So you think he's the killer?"

Rascal shrugged, holding his door. "Not sure. But running doesn't make it look good." His brows pushed together. "Wait here." With a slam that shook the truck, Rascal shifted into his wolf and disappeared.

"Not a chance," Wynona muttered, getting out of the truck. She brought her magic to her fingertips and headed toward the entrance of the alley. She could protect herself now and she wasn't about to let Rascal take down the nightmare alone.

## CHAPTER 19

Wynona couldn't see anything down the street. In fact, it was eerily quiet, as if all the inhabitants could tell that something was about to go down. She slid along the side of the building, then stepped out into the open with a lunge.

*Act casual,* she reminded herself, then laughed lightly. "I'm such an idiot." Putting her chin high, she slowly worked her way back toward the apartment building she and Rascal had just left.

A shout caught her attention and Wynona froze as a body came barreling around the corner, followed quickly by a wolf, who was snarling and gaining ground.

Echoe looked over his shoulder and tripped, hitting the pavement with a cry. The briefcase in his hand bounced away and broke open, money flying into the air like confetti.

Wynona's eyes were open wide as she watched it begin to litter the street and sidewalk. "Oh my…" Her attention came back to the fight when Rascal whined. Snapping her gaze down, she gasped at the sight of Rascal limping as he paced around Echoe.

Echoe had climbed to his feet, his muscles bulging and…

Wynona blinked. He was *growing*. His clothes began to tear at the seams as Echoe's body shifted and Wynona knew deep in her gut that she was about to see a nightmare come to life. A rage and protectiveness she had only felt twice before overtook her common sense and she threw a hand toward the creature, not quite knowing what she was doing.

Purple magic flung into the street and landed on Echoe like a thick net. Wynona's fingers stayed outstretched and she watched herself from a sort of detached state as she manipulated the blanket until Echoe fell to the ground with a grunt. The netting pinned him to the pavement and she could feel his struggles for freedom, but eventually they ceased.

Slowly, she walked toward the scene, still holding her magic in place and watching for any signs that the creature was going to break free.

"He can't breathe, Wy!" Rascal shouted, back in his human form. A cut on his arm was bleeding, but he was looking at Wynona, willing her to understand him. "Wy? Did you hear me? He can't breathe! I'm safe. Let him breathe!"

Wynona shook herself, the words finally penetrating, and she immediately lowered the blanket of magic to not cover his face. She found herself panting in exertion the same way Echoe did once he could reach air again.

"You…" The shifter tried to speak as Wynona grew closer. His eyes were wide and his clothes hung from his frame now that he'd gone back to his normal size. "The money is mine," he wheezed. "You…you take it from me."

"You shouldn't have tried to run," Rascal grunted, pulling a hag's thread from his pocket. "His hands please, Wy."

Wynona pulled her eyebrows together as she manipulated the magic to lift his hands in the air and make them available for Rascal to tie up. Once it was done, she felt the thread tugging on her magic and Wynona let it loose.

Breathing heavily, she bent over, hands on her knees as she fought to fill her lungs with enough oxygen.

"I'm putting him in the truck and calling for backup," Rascal stated firmly. "Don't you dare move this time, do you hear me?"

Wynona glanced up to see how brightly his eyes were shining and she nodded her agreement. His wolf needed her safe in order to calm down. She understood that and would comply. Just like her witch side had needed him safe only moments before.

*I think we need to get control of that witchy side,* Violet chimed in.

Wynona closed her eyes. *I could have used you here, Violet. Maybe you could have bitten my ankle before I got too carried away.*

*Eh...it wasn't too bad this time,* Violet offered. *At least you didn't eat anybody. That's my job, after all.*

A small smile tugged at Wynona's lips, but she couldn't quite bring herself to laugh at her blood-thirsty familiar. Every time Rascal's life was threatened, Wynona found herself in a dark place. Panic and fear seemed to push her conscience from her mind and the black side of her powers took over. The strength of what she could do was thrilling, in an odd way, but the fact that Wynona felt like she had so little control was not.

"Wy?" Rascal was slowly approaching her as if she were some kind of wild animal. "Are you back?"

Wynona straightened, winced at the pain in her head and nodded. "I'm fine." She looked at his arm and whimpered. "But you're not."

He shrugged and stepped up to wrap Wynona in a hug. "I'll be fine. It's only a scratch and we shifters heal fast." Burying his face in her neck, Rascal growled low. "You were supposed to stay in the truck."

She huffed, grasping the back of his shirt like a lifeline. "I can't stand back if I think you're in danger, Rascal. Don't ask it of me."

Rascal groaned and kissed her neck. "You're going to be the death of me, witch."

"I'm not trying to be," Wynona whispered hoarsely, pulling him closer. "But I can't let you go. Not if I can help it."

Rascal pulled back and cupped her face with his large, warm hands. The glow in his eyes was much warmer now. "I'll guess we'll just have to protect each other, huh?"

Wynona nodded, biting her lip when he wiped a tear from her cheek. "We should probably clean up the money before other creatures get brave enough to come steal it," she said softly.

Rascal kissed her forehead, then spun her in his arms, still holding her close. "I'm not ready to let go. Why don't you use your witchy skills to clean up while I use mine to hold you close."

The laughter managed to emerge this time and Wynona leaned back against his chest, letting him hold a good portion of her weight. With a flick of her fingers, the money began to float back toward the briefcase and neatly stack themselves into rows until the lid closed with a quiet click.

"Do you think he killed Mr. Braxet?" Wynona asked, hearing sirens in the distance.

Rascal grunted. "I don't know. But something's not right here. And how would he have done it? The guy's too big to have snuck in."

Wynona nodded. "It does seem like someone would have seen him if he was trying to get in or out of the interrogation room."

They turned when the sirens grew louder and Rascal waved down the police cars, finally stepping away from Wynona. She felt cold without his touch, but all in all, she was simply grateful he was still there. If anything ever happened to him, Wynona wasn't sure what she'd do.

*All the more reason to get in control,* Violet snapped. *Those are YOUR powers. Quit giving them away and accept yourself for who you are.*

Wynona didn't respond, but she replayed the words in her head all the way to the station. Was this truly who she was? A cold, emotional creature with too much power? Or could she somehow combine her two sides? Keep the power, but also keep the conscience?

*I don't think I'd be happy with anything else,* she thought softly.

*Then let's get it figured out,* Violet said. *Come back to the house when you're done. We'll practice. And if we're lucky, Lusgu will be in a chatty mood.*

Wynona snorted at that. The landscape flew by as they drove back to the station. She was glad they'd put Echoe in one of the squad cars. Wynona definitely wasn't ready to see the fear in his eyes again as he watched her.

No one would believe that a witch like her had scared a nightmare shifter. They were supposed to be some of the most frightening creatures in the paranormal world. Yet *he* was scared of *her*.

Rascal reached over and took her hand, interlocking their fingers and resting them on his thigh. "I don't think I said it before, but thank you," he said.

Wynona gave him a wan smile. "I'm sorry I got out of control again, and almost killed him, but I'm not sorry I kept you safe."

Rascal brought their hands up and kissed her fingers. "You did great. And this time Violet didn't have to attack in order to bring you back. I think we're making progress."

Wynona rolled her eyes. "Yeah...she and I have been talking."

"I'm gonna guess she wishes she was here."

"She did say that she was glad I hadn't eaten anyone, that was her job."

Rascal chuckled and shifted in his seat. "She's fierce for being so tiny."

"Don't call her that, or she'll take a bite out of you," Wynona warned him. Rascal's smile kept her feeling relaxed the whole way to the station. "Do you think there's a chance I can merge these two sides of me?" she asked quietly as he helped her down to the pavement.

"Two sides?" Rascal asked.

"Yeah...the emotional powerhouse and the one I try to be every day," Wynona clarified.

Rascal shrugged. "Sweetheart, they're already you. You just have to decide who you want in charge."

Wynona mulled that over as they walked inside. She waved at Amaris, who gave her a tentative smile, then followed Rascal back into one of the open interrogation rooms. Sitting in the back corner, Wynona planned to wait this one out. All she wanted to do was listen.

It took another twenty minutes before they were all set up and Echoe was sitting across from Chief Ligurio and his laptop. Rascal had his normal spot standing next to Wynona's side. She was grateful for his confident presence and she let him calm her as she went through his and Violet's words. They made it sound so simple, but Wynona felt like it was anything but.

"Where did you get the money?" Chief Ligurio asked casually.

Wynona shook herself slightly, realizing the conversation had started without her.

"It is mine," Echoe said wearily, his head drooping over his chest. "I earn it."

"Was it paid to you?" Chief asked.

Echoe closed his eyes and sighed. Slowly, as if it took great effort, he lifted his head and stared down the chief. "I work for years with barely any pay. I cannot eat if I want to sleep. I must choose." His jaw clenched, but his muscles didn't bulge the same way they had at the apartment.

Wynona noticed the hag's thread had been kept on the shifter's wrists, more than likely because Daemon wasn't there to keep Echoe from using his magic.

"I. EARN. IT!" Echoe bellowed. The veins in his neck popped, but his body didn't grow any larger and Wynona let out a breath after his voice stopped echoing.

Chief Ligurio waited a beat. "And did you kill Braxet in order to get your money?"

Echoe whined and slumped, like an animal who had lost the will to live. "I take bit by bit," he whimpered, the sound completely at odds with his size. "I hide. I save. When enough…I planned to leave."

"And did you kill Braxet so you could take the money?" Chief Ligurio said in a harsher tone.

Echoe shook his head, a low keening coming from his mouth. "No…I take. I save. I leave. His death let me take more. No one know the combination but me." His dark eyes were filled with sorrow when he finally looked up. "I always there. Mr. Braxet not think I watch, but I watch. I not stupid. I know. I memorize numbers and take money. Small amounts so he would not see." Another cry slipped from wet lips. "But with him gone, I take more. It taking too long. I take and I leave. I want to be free. I want to eat and sleep. Not choose."

Wynona hadn't realized she was crying until Rascal put a hand on her shoulder. She quickly wiped at her face. *I believe him.*

Rascal sighed. *Me too. But now we're down two suspects and no evidence toward anyone else.*

Wynona looked up and gave him a nod. "We'll figure it out," she whispered as softly as possible. The rest of the conversation with Echoe was lost on Wynona. She didn't need to hear more. Echoe might not have been bruised and broken physically from his life with the circus, but Tororin Braxet had dealt out his own abuse in his own way.

Her worries and pain for the creatures locked away at the circus only heightened at the sight of the emotionally broken creature in front of her. Somehow, they would get to the bottom of this. They would find Mr. Braxet's killer and hopefully with the case solved and the owner gone, something could be done to help the ones left behind. Because at this point, she didn't doubt for a moment that they really were cursed.

## CHAPTER 20

"Can we go to the interrogation room?" Wynona said softly to Rascal as they were all filing out of the one with Echoe.

Rascal looked around, then nodded. "Give me a second. Chief has the key."

Wynona stood at the side of the hallway, twiddling her thumbs as Rascal disappeared for a few minutes before coming back. He dangled a keyring with a grin.

"Alright, Detective Le Doux. Let's see what you can find."

Wynona rolled her eyes, but grinned and pushed her shoulder against his as he walked up to the door.

With a quiet click, Rascal opened, lifted up the caution tape and stood back so Wynona could enter first.

She flipped on the light and noted with frustration that the room was all but empty. Absolutely nothing, other than the dark stain on the table, said that there had been a death there.

Rascal clasped his hands behind his back and walked the perimeter of the room, his head moving from ceiling to floor and back. "I just don't see how anyone could have gotten in, killed him and gotten out so quickly."

Wynona nodded, squishing her lips to the side. "It's a problem for sure. But it just seems too convenient that he killed himself. Nothing in his life said he was suicidal."

"Maybe the divorce had him depressed?"

Wynona paused to let the thought percolate, but it simply didn't ring true with what she knew about him. "I don't see it," she said. "He seemed eager to offer me a contract. He was excited to expand. None of that says he was struggling with his wife getting ready to leave." Wynona tapped her bottom lip. "Plus…I'm guessing that he and Mrs. Braxet hadn't been getting along for a long time. She had obviously turned her attention elsewhere. Maybe Mr. Braxet had done the same."

Rascal nodded slowly. "That's a good thought. Maybe we should ask around at the circus and see if there was a girlfriend."

"Bud would probably know," Wynona said.

Rascal scowled, but nodded. "He probably would."

A smile tugged at Wynona's lips, but she held it back. His jealousy really shouldn't have been funny, but the way Rascal pouted was more enjoyable than it should have been. She blew out a breath and put her focus on the table. There had to be something there. "Did Mr. Braxet come to the station with anything? Any belongings that were confiscated?"

Rascal's eyebrows went up. "You know…I think there was. Do you want to go to the basement with me? Or wait here?"

Wynona pinched her lips together. "I love Yetu, but this time I'd like to keep searching." She smiled. "Tell him I said hello."

Rascal grumbled and rolled his eyes. "I'll hear about this for weeks, you know. You're one of his favorite people."

Wynona laughed softly as she watched him leave. Once the door was closed, the room was eerily quiet. On impulse, she turned on her magic vision and scanned the space. It just seemed so weird that a crime could be committed so quickly without using magic.

Wynona went over every square inch of the table. Nothing. Absolutely nothing.

"Here it is," Rascal said, coming back through the door.

"Looks like you were in and out quickly," she said, keeping her eyes on the table. Something was bugging her.

Rascal snorted. "I'm surprised the roof didn't collapse on my head. You really need to go say hi yourself next time."

Wynona grinned. "Will do." She went back to the table. "Rascal?"

"Hm?" His attention was on the bag as he pulled out items and began arranging them on the floor.

"Does magic ever get used in here?"

"Sure. Not every person interrogated is cuffed or held at bay with Skymaw."

"Then why is it completely cleaned of magical residue?"

Rascal looked up. "I don't follow."

"You know how a gun with no fingerprints is suspicious?" Wynona pressed. "Because there should be prints at least somewhere?"

A low rumble left Rascal's chest as he stood and came over to her side. "Got it. Someone wiped it clean. We talked about this in the beginning, but never pursued it."

"Who can do that?" Wynona asked. "What creature has the ability to wipe a magical signature?"

Rascal shook his head. "Just a sec." He pulled out his phone. "Chief? You need to come to the room." He paused. "Yeah. Okay." Rascal hung up. "He's finishing up something, then he'll be over."

"What are you thinking?"

"I'm thinking this proves foul play," Rascal said, pushing a hand through his hair. "I don't know who can clean magical signatures, but it's definitely not an incubus. We both know where their powers lie and it's not in clean up."

Wynona pursed her lips. "True."

"You're not convinced?"

Wynona shrugged. "He was dead. I don't think Mr. Braxet could have cleaned it up. But I'm still a little lost. I had no idea that kind of thing was possible." She looked over at him. "I do, however, agree that this means someone was here."

Rascal nodded. They both turned when the door opened.

"What did you find?"

Rascal nodded at Wynona.

"There's no magic in the room," she said.

Chief Ligurio's eyebrows went up. "And? I thought we knew no magic had been used in his death."

"None. As in, someone wiped it clean like they would fingerprints on a gun. I discussed it with Daemon the day of the murder, but then everything went haywire and we haven't spoken about it since."

Chief Ligurio huffed and put his hands on his hips. "So it was murder."

Wynona nodded. "We think so. Neither of us believe incubi are capable of that skill, not to mention he wasn't alive to have wiped it clean."

"Unless he did it before he died?"

"But why? What would have been the purpose?" Wynona asked. "There would be no reason to spend time on that."

Chief Ligurio nodded. "Maybe so, but our suspicion doesn't quite prove it in a court of law."

"Understood," Wynona affirmed. "However, it does mean we know for sure that we're looking for another person."

"Which we were kind of assuming anyway," Rascal added.

Wynona gave him a grudging nod.

"How do we figure out what creature has that ability?" Chief Ligurio asked.

Wynona and Rascal were both silent. "We need some kind of encyclopedia that has creatures sorted according to powers," Wynona muttered.

"Maybe you should write one," Rascal said with a grin.

"Right. Because I have so much time on my plate." She gave him a challenging look. "Are you wanting me to spend time on our wedding or on writing a book?"

"I'm sure you'd hate writing anyway," he said quickly.

"That's what I thought," Wynona said triumphantly.

Chief Ligurio cleared his throat. "Anyway. Was there something else I should know?"

Wynona shrugged. "No, but Rascal did bring up Mr. Braxet's things from the evidence locker. I thought we should look through them."

"Ah..." Chief Ligurio nodded slowly. "I'm guessing you didn't go down and that's why Yetu bellowed enough to shake the walls."

Wynona threw her hands in the air. "I don't know what you're talking about! I didn't hear a thing!"

Rascal tapped his ear. "Super hearing. It's the one thing I have that you don't."

"I can't shift," Wynona pointed out.

"Yeah, well...I wouldn't be surprised at all if one morning you woke up as something else," he said wryly.

"With the way you discover powers, it's a little too likely," Chief Ligurio added, walking across the room. "What was in the personal belongings?"

Wynona followed. "I haven't looked yet." She squatted down. "What's this?" The pile contained normal possessions, such as a wallet and business cards. But a small, thin box was among the pile as well and Wynona didn't recognize it as anything stereotypical.

"Not sure," Rascal murmured. He pulled gloves out of his pocket and snapped them on, then picked up the box.

"Got a pair for me?" Wynona asked.

Rascal pulled up another set and held them out without looking her way.

Wynona worked them on, then patiently waited while Rascal turned the box over and over.

"I can't see how to get inside of it," he muttered.

"No buttons or secret levers?" Chief Ligurio questioned.

Rascal shook his head, then held it out. "Look for yourself."

Wynona took the offering. The box was surprisingly heavy considering its size. At maybe two inches by four inches and slim from front to back, she had expected it to barely weigh anything at all. "It's not some tool that men use, is it?" she asked. "Not something that can open a locked door or jack up a tire?"

Rascal chuckled. "Not one that I've ever seen."

She shrugged at his smirk. "Sorry. I'm not familiar with tool sets."

"Is it magical?" Chief asked.

Wynona groaned. "Why didn't I think of that?"

"Well, we thought of it now," the vampire snapped. "Take a look."

Wynona blinked until her vision went slightly purple around the edges and sure enough. There was magic all over the tiny device. "Oh my…" She turned it around. "It's…solid. There's magic all around this as if…"

"As if…" Rascal pressed.

"As if the magic is keeping it from opening," Wynona finished. She drew a finger along the sides, testing to see if the magic reacted to her presence.

"Anyone know how to counteract incubus magic?" Chief grumbled.

"It can't have been Mr. Braxet's magic," she stated. "With him gone, the spell would have faded."

"Then whose is it?"

Wynona shook her head. "I have no idea, but…" She hesitated.

"What?" Rascal asked warily.

"I'd like to see if it reacts to my magic," Wynona said guiltily. "But that means I'll need to touch it without gloves. Can I contaminate the evidence that way?"

Chief Ligurio pinched the bridge of his nose and stood upright. "Fine. Do what you need to."

"Do we need to back up for safety?" Rascal teased.

"You might actually," Wynona said without humor. "I never quite know how these kinds of things are going to go."

Rascal scowled. "Not funny."

"It wasn't meant to be," she retorted.

"You're not risking yourself over this."

Wynona gave him a pleading look. "Rascal…" she cooed. "We need to figure this out. For the circus members, for the people under suspicion who are innocent and most importantly…for ourselves."

"And how does you getting hurt help us?" he ground out.

She shook her head. "Let's put this case away so we can move on, huh? Give me a chance."

"I don't like it."

"I know," Wynona said. "And I'm grateful you care. But I also know you'll take care of me no matter what happens."

Growling, Rascal sat down. "Go on, then. Touch it."

"You're not going to move away?" Her eyes widened.

"If you're here, I'm here."

Chief Ligurio snorted and scooted back.

Suddenly feeling as if she were taking her life in her hands, Wynona set down the box to remove the latex gloves. Her hand hovered a moment before picking the box back up. A small shock caused her to jump, but it didn't hurt enough to stop her. Keeping it in one palm, Wynona brought her magic to the point of a finger and brought the two objects together.

She gasped when she saw the deep red magic begin to sizzle at the contact, but her purple magic was winning without much effort, so Wynona kept pushing. Her finger was now touching the box and the small shock from before had turned into something decidedly uncomfortable, causing her to grit her teeth.

"What is it?" Rascal demanded, his eyes going from the box to her and back.

"It stings a bit," Wynona admitted, still focused on the task. "But I'm kind of…burning…the other magic away, so hold on." She could hear Rascal's breathing getting heavier and heavier, but Wynona tried to put it to the back of her mind. She was almost…*there*! "Ah-ha!" she cried, right before yelping and dropping the box on the ground.

What had only been a few inches in diameter was now the size of a paper file, like the ones kept in the records office down the hall.

"Well, well, well…" Chief Ligurio drawled, bending to pick up the container. "Just what was he trying to hide?" With the box enlarged, it was easy to lift the two pieces apart and Wynona watched the vampire shuffle through some papers contained inside.

"Are you going to share what you're seeing?" she asked, taking Rascal's offered hand to help her to her feet.

Chief Ligurio smirked. "Remember how the partner said anyone would want to kill Braxet?"

Wynona nodded.

Chief's smirk grew wide and his eyes flashed in triumph. "We just discovered why."

## CHAPTER 21

Wynona felt as if her jaw would never quite pick up from off the ground. But somehow, she couldn't quite keep it from falling every time they turned another page in the box they'd discovered among Mr. Braxet's things.

The incubus had been blackmailing nearly every person who worked at the Cursed Circus. The creature's death seemed almost normal after everything they had read.

Wynona leaned back in her seat, stretching her neck after staying in one place for far too long. "This is ridiculous," she muttered. "How in the world did he discover all these things?"

Rascal slowly shook his head as he continued to glance through papers. "I don't know, but he obviously had his ways." He snorted. "Get this. Someone named Cintrine Fernsand was being blackmailed because she ran away from home as a minor." Rascal rolled his eyes. "Unless she's still a minor, that wouldn't be a threat anymore. I wonder how he's still keeping her in line."

Chief grumbled. "All it takes is for a creature to be ignorant of the law," he said. "If the girl still believes she can be taken back to her parents, then Braxet wins."

"Providing she wants to stay away from her parents more than she wants to pay Mr. Braxet his price for silence," Wynona pointed out.

Chief nodded. "True. As soon as she's not scared of her parents, he holds no power."

"This blows our suspect list into the stratosphere," Wynona groaned. "Any one of these creatures could have killed him."

"No," Rascal corrected. "They might have had motive, but only a few had access during the time of the actual murder," he pointed out. "Really, what we need to do is find what he had on his ex-wife. Her *unavailability* is still frustratingly suspicious to me."

Wynona sighed. "I don't like her disappearing either, but I still don't see the point in bribing me to declare it a murder, if she did the murdering. Wouldn't she have just set up the crime scene to be clear what it was? That way she didn't lose the money."

"It all gives her plausible deniability," Rascal argued.

"It's an awful lot of work," Wynona muttered. "There had to be easier ways than to fake a divorce. Then stage a murder into a suicide. Then kidnap me and try to pretend to bribe me into finding the real killer so she can collect the money." Wynona shook her head, her hair falling into her face. "There are too many steps to be feasible."

"Which is exactly what she wants you to think."

Wynona laughed and rolled her eyes. "I agree she shouldn't be hiding. But I don't think she did it."

"Half our suspects aren't suspects anymore, then," Chief snapped. "Nasille is dead. We're following your lead on the ex since we can't find her anyway. The bodyguard was embezzling, but doesn't appear stable enough to have planned a murder, though I'm not ready to completely write him off yet. And the secretary has an alibi that can't truly be corroborated, or denied." Chief Ligurio sighed. "You realize that leaves only…"

Wynona stiffened. "It leaves someone from the station. In particular, Daemon, who was watching Mr. Braxet."

Chief hesitated before nodding.

"I don't like it," Rascal growled.

"And I do?" Chief snarled back.

"You both know that Daemon is innocent in this," Wynona said fiercely. "There has to be someone we're missing."

"Sure…" Chief said sarcastically, waving at the pile of papers. "A thousand of them. But none were here when the death occurred."

"Neither was Daemon," Wynona said tightly.

"Wy…we're on his side," Rascal said softly. "Neither of us want him to be involved."

"Then quit looking in his direction," she said, leaning forward. "I feel like we go through this every time we're working on a case. You're always willing to believe the worst in creatures, even those you know and love."

Chief closed his eyes and shook his head, leaning back in his seat before pinning Wynona in place with his red eyes. "Ms…Wynona… one thing you learn when you've worked in this job as long as I have is that no matter how wonderful a creature seems, or how much you like them…everyone….*absolutely everyone*…is capable of murder." He learned his elbows on the desk and steepled his fingers. "And that includes you and myself. All it takes is the right amount of desperate motivation."

Wynona's pulse was speeding and there was a rushing sound in her ears. "I don't believe that," she said hoarsely.

Chief glanced at Rascal, who gave Wynona a pitying look and shrugged. "We've seen it," Rascal said gently.

"And I believe there are good creatures out there, who would rather die than kill. They put others above themselves and would do that to the end."

Chief huffed. "Believe what you want, but all we're doing is following evidence."

"Then we need new evidence," Wynona said stubbornly.

"You're more than welcome to find it," Chief Ligurio invited, spreading his hands wide.

"Thank you," Wynona said, standing up. "I think I will." She shuffled through the papers. "Where was the one about the girl?"

Rascal pulled it out and handed it to her. "Why that one?"

Wynona gave him a humorless smile. "Because she's probably still younger than everyone else, and often that makes a creature more impressionable."

"Or easier to scare into talking," Chief Ligurio added.

Wynona glared, but didn't respond, knowing he was right. Someone afraid of being caught by the police, especially someone young, would probably be willing to talk more than a hardened criminal. "I'll let you know if I find anything."

"I'm coming," Rascals said, standing up.

"No," Wynona argued. "Stay and get some work done. A girl to girl chat will probably work better."

"I don't want you there by yourself," he said, not sitting back down.

"And I don't want you scaring her."

Rascal let out a low growl. "Then I'll wait outside the door, but there's no way I'm letting *Bud* get you alone or getting a call that you fainted because your senses were overloaded by the animals, Wy. Don't ask me to do it."

Shame filled her, but Wynona wasn't quite ready to let down her pride yet. She'd had this argument with these men too many times and she hated how often she gave in just to keep the peace. She'd stood up to Violet and Lusgu. Wynona could stand up to Rascal and Chief Ligurio as well. "Fine. But you *will* stand outside."

"I said I would," Rascal ground out. Before anyone could say another word, he stormed to the door, his hair standing on end and his eyes glowing. Yanking on the handle, he held it open for Wynona, ever the gentleman despite his anger.

Clenching her hands at her side, Wynona walked past him, trying to look unaffected by his anger, though she could feel it pulsing through her veins. She would never admit that she had to strengthen the wall in her mind, because his emotions were enough to knock her to the ground. That wouldn't bode well right now.

The ride to the circus was awkward. Extremely awkward. Wynona shifted her weight for the twentieth time, realizing that she hadn't been this uncomfortable around the wolf since before they'd officially met. *And even that might not have been quite as bad.*

*That's because soulmates weren't meant to fight.*

Her neck hurt with how quickly she snapped in his direction. "How did you hear that? My wall was up."

Rascal glanced her way. "You muttered it under your breath."

Her eyebrows went up. "But you answered in my mind and it was clearer than usual with my wall up."

Rascal nodded. "I sent it intentionally, maybe that had something to do with it."

Wynona slumped against the seat. "I don't like being cross with you."

"Me either, but it's not a bad thing for you to stand up for yourself once in a while either." He grunted. "I know my wolf and I get a little overbearing sometimes."

"Doesn't mean I have to be rude about it," she said softly.

"You weren't. Just firm." He pulled into the parking lot. "Let's forget about it. Ultimately, we're on the same team. I don't want Skymaw to be guilty any more than you do, so let's go prove he's innocent."

Wynona nodded. She could handle that. "Sounds good to me." She opened her door.

"Don't you dare."

Wynona chuckled and waited for him to come around, lift her down, then take the time to steal a short, fierce kiss. "Frustrated or no, I'll always take care of you," he said in a gravelly tone.

Wynona traced her finger along his jawline. "I know."

Nodding firmly, he stepped back and took her hand. Wynona took the few moments they had before arriving inside to reinforce her barrier. She still winced, however, at the level of the noise, though she was able to keep from collapsing at the emotional load.

"Does it hurt your ears?" Wynona asked, knowing Rascal's ear's were so much more sensitive than hers were.

Rascal scowled. "Can't say it's enjoyable, no."

"Let's get this done quickly." Wynona took off, Rascal at her side. They hurried down into the center ring and walked around to the back. The noise grew louder and a muscle in Rascal's jaw began to twitch. "Are you going to make it?" she said, leaning in so he could hear.

He nodded, but his jaw didn't unclench even the slightest amount.

Wynona pinched her lips and began to scan the area. She didn't recognize many of the creatures in the cages. Wynona truly did need an encyclopedia in order to figure them all out as well as their powers. She did, however, see the demon who had glared at her before.

In fact, he was glaring at her right now. Gulping down her fear, Wynona walked forward with her head held high. "Hello," she said clearly, trying to speak over the noise. "I'm Wynona Le Doux."

"I know who you are," the creature sneered. His eyes flashed a deep, crimson red and Wynona had to lock her knees to keep from backing up.

She had no idea why this creature was at the circus, but something about him felt decidedly...wild. A heated presence at her back let her know she was no longer alone and Wynona was able to relax just slightly.

Rascal's chest was shaking with anger.

Wynona reached back and grasped his hand. "I've been hired by the police to help solve Mr. Braxet's murder." She tilted her head to the side, giving the demon a smile she hoped would help put him at ease.

If his continued sneer was anything to go by, it didn't work.

"Do you know where we can find we can find Ms. Cintrine Fernsand?"

The demon's face grew tighter. "Why do you want her?" he said, his voice starting to rumble. A glow, decidedly like shifting lava, was beginning to show through cracks in the creature's skin. When heat began to emanate from his being, Wynona felt her worry spike.

"Wy," Rascal snapped, pulling on her arm. "Get behind me."

Wynona let him pull her half a step, before she dug in her heels. "No," she said, shaking herself. "I can protect us."

"Wy," Rascal warned, the tone more urgent than before.

The air between them and the demon was starting to shimmer, but Wynona pushed back her panic. She couldn't run and hide every time her safety was threatened. This was exactly what her powers were for and if she was going to keep fighting for her independence and the freedom of her friends, she needed to stand up to the bullies.

This demon was definitely a bully.

Waving her hand, Wynona put up a purple shield. When a blast of heat nearly obliterated it, she grit her teeth and strengthened it until it was almost as thick as a brick wall.

The demon's heat wavered slightly as his eyebrows shot up, in surprise. He didn't stay back for long, however, his brows furrowing together as the heat increased.

When the wooden threshold of the door began to blacken, Wynona knew she needed to do something. Stealing an idea from Celia, when the sisters had fought the demon who burned down the tea shop, Wynona used her magic to cover the demon completely. Her fingers were flexed widely and beginning to ache as she carefully opened a slit, ignoring the demon's bellow of rage. Siphoning out the oxygen, she watched her quarry stumble, his eyes starting to roll.

It wasn't until he had fallen to his knees that the flames began to go out and Wynona could feel a difference in the heat from inside the capsule she had created.

"Please! Stop!" a feminine voice shouted. "You're going to kill him."

Wynona ignored the sound. She was concentrating so that exact scenario *didn't* happen, but if she looked away, she could miss her cue. A struggle behind her let Wynona know that Rascal had stepped in.

*Just a moment more,* she thought, watching the demon slowly slump. Finally, his eyes rolled back in his head and he collapsed to the floor, his head hitting with a loud thud while the cracks in his skin closed up, leaving black scars on his body like vines up a trellis.

Wynona immediately opened the shield, then rushed over to check on the body. She reached for the pulse in his neck, but stopped, easily able to see that his chest was rising and falling. Relief coursed through her and Wynona stood up, looking back at Rascal with a tired smile. "He'll be okay," she whispered hoarsely.

Rascal let go of the woman he'd been holding back and reached for

Wynona. She gratefully collapsed against his chest, letting him hold her up for a few moments while she caught her breath.

"Those shields seem to be a specialty of yours," Rascal whispered into her hair. "I never thought of you using them for offense instead of defense, however."

Wynona chuckled. "Me neither. But Celia's little lesson on air and fire came to mind, so I put it into action."

He huffed. "This might be the first time I've ever been grateful to her."

Wynona smiled, then focused on the woman for the first time. Her long blue hair billowed in waves, moving as if she were underwater and to Wynona's surprise, the woman's skin was blue as well.

Long, tapered fingers caressed the side of the demon's face and traced a few of the fire scars that were slowly fading. Wynona winced as she watched them. They looked like they hurt.

Bright brown eyes, completely at odds with the blue face and hair, looked over at Wynona.

"Ms. Fernsand, I presume?" Wynona asked with a sudden hunch.

The woman blinked.

"Despite what he thought," Wynona nodded toward the demon, "I'm not here to hurt you. His protection was completely unneeded."

Tears filled the woman's eyes and she looked back down at the body. The demon began to stir and she gasped, leaning in and touching his cheek. "Tag?" Ms. Fernsand whispered, her voice rippling like the water she seemed to be made of.

The demon blinked, the fire gone out of his eyes. When those black eyes landed on Ms. Fernsand, they softened and he almost smiled, until realizing he wasn't alone. His glare returned and he climbed shakily to his feet, standing between the two parties.

Wynona put her hand up. "Stop," she said, standing back on her own two feet. "I don't want to have to knock you out again, but we need to speak to Ms. Fernsand. I'm not here to hurt her or cause any distress. I'm just looking for answers."

"How do you know answering questions won't cause her distress?" the demon challenged.

Rascal growled and stepped forward.

"Please," Wynona said softly. "We're not the enemies. We're trying to put the enemy behind bars. And I have questions for Ms. Fernsand, and probably ones that you can help with as well." Wynona clasped her shaking hands together. "How about we do the interview all together? Will that help you feel better?"

Tag hesitated and looked over his shoulder.

Ms. Fernsand nodded.

Tag looked back. "Tagthoth Brolmuthan," he said in that gravelly tone. "You may call me Tag."

Wynona nodded. "I'm Wynona Le Doux. This is Deputy Chief Strongclaw. Now…where can we meet that will be a little quieter?"

Ms. Fernsand stepped forward. "We can meet in my dressing room." She hesitated. "And I'm guessing you want to know about my affair with Tor?"

It took every ounce of control Wynona possessed to keep from stumbling over her own feet, while Tag growled loud enough to wake the dead. "I think that would be a very good place to start."

## CHAPTER 22

Wynona looked around as they stepped into Ms. Fernsand's room. It was a direct reflection of its owner, with blue, water themed costumes and furniture crowded inside a tiny space.

Ms. Fernsand grabbed a couple of costumes off the back of a couch. "Sorry," she said in that soothing murmur. "I wasn't expecting company."

"It's fine," Wynona assured her. "We don't mind standing."

"No, no," Ms. Fernsands said quickly. "Please…sit. I'll make tea."

Rascal snorted quietly and Wynona gave him a look. It wasn't Ms. Fernsand's fault that Wynona was a bit of a tea snob. Grabbing Rascal's hand, she walked past Tag, who stood guard next to Ms. Fernsand, and gingerly sat on the edge of the couch. Rascal, of course, stood at her side, making Wynona feel awkward being the only one down on her level.

The cups trembled slightly when the blue woman brought them over. "Careful, they're hot." She closed her eyes. "Of course, they're hot. You knew that. I just…" Pinching her lips together, Ms. Fernsand wrapped her arms around middle and folded into herself a little.

Tag reached out, but halted at the last moment. "It's going to be okay," he assured her.

"He's right," Wynona said. "But I would like to get right to the point." She waved toward a chair. "Why don't you sit down?"

Ms. Fernsand followed directions and Tag stood with the same military precision that Rascal did.

"We knew that Mrs. Braxet was unfaithful to her husband," Wynona began carefully, watching Ms. Fernsand's reactions. "But we weren't sure of his own actions."

Tag snorted. "Her affairs were more than likely a reflection of his own."

"Tag," Ms. Fernsand scolded.

The demon shook his head. The scars had completely healed at this point and Wynona had a million questions about them, but decided it was *not* the time to ask. She'd never seen anything like his split skin and flowing lava. Heat was definitely a demon thing, but not usually within their very veins.

"He was an incubus," Tag snarled. "What did you expect?" His muscles bulged slightly. "He took his turns with every female in the circus."

Wynona knew her jaw had to have dropped again. Mr. Braxet was proving to be a disgusting piece of work, even after his death. No wonder he'd thought nothing of using his powers in trying to convince her to come work for him. It must have been a blow to his ego that she hadn't responded.

"Take it down a notch," Rascal warned.

Tag's eyes flared for a moment before he visibly calmed and nodded. "It wouldn't have been so bad if the women had actually wanted to be involved," he muttered.

Wynona turned to see a very pale Ms. Fernsand. "Did he coerce you into this relationship?" Wynona asked.

Ms. Fernsand's eyes were looking at anything but Wynona as she shrugged. "He was…liberal with his powers, if that's what you're asking."

Tag growled again. "He took what he wanted, when he wanted it.

And sometimes, like in the case of Cintrine, he kept favorites for a time." His lip curled. "It was a way to punish me." His eyes softened as he looked down, shame practically oozing from his pores.

Ms. Fernsand shook her head. "It wasn't your fault."

Wynona put her hands in the air. "I'm sorry. I'm not trying to seem heartless, but I really do need to get some things clarified." She leaned forward. "May I call you Cintrine?"

"Cindy is fine," Ms. Fernsand said softly.

"Cindy." Wynona nodded. "How long have you been in love with Tag?"

The two looked shyly at each other and Wynona realized she might have let the kitten out of the cauldron a little too soon. "Uh…we…"

"Since we met," Tag interrupted. He glanced at Wynona, then wiped the tender look off his face. "But we've never had a chance to be together."

"I'm sorry," Wynona said sincerely. "That had to be hard."

"So is being cursed," Tag spat back.

Wynona nodded, knowing he was trying to bait her. "I know. I was cursed for most of my life."

Tag blinked and Cindy gasped.

"You're President Le Doux's daughter," Cindy whispered. "The one who has no powers." She paused. "Or didn't."

Wynona nodded. "My grandmother cursed me and the curse broke when she died," she stated matter of factly, but the old feelings of hurt still lingered. They were much more manageable than before, especially since Wynona understood the reason behind it, but it didn't truly take it all away.

"Only death can break a curse?" Tag asked, his voice softer than before.

Wynona shrugged. "I'm not sure. But it's one way." She frowned. "Wait…are you saying you weren't born cursed?"

Tag shook his head. "No. Unlike most of the creatures here, mine was placed on me a few years ago."

"Do you mind if I take a look?" Wynona asked.

The demon frowned.

"I can see magic," Wynona explained.

His dark eyebrows shot up. "Have at it."

Wynona blinked until her vision appeared and she knew Cindy's gasp was due to her purple, glowing eyes. The woman seemed easily startled, and it brought Wynona to a question. *First things first.* She studied Tag, who was standing with his legs apart and arms folded over his chest. "Yes...that's a nasty one," she murmured. Black, thorny vines wrapped his body and if Wynona had to guess, she would say that the splits in his skin when he got angry were in the exact same spots as the vines. They oozed slightly, giving away the fact that the magic that created them was anything but light and joyful.

Wynona turned to Cindy, but other than the glow of inner blue magic, nothing stood out. *Not an outside curse then.* Wynona blinked back to her regular vision. "Cindy, tell me about you."

"I...what?" Cindy glanced up at Tag.

"What kind of creature are you? I can see you have magic, water magic, I'm sure, but no outward cursing. What brought you to the circus?"

Cindy's face fell. "I'm a water elf."

"Water elf?" Wynona clarified. "I've never heard of it."

Cindy shrugged. "My mother was an elf and she had an affinity with water. When she...when she became pregnant with me...something went wrong."

"Was your father also an elf?"

Cindy shook her head, her eyes on her lap.

Wynona nodded. So another mixed pair brought an odd result. There seemed to be several of those in the circus. "And what are your powers?"

Cindy looked up at Tag, who nodded at her. Holding out a trembling hand, her fingers slowly turned to water, falling to the floor until her entire body had disappeared. Instead of a puddle, the water had absorbed into its surroundings and she seemed to have completely disappeared.

"Can she still hear us?" Wynona asked, slightly alarmed.

Tag nodded. "Yeah. But she can't answer until she's corporeal again."

"Thank you, Cindy," Wynona called out. "You may come back now."

"Hang on," Tag grunted. "It takes a bit of work."

Wynona let out the breath she'd been holding when Cindy was finally back in her chair. The elf looked exhausted, but was in one piece. "I'm guessing the brown eyes come from your father?"

"I suppose they do," the elf murmured.

Wynona nodded. Rascal tapped her shoulder, handing Wynona the folded papers. "Oh yes, Cindy... We wanted to ask you about why Mr. Braxet was blackmailing you."

Tag stepped forward, his skin immediately turning red.

"Hold on, Tag," Wynona said without anger. "We know he was blackmailing you as well." The demon's muscles were strained tightly and Rascal was shifting behind Wynona. She needed to cool this down quickly before they had another fire on their hands. "He's gone. He can't hurt you or Cindy anymore and we're here to help."

"Whoever killed Braxet should be sainted instead of put behind bars," Tag snarled.

"I'm realizing more and more that he was far from a good creature," Wynona said, still careful to keep her voice calm. "But killing someone is against the law. I'm very sorry for everything you've gone through and I'm delighted you've been freed in a small way, but without law and order, the world would be chaos. We can't let someone go free for this."

Tag didn't move until Cindy's hand landed on his arm. The contact between the water elf and the demon caused a heavy sizzling and steam filled the room, but Tag shut himself down quickly at her move. "Sorry," he muttered.

Cindy gave him a small smile. "It's fine."

Wynona put two and two together and realized that Mr. Braxet might not have been the only issue between the two becoming a couple. "Why were you afraid of your parents knowing where you are?" Wynona asked. "It said you ran away from home. Do you realize that as an adult, there's nothing they can do to force you to go back?"

Cindy nodded, her eyes once again on the table. "I know...but it...I don't think my father knew I existed."

"Do you know who your father is?"

Cindy shrugged.

"Are you afraid of him?" Wynona pressed.

"I'm not sure of anything," Cindy said, a little more snap in her voice than before. "And I'd rather not have Tor dump information in someone's lap that may or may not be true, just to spite me for not following his rules."

Wynona leaned back. Evidently that was a touchy subject. "And you, Tag? I remember yours said you were being blackmailed because you took on a witch and then disappeared."

He raised a challenging eyebrow at her. "If you mean that a witch captured me and experimented on me, leaving me with this curse, then yes, I suppose that's accurate."

Wynona narrowed her eyes, though her heart sank at his words. Why were witches so elite? Why did they think they were above the law? It made Wynona sick. "So, Cindy was the real hold on you." It wasn't a question and she didn't need Tag to answer. Sighing, Wynona turned to the elf. "I need your alibis for the day of the murder."

"What?" Tag bellowed.

Wynona stood up and Rascal stepped in front. The room was getting hot again. "Mr. Brolmuthann, I told you I was here in an official capacity. Both of you have given me reasons as to why you would wish Mr. Braxet dead. I'm simply trying to put together a scenario and if I know you weren't involved, it makes my job easier."

"If I'd had the opportunity, I'd have killed Braxet years ago," Tag said tightly.

"Tag, don't," Cindy warned.

"But we're not allowed to leave the grounds, Ms. Le Doux. So unless you can magically break a barrier that keeps us here, or somehow put Braxet's murder somewhere other than the police station, then we're not much help to you."

"None of you can leave?" Wynona asked, frowning.

"None of the performers," Cindy clarified, giving Tag a look. "A few of the regular employees can."

Wynona nodded. That explained Echoe living elsewhere and might have even been part of his motivation, so he felt less like a prisoner. But she could also understand why the circus wouldn't want to make it optional for some of the creatures to leave. Many of them were unable to control themselves, after all. The fact that it covered every performer was disheartening, however.

"Thank you so much for your time," Wynona said. "Tag, if I can think of anything to help you with your curse, I'll let you know."

Tag's nostrils were still flaring, but he nodded at her. The demon and elf didn't follow Rascal and Wynona as they slipped out and Wynona was grateful. She didn't want to make more small talk, just get out of there as quickly as possible and go back to the drawing board. Without being able to look at the blackmailed performers, their list of suspects had gone right back to ground zero and it broke her heart. Because the only one left was Daemon.

## CHAPTER 23

"We'll figure it out," Rascal assured Wynona as they drove to her house. He reached over, his hand resting on her thigh.

Wynona grabbed his hand and squeezed it tight. "It's just not right," she snapped. "No one should be allowed to treat others like that. Why haven't we figured out yet how to break curses? You'd think that would be big business for someone."

"Maybe that's how you'll make your fortune," Rascal teased.

Wynona gave him a small smile in return. "If only. All these stupid powers and yet I can't figure out how to break a curse." She blew a raspberry. "In fact, I can't even find the right counteractive spell in Granny's grimoire. I'm useless."

"Hey," Rascal said in a stronger tone. "None of that now. We don't have victims in this relationship, Ms. Le Doux."

Wynona did laugh this time. "You're right. I'm sorry."

Rascal cocked his head. "Eh? What was that?"

Wynona's smile widened. "You're right, dear Wolfman. I was wrong."

"Thank you very much," he said primly. "I'll tuck that one away for when I need to win an argument after we're married."

"Not for before we're married?"

He flashed a toothy smile. "Nope. It'll be more important afterwards. Our time married will last longer than our time engaged." He pursed his lips. "I hope."

Wynona patted his hand. "It will. I promise we won't take that long. As soon as this case is over, we'll get the plans finished."

Rascal snorted, then put the truck in park. "Promises, promises," he muttered.

Wynona shrugged. "Sorry. No rushing the bride. It'll be the only time I get to do this."

"It better be." Rascal raised a challenging eyebrow at her, then hopped out of the truck. Jogging around, he opened her door and helped her down. A long kiss later, he released her waist and shut the door. "Now…let's go research curses."

Wynona followed behind, her pulse still racing from their romantic moment. The urgency to get this case over with was growing, and not just to see a murderer brought to justice.

"Violet?" Wynona called out as soon as they walked inside. No scampering or mental call followed Wynona's greeting, so Wynona tried again. *Violet? Where are you?*

*With Lusgu. We're at the shop. Are you home?*

*Yep,* Wynona responded. *I'm going to do some research in the grimoire.*

*Great. We'll be back soon. Lusgu's cleaning the bathroom to within an inch of its life.*

Wynona smiled. "They'll be here soon," she told Rascal.

He nodded. "I heard."

"Stay out of my head," Wynona sang out as she walked toward the kitchen.

"Make me," Rascal mimicked.

Wynona smiled and shook her head. A minute later there were two steaming cups of tea and she went to retrieve the grimoire. The book felt extra heavy in her hands, though Wynona was unsure why. Her heart fluttered slightly and Wynona paused to pay attention.

"Wy?" Rascal called.

She could hear his footsteps coming down the hall before he stood in the doorway.

"What's going on?" he asked. "I can feel something off."

Wynona held up a finger, pinching her lips together. She wasn't sure what was going on, but she was determined to figure it out. The palpitations of her heart didn't hurt, and the book wasn't uncomfortable to touch…but something was definitely different.

After several long seconds of nothing, Wynona blew out a breath. "Sorry. I'm not sure what that was about," she admitted, tucking some hair behind her ear. "But my heart felt a little funny and the book felt heavier." Wynona scrunched up her nose. "That sounds weird, but I'm not sure how else to describe it."

"Does anything hurt?"

Wynona shook her head. "No, but something happened. I just don't know what it means."

Frowning, Rascal held out his hand and Wynona took it, letting him lead her to the kitchen. "Sit," he commanded. "I'll get you something to eat."

"I'm really not hungry," Wynona said over her shoulder.

"Too bad," Rascal responded. "Let's get your blood sugar up a bit, just in case."

Shaking her head with a smile, Wynona put the book on the table, careful to keep the tea where it couldn't spill on anything, and opened it. A puff of air hit her in the face and she gasped.

"What now?"

Wynona shook her head. "I don't know!" She splayed her hands to the side. "It's almost as if…" Wynona's eyes widened. "Granny? Are you here?" Immediately, Wynona turned on her vision. When a ghost was in invisible mode, it was the only way she knew how to see them.

Granny had crossed over a long time ago, but maybe she'd found another way to visit? Could the grimoire give someone that kind of power?

"Do you see anyone?" Rascal asked, his voice tight.

Wynona slumped in her seat and blinked her eyes back to normal. "No. But I thought maybe she was leading me to an answer."

Rascal squeezed her shoulder. "It was a good thought. Though I've never heard of a creature coming back from the other side."

Wynona blew a piece of hair out of her face. "Me neither." Resigned that her overactive imagination was just messing with her, Wynona began to flip through the pages. It still amazed Wynona that for a woman as good as Granny was, she had a few dark corners that were a little…more than Wynona wanted to take on.

She skimmed quickly through the front section, where she had looked the other night when she and Lusgu were working. Once the spells and incantations looked new, Wynona slowed down.

"Eww…" she muttered.

Rascal set down a plate with bread and cheese on it. "What'd you find? A spell to turn someone into a slug?"

"Haha," Wynona retorted. "No. This one was for preserving body parts."

Rascal's thick eyebrows went up. "For what purpose? Like, to keep a creature alive? Or to keep the parts fresh until they can be used for something."

"The latter, I think," Wynona said with a grimace. "She's talking about jars and preservation, so I'm pretty sure the body isn't still moving at this point."

Rascal gave a dramatic shiver. "Remind me not to cross your grandmother."

"Too late."

He smirked and went back to the kitchen.

Wynona ignored his rummaging and put her focus toward the book. "Here's one for talking to loved ones," Wynona said softly. Her hand rested on the page as she thought of the woman who had created the spell. "I doubt it works when they've crossed the veil though."

Rascal grunted.

Wynona tapped a finger, lamenting her loss for a few moments, before slowly pulling her hand back in order to move on. "Oh!" she cried, shoving away from the table a little.

"What? Where?" Rascal was at her side in a moment, his head jerking everywhere. "Wy! What's going on?"

Wynona pointed a trembling finger at the open page. "It...it moved with my fingers."

"What?"

Wynona couldn't seem to look away from the book. She was absolutely positive, though the idea should have been a reason to call her insane, that the page had lifted with her finger, caressing her as she pulled back.

"I'm totally lost," Rascal said, scratching behind his ear. "The page moved? Did it just get stuck to your hand?"

Wynona shook her head. "Watch." She was terrified to do it again, but it wasn't like it was bad...in fact, it had felt sort of nice. Like a pet wanting more attention. She hovered her hand over the page, then dropped one finger, slowly drawing it down. As she lifted her finger back up, the page came with it, as if seeking for a longer connection.

"That's..." Rascal coughed and held onto the back of her chair. "Is that a witch thing?" he asked, his voice higher than normal.

Wynona shrugged. "I don't know. I've never been taught the art of grimoires. I thought they were simply books or journals. They contained magic spells, which have power, but I never realized the book itself might have powers." A shudder wracked her body.

"I don't know why I didn't think of that," a husky voice grumbled.

Wynona's head swiveled. "Lusgu! Is Violet with you?"

Violet's scampering was loud as she ran across the floor and climbed up until she reached Wynona's shoulder. *You have to feed it,* Violet stated knowingly.

"What are you talking about?" Wynona shouted.

Lusgu sat down with a heavy grunt. "It's my fault," he snapped. "I should have realized you'd need to be accepted before anything could happen."

"Okay..." Wynona put her face in her hands. "Accepted? Feedings? What in the paranormal world are you two talking about and why do you know this and not me?"

"You just said no one ever taught you about them," Rascal said softly. His eyes narrowed. "But I have no idea how the brownie knows anything. Grimoires are a witch thing."

Lusgu scowled. "Some of us make a point of gaining knowledge even outside of ourselves."

Rascal huffed.

Lusgu turned his black eyes to Wynona. "Grimoires are strictly a female witch tool. Over time, the more spells that are put inside, the more alive the book becomes. It's basically the witch's child, though one filled with their heart's desires and knowledge, rather than their DNA."

"And the ones that are…evil?" Wynona asked. "Are the books actually evil? Not just the spells?"

Lusgu nodded and sighed. "They are what they were created to be."

Wynona's eyes went back to the book. "Not all of Granny's spells were completely free of darkness," she whispered.

"No creature is completely one way or the other," Lusgu grunted. "I should think you of all creatures would know that. You've put murderers behind bars who did good things in other areas of their lives."

Wynona slowly turned and looked at Rascal. This was the exact conversation she, Rascal and the chief had had earlier.

Rascal gave her a sympathetic smile. "It's all in the choices, Wy. It's how I wasn't ticked off or scared that a Le Doux was my soulmate. I'd seen your choices." He shrugged. "But given the right motivation, any of us will turn another direction."

Another shiver rocked her and Violet nuzzled under Wynona's ear. "Violet said I'm supposed to feed it," Wynona said hoarsely. "What exactly does that mean?"

"There are two ways," Lusgu explained. "Add your own spell, or give it some of your magic."

Wynona jerked back. "Excuse me?"

Lusgu rolled his eyes. "Just push a bit in so it can read you. It won't need more after that. Once the book has fully bonded, you'll be able to see more and it will respond to simple commands. If it's reacting when you touch it, then it wants to bond with you."

"Do you think it would help us figure out your curse?" Wynona asked.

Lusgu hesitated. "I don't know. Saffron wasn't..." He began to choke and Wynona realized she was asking questions he was unable to respond to.

She sighed. "Yes or no. Could it possibly help?"

He nodded.

Wynona looked at Rascal, who was scowling. "Are you alright with me doing this?"

"Not if it's going to hurt you."

Wynona nodded. "I don't really want that either. My life is complicated enough as it is." She twisted so she could see Violet. "Any ideas? Is it safe?"

*Witches do it all the time. As long as you trust Saffron, it should be fine. I wouldn't recommend trying to take on a grimoire from an unknown witch.*

Wynona chuckled darkly. "Trust Granny? That's a loaded question."

Lusgu grunted.

Wynona took a couple of cleansing breaths. "Okay..." she whispered. "I think I should do it. If witches have been doing it for centuries, then it should be fine and the book hasn't hurt me yet." She glanced at Lusgu. "Maybe it'll help me help others and that's all I've wanted to do anyway."

Rascal growled softly.

Wynona could feel the anxiety emanating off of him, but she felt compelled to do this. Not just for Lusgu, but also for herself. She was a witch. An untrained, powerful witch. Tools such as a grimoire would surely be a help to her as well, and maybe it would put her on a better path to handling her own talents and abilities.

It was definitely worth a shot.

Laying her hand on the page, Wynona closed her eyes and called her magic up. The book immediately began to vibrate and she could almost *feel* its eagerness. Slowly, she worked the magic down her arm. She didn't want to smash a large blast into the book, but she wanted it to know who she was.

Her hand shook the closer the magic came to the book and when the two finally touched, Wynona gasped. Her eyes flew open to a world colored in shades of purple. Trails of mist floated from the book that Wynona somehow recognized as Saffron's residue.

*We see you... Welcome, sister...*

Wynona gasped. It wasn't true words, but a definite sense of belonging. This grimoire had not been Saffron's first. She had joined with it the same way Wynona was joining with it. A feeling of connection and family filled her chest until Wynona wanted to weep.

A sudden thought flitted through her mind and Wynona felt compelled to obey. Lifting her hand, she let it hover in the air over the grimoire. Pages began to flip, slower, then faster until a section opened toward the end of the book. The page it stopped on was almost completely blank except for a small verse in the center.

**Piece by piece**
**Until undone**
**Unspool a yarn**
**The witch has won**
**The strong will win**
**The strong will lose**
**A family split**
**His will refuse**

"What the he—" Rascal cleared his throat. "What in the paranormal world is that supposed to mean?" he ground out.

Wynona slumped in her seat, her energy spent. "I have absolutely no idea."

## CHAPTER 24

Wynona didn't want to open her eyes. She was comfortable and warm, Rascal's arms were around her…and the outside world was a disaster. It was far better to just shut it all out by pretending that it didn't exist.

Rascal chuckled, causing her to bounce against his chest. "I don't think it works that way."

"It does if I say it does," Wynona murmured, keeping her eyes closed.

*Please don't make me be the grownup in this conversation,* Violet whined. *That's not nearly as fun.*

Wynona rolled her eyes behind her closed lids. "Violet…that's ridiculous and juvenile."

*Exactly my point.*

Rascal chuckled again and Lusgu grunted as he walked past. Wynona cracked her eye open just enough to see the broom following in his wake. She was coming to understand that cleaning was a way he found control. *And he must need it when his life is ruled by a curse I can't break.*

"Hey now," Rascal chided. "You'll get there. That was your first try at the grimoire. I'm sure you'll figure something out soon."

He kissed the top of her hair and Wynona wanted to simply melt into a puddle. Right now life was perfect. But as soon as she sat up and opened her eyes, she'd be back in a world where a murderer was on the loose, an entire circus of performers were trying to recover from being abused, one of her good friends and employees was cursed and another friend was being accused of murder.

"Okay..." Rascal began. "Let's talk it all out. What suspects do we have left?"

Wynona groaned and sat up, rubbing her forehead. "If none of the performers could leave the grounds, then that leaves only someone at the station," she said softly.

"So we have Daemon," Rascal stated matter of factly.

Wynona slumped. "Yes."

"Anyone else?"

She shrugged. "I don't know. Again, anyone could have gone in during the couple minutes he was gone."

"In other words, the whole station," Rascal muttered, pushing a hand through his hair. "But how did they get out? That's the real question. And did Braxet know them? Without a fight scene, it seems to me that he probably didn't feel any fear from the perpetrator's presence."

"Good point," Wynona murmured. She leaned her elbows onto her knees. "And Daemon might have had opportunity, but he has no motive."

"Other than knowing Braxet attacked you and we've suspected him of dirty dealings in the past."

"But is that enough to make Daemon break the law?" Wynona looked over her shoulder. "I don't think that's a strong enough tipping point for a good officer."

Rascal pursed his lips and nodded. "I agree. But the time frame is hard to shake off."

"Could someone have gone in and not come out?"

Rascal stiffened. "What do you mean?"

"I mean..." Wynona was talking slowly, working through the thought even as she spoke. "I mean, what if the murderer slipped in, killed Mr. Braxet, but never actually left?" She sat up and looked at Rascal with wide eyes. "What if they were in there the whole time?"

"But if he was still in there when Skymaw came back, then he would have been there when we went inside." Rascal frowned. "There's no other way out of that room. We should have seen them when we went in."

"But could we have missed someone? Is it possible?"

Rascal grumbled. "I guess. But my senses are pretty sharp. Why didn't I smell them?"

Wynona twisted on her hip, the idea gaining momentum in her mind. "You weren't looking for them! Tons of officers go in that room. You wouldn't have even been thinking about a smell. Smelling any of your other officers would have been normal!"

"Whoa...slow down," Rascal said, putting his hands in the air. "It's highly unlikely that an officer was in there. Where would they have hidden? We opened the door widely and there was no one there except the body."

Wynona chewed on her bottom lip. "I need to see the room again."

Rascal groaned and leaned back against the couch. "You're not going to let this go, are you?"

Wynona shook her head. "No. I really think we're onto something. It would make so much more sense. There's no way Daemon killed him, but I do think there's a way he accidentally shut the murderer in the room."

*I'd listen to her,* Violet said as she smoothed out her fur. *Despite being too stuck on the rules, she does usually have a point.*

"Hey!" Wynona cried. "You better remember who feeds you cookies."

Violet sniffed. *Threats are beneath you, Wynona.*

Rascal laughed out loud while Wynona glared at her familiar. Sometimes the mouse absolutely drove her crazy.

"Come on, sweetheart," Rascal said, standing and taking her hand. "Let's go have a look. I know full well you won't sleep tonight unless we figure this out."

"Well, think of it this way," Wynona said as they walked toward the door. "With one less problem to solve in my brain, I can put my energy toward solving the others that won't go away."

"The next one better be when we're getting married," Rascal grumbled. "That would be the easiest fix of all."

"Only because you want to elope."

"See?" he said, opening the side door to the truck. "Easy. No clean up, no invitations, no family or friend's drama. Five minutes with a Justice of the Peace and bam! Husband and wife."

"Yeah," Wynona drawled. "What a story that'll make for our kids."

Rascal leaned in, a smirk on his lips. "There's nothing more romantic than an elopement," he said, his eyes focused on her mouth.

Wynona tried to hold back her smile, but she was failing miserably. "How do you figure?"

His hand went to the back of her neck and he slowly pulled Wynona's face forward until their lips were millimeters apart. "Because it'll let our kids know just how much I love their mother and can't wait to make her mine."

The kiss was probably meant to last only a second, since they were leaving, but with a throaty growl, Rascal cupped her face fully and extended it until they were both struggling to breathe normally.

"Ah, sweetheart," he groaned, taking one last taste of her. "You're killing me."

Wynona shook her head. "The feeling's mutual."

Chuckling and shaking his head, Rascal winked and closed the door, then headed around to the driver's seat.

The station was quiet when they arrived and the front desk was empty. "I guess we don't have to worry about anyone disturbing us during our investigation," Wynona said with false cheer.

Rascal nodded. "That's because everyone else is smart enough to be home and going to bed…" He glanced sideways at her. "With their husbands and wives."

Wynona smacked his bicep. "Soon! Okay! I promise!"

"Heard that one before." He stopped and unlocked the interrogation room. "Your room awaits, m'lady."

Putting her nose in the air, Wynona sauntered past him, enjoying his smile at her antics. Once inside, she paused. "Okay... If I were a killer...and I was trying to hide, where would I do it?" She turned a slow circle, eyeing every corner of the room. It was one large box. No filing cabinets, no closets, no furniture other than the table and folding chairs that stood in the center.

"I don't see it, Wy," Rascal said, his tone serious. "There's nowhere to be but visible."

"Do any of the officers have the ability to hide themselves?" Wynona asked desperately. She couldn't be wrong about this, she just couldn't! There had to be a way for someone to hide.

"We don't have any ghosts on the force."

Violet's purple nose came up over the edge of Rascal's pocket. *What if they were too small to see?*

Wynona blinked. Something was on the edge of her mind. Some piece of information that she couldn't quite grasp. "What shifters do you have?" she asked, trying to find something to trigger her thoughts.

"A griffin, myself, I think we've got a lion, a tiger and a bear."

Wynona glanced at him and Rascal winked. "Funny."

"I thought so." He took in a slow breath. "But seriously, the only shifters we have are predators. None are small enough to hide in here. Not to mention, I think Skymaw's black hole abilities would have negated their ability to shift."

Wynona rubbed her forehead. "This is all so complicated." She looked up and stopped.

"What?" Rascal asked. "Your face just said you thought of something."

"Rascal, would you go out in the hall and in a minute, open the door, look around and then shut the door again?"

Rascal scowled. "You really think you found something?"

Wynona nodded, turning to focus on him. "I think I did."

The wolf sighed. "Fine. Come on, Vi. Let's go."

As soon as the door was shut, Wynona walked to stand against the wall behind the door. When Rascal swung it open, he shouldn't be able to see her unless he purposefully stepped in and looked back.

Rascal opened the door and was quiet. "Okay, Wy. I don't..." He trailed off and smirked as he spotted her behind the small pane of one-way glass in the door. Just big enough to be able to check on the occupants. "Gotcha."

Wynona thought frantically. "Try again."

Rascal rolled his eyes. "I can clearly see you."

"No, no. Try again. Seriously."

Sighing, Rascal went back out.

Wynona squatted down and waited. Sweat trickled down the back of her neck and her thighs were burning by the time Rascal opened the door, but she waited him out, angling her body so the door didn't hit her.

She heard his footsteps and several moments of silence before he poked his head around the door. "You were definitely harder to see that time."

Wynona stood, stretching out her legs, her mouth tugging into a smile. "If you hadn't known to look, you wouldn't have seen me, would you?"

Rascal made a face.

"Daemon didn't look behind the door, did he?" Wynona continued to press. "Because he wouldn't have thought he needed to. He opened the door, glanced around like you did the first time, and called it good."

Rascal put his hands on his hips. "Probably."

*That's it. The officer squatted down,* Violet squeaked.

Wynona nodded. "That, or they're simply that small."

Rascal smiled sadly. "I guess it's time to pull out the officer files," he said grimly. "And start seeing who might have a previous connection to Braxet."

"I'm sorry," Wynona said softly.

"We knew this might be coming," Rascal stated. "It was always a possibility. But just like I was pretty sure we'd prove Skymaw innocent, I hoped it wouldn't really come down to it." He huffed. "Nothing for it. Come on, Wy. There are too many to tackle tonight. We'll come back first thing in the morning."

Wynona didn't speak as she took his hand. There was nothing she could do to take away the sting of knowing one of his friends and coworkers had committed a crime such as this. Wynona knew very well what betrayal felt like and she hated that Rascal was getting a taste of it as well.

## CHAPTER 25

"I need more tea for this," Wynona murmured as she eyed the stack of files on Rascal's desk.

He snorted a laugh. "There's not enough tea in the world for this." Grabbing a chair, he pulled it up to the desk and invited Wynona to sit down. "Only way to eat a griffin is one bite at a time. Let's get going, Witchy Girl."

Wynona stuck out her tongue and Violet snickered. "Don't think I'm not putting you to work," Wynona told her familiar.

Violet's glare was far from intimidating.

Smiling, Wynona set the mouse down on the desk. "Okay. Here's one for you," she said, opening a folder. "And I'll take a look at this one."

"What exactly should we be looking for?" Rascal muttered. "I doubt any of these are going to say, 'Has had dealings with the Cursed Circus.'"

Wynona nodded. "True. Let's look at species and abilities right now. We can look for the connection later. We need officers who aren't tall and have the ability to be overlooked."

"Without magic," Rascal said wryly.

Wynona made a face. "Without magic."

Rascal leaned back in his seat. "It's a crazy order. I'm not sure I know of any species that can do much without magic."

"We've got to try."

"Right." Rascal leaned forward and began skimming the file. "Huthor is a six-foot-two vampire. I don't think that's who we're looking for."

Wynona grinned. "Probably not. He's too tall."

"Agreed." They were quiet for a few minutes while they both continued to look.

"Here's a fox shifter," Wynona murmured. "He's a predator, but the kind that sneaks around. Perhaps he's one to look at?"

Rascal nodded. "Sounds plausible."

Wynona set the folder aside and moved onto the next one. Hours passed and by the time lunch rolled around, Wynona's stomach was grumbling, Rascal was getting grouchy, Violet was asleep and they had a stack of half a dozen officers that might fit the bill.

"I think we need to get lunch before we do anything else," Wynona said as she stood and stretched. "We'll both think better if we have a small break."

"I haven't thought about it much," Rascal admitted as they walked out of the station. "But your re-grand opening is in a few days. Have you been able to get ready for it at all? I feel like you've been spending all your time on this instead."

Wynona blew out a breath. "Time? I don't understand what that means."

Rascal gave her a rueful grin. "That bad, huh?"

Wynona tilted her head back and forth. "It'll be okay...I think. I already had all the orders for food and such ready to go. I'm sure Lusgu has made sure the shop is spic and span and mostly I'll need to show up. I have some appointments for custom orders and those will, of course, take priority, but otherwise, I'll just be mingling and doing my normal thing."

"Do you think you'll try to hire help again?" Rascal gave a chin tilt to another officer as they walked past.

Wynona didn't hear the question at first. Instead, she found herself studying each and every creature they walked past. They only had a handful of names. But which ones were they? Was she looking at the very officer that killed Mr. Braxet?

"Wy?"

She jumped out of her reverie. "Yeah?"

Rascal sighed. "Not everyone in here is a killer."

"I know that."

Rascal raised an eyebrow at her. "Do you? Because this is my team. They're family to me. Yes, I know we're having to weed out an interloper, but the rest are good creatures doing their best to help society be safe."

Wynona stopped walking. "Rascal...I know that. I wasn't judging them. Of the two of us, I'm usually the one fighting for the fact that most creatures are good."

Rascal scrubbed his hands up and down his face. "I know," he muttered. "But you looked scared...and I can't take that. Mole or not, you don't have anything to fear from this station."

Wynona's muscles relaxed a little. "I know," she whispered. "I do. But I also know that somewhere in this crowd, someone reached their breaking point, and I suppose it worries me that they might reach it again."

Nodding his understanding, Rascal took her hand and led Wynona toward the front again. He nodded and grunted at others as they walked, but didn't stop to speak.

Wynona, however, kept looking around, trying to decipher the inner workings of every creature in the building. Instead of shifty, murderous intentions stopping her progress, however, it was a set of brown eyes. "Rascal...wait!"

He stopped. "What?"

Wynona tilted her head around. "That officer. The dwarf."

Rascal nodded. "Officer Frostjaw?"

"Frostjaw?" Wynona whispered.

Rascal nodded. "Yeah." He scratched his chin. "I think his file is in the pile of possibilities, though I'm guessing it's mostly due to his size." Rascal's golden eyes looked at Wynona. "What did you want to know about him?"

Wynona frowned. "I'm not sure it matters, but...can we go speak to him?"

Rascal shrugged. "Sure." He navigated the crowd. "Frostjaw!"

The smaller officer spun, his bushy eyebrows high on his forehead. "Deputy Chief." The petite officer eyed Wynona. "Ms. Le Doux."

Wynona gave him a tentative smile. "Hello, Officer Frostjaw. I don't think we've formally met."

The dwarf nodded and they shook hands.

Wynona noticed there was dirt under his fingernails and dust on his boots. He appeared to be a creature who spent a great deal of time in nature, which made sense considering his species.

"What can I do for you, Deputy Chief?"

Rascal turned to Wynona.

"Have you ever heard of a Ms. Cintrine Fernsand?" Wynona asked. She kept her eyes on his face. There was something about his eyes that had caught Wynona's attention. They were wide and brown. And while many creatures had brown eyes, the shade was slightly lighter than usual. Just like Ms. Fernsand's.

The dwarf frowned. "Fernsand?" He shook his bearded head. "No. Should I have?"

Wynona sighed. Nothing in the officer's demeanor said he was lying. *I'm grasping at straws,* she thought.

*Eye color isn't a crime,* Violet added. *I think you're just tired.*

"Thanks," Rascal said, breaking into the conversation. "We're working on some clues for the Braxet case and thought maybe you might know one of our witnesses."

The dwarf made a face. "Witness? I didn't realize there were any witnesses in that case."

Rascal waved him off. "Doesn't matter. Thanks. We'll talk to you later."

Wynona walked out with Rascal tugging on her hand. *Sorry,* she sent him. *I must be getting paranoid. I'm seeing clues everywhere.*

Rascal squeezed her fingers, but didn't speak until they got outside. "I saw his eye color too. But brown isn't unusual for a dwarf. It was Ms. Fernsand who was different."

Wynona nodded and climbed into the passenger seat of the truck. "I know. Again, sorry."

Rascal gave her a quick peck and closed her door before going around to his own side. "Where to?" he asked, revving the engine.

"Whatever sounds good to you," Wynona said. "If you want to go to the tea shop, I'm sure I can pull something together. Or we can grab something quick."

"I want this mole business over with as quickly as possible, so though you know I love your cooking, I'm going with fast food today."

Wynona's stomach simultaneously roiled and rumbled. "That's fine." She was so sick of this whole affair. Sick of not knowing the truth. Not knowing who they could trust. Not knowing why or how Mr. Braxet or Mr. Nasille were killed, or how the two murders were tied to each other.

Sick of being kept from Rascal, or always feeling like she had to put him off about their wedding. Sick of not understanding her powers and not being able to help those she wanted to help. Or not being able to fix Lusgu, or understand why he was so cranky or secretive.

*I think maybe you need a nap more than you need food,* Violet mused.

Wynona sighed and let her head fall back against the seat, closing her eyes. "Maybe I do."

Rascal's large, warm hand landed on her knee. "It'll all be over soon," he said soothingly. "We're closing in, even if we're not happy with the direction this is going."

"I hope so," Wynona said, keeping her eyes closed. "I'm reaching my breaking point, but I don't really feel like I have a choice but to keep going."

"We've narrowed it down to an officer, that's progress," he reminded her.

"Yes, but which one? And how can we figure out their connection to the circus? Anyone willing to kill a man would also be willing to lie to cover it up."

"Your brilliant plan last night showed us that it was someone small enough to fit behind the door and be easily ignored. We'll get there." Rascal squeezed her leg. "We'll get there."

Wynona gave him a sideways glance. "You're awfully calm about it being someone in the station."

Rascal shrugged and put both hands back on the wheel. "I wouldn't say I'm calm. Resigned might be the better word. In my business, you don't make it a career without understanding that at some point, someone's going to break."

Wynona shook her head, compassion helping soothe the worry in her stomach. "I'm sorry."

He shrugged again. "It is what it is. I don't like it, but I can't do anything to stop it either. All I can hope to do is correct it." He gave her a tired smirk. "I'll probably go crazy when it's over. You can feed me a steak and make it all better."

Wynona laughed softly. "Let's start with lunch."

"Agreed."

Half an hour later, Rascal was slowly driving down the street to the police station when movement in the parking lot caught Wynona's eye. After realizing what was going on, she said, "Rascal, pull over." She waved her hand when his fingers moved to the siren switch. "No. Quiet. Just pull over."

"You're no fun," he muttered, pulling into a parking spot along the street. Putting the truck in park, he twisted in his seat. "What'd I miss?"

Wynona took off her seatbelt and twisted so she could see out the back of the truck. "Officer Frostjaw was getting in a patrol car."

Rascal frowned. "So?"

Wynona watched the patrol car pull out of the lot and turn toward the road out of town. "So…he stole the keys to the car from another officer." She looked at Rascal. "I watched him walk by someone else and slip them from his pocket. I don't think he wants anyone to know where he's going and he turned toward the outside of town."

Rascal pulled out, jerking the wheel when he almost hit another vehicle. "Then I guess we better figure out where he's taken that stolen police car, hm?"

Wynona nodded. "I think we better."

*Ooh...now we're getting somewhere,* Violet added. *But what if he's just visiting his mother or something?*

Wynona pursed her lips. "I don't think most officers steal cars to visit relatives."

*Unless they're really terrible relatives.*

Wynona shook her head. "I guess there's only one way to find out."

## CHAPTER 26

Wynona shifted in her seat. With every passing moment, she grew more and more certain that they were headed to the Cursed Circus. The officer had done a bit of weaving through the outskirts of town before finally taking the right road, but the destinations he could be headed towards grew fewer and fewer.

Rascal's face was tight, the pulse in his jaw ticking.

"Are you going to be alright?" Wynona asked.

He nodded curtly. "I'll be fine."

She rubbed his shoulder. "Do you think there's a chance he's going for something other than the case?"

"Not after we mentioned Ms. Fernsand," Rascal ground out. "He *asked* about her being a witness, pretending not to know her. I stayed vague about the answer because I didn't want too much information floating around the office. Not when we're trying to investigate a mole. If Frostjaw didn't know anything…he wouldn't be headed there now. There'd be no reason for it."

"I'm sorry," Wynona repeated. "We need to make sure we get the evidence we need though, before arresting him." She pinched her lips together. "I can't really figure out why though. There's been no indication of his involvement with Braxet. Why would Officer Frostjaw kill him?"

Rascal growled. "I don't know." He pulled off to the side of the country road, parking into the treeline. "We walk from here," he stated.

Wynona nodded and waited for Rascal to come open her door, though she was anxious to get this over with. Her nerves were twitchy and she wondered how Rascal could appear so calm.

"Practice."

"Stop reading my mind," she said in exasperation.

*Then I suggest you stop speaking it out loud.*

Wynona groaned softly as she stepped over a fallen log. "Tell me I didn't speak out loud again."

*Okay...I won't tell you.*

Pulling in a long breath, Wynona blew it back out. *Focus,* she reminded herself. *There's time for being an idiot later.*

Violet snickered and Wynona glared at Rascal's pocket.

"Around this way," Rascal said softly, leading Wynona around the edge of the forest opening. "I want to see where he parked before we go inside."

It took another ten minutes for them to walk around the circus property to see the squad car parked in the back and near the garage. It looked like Frostjaw was familiar with the layout of the property, telling Wynona the dwarf had been there before.

Another growl slipped out from Rascal's throat. "He should have said something."

"You're right," Wynona whispered. "But the fact that he didn't tells me that his involvement with them might not be a simple thing."

Rascal clenched his jaw. "We'll see."

"Do you think he was involved in Nasille's murder as well?"

Rascal's lips thinned. "I don't know, but having them both die in similar ways that close together is suspicious. I still don't see the connection though."

"Me either." Putting her focus back on the compound, Wynona

followed Rascal up to the garage. She waited while Rascal slipped through a side door and waved her inside.

Cars were lined up, but the inside was far from the pristine space Mr. Nasille had kept it. Other than the space roped off as a murder scene, the entire inside of the garage was a mess. Tools were everywhere and cars were in various states of disrepair. It appeared as if a storm had blown through and no one had bothered to clean up.

*Oh my goodness,* Wynona thought.

Violet chittered.

"Nasille was complaining about imps, wasn't he?" Rascal murmured, his ears twitching. Golden eyes searched the area like a laser beam. "I don't hear anyone."

"Hang on." Wynona turned on her magic vision and whistled under her breath. "It's still layered in multiple spells, but nothing looks new to me." She shrugged. "To be perfectly honest, however, I'm not sure I'd know if something was new."

"Look at the tools," Rascal suggested. "Are they covered in magic?"

After surveying the room carefully, Wynona walked up to a few metal tools lying on the floor. She thought one might be a wrench, but she had no idea what the others were used for. A soft brown emanated from them, in speckles, as if tiny, magical hands had been handling them. She straightened. "Yeah. It's brown, so it's an earthy magic, as best I can tell. The spots are small and light, so I think you're right. It's probably residue from the imps."

Rascal nodded sharply and tilted his head toward the building. "Frostjaw isn't here. Let's go inside."

Wynona followed him back into the crisp, afternoon air. She kept a hand on his back, as if to reassure her that he wasn't running off and leaving her. Even with her shield up, she could feel the anger beginning to roll off him in waves. The weight of the other animals at the circus was also heavy, but Rascal's was the most potent.

With each passing moment, his emotions grew stronger and stronger. When they finally caught up to Frostjaw, Wynona was worried she would have to hold Rascal back from hurting the other officer.

"Wait here." Rascal pulled on a side door, but it didn't budge. "Is it magically locked?" he asked her.

Wynona changed her vision and shook her head. "Not that I can see."

Without a word, Rascal pulled out some tools and broke the lock, letting himself inside.

Eyes wide, Wynona followed. Her fiance was growing more dangerous by the second.

Sniffing, Rascal walked down the dark hallway, then paused. "The main hallway is that way," he said, sniffing again. "We're going up."

"Up!" Wynona squeaked, then covered her mouth.

"Up." He studied the ceiling. "Can you use your magic to lift me into that vent?"

Wynona grimaced. "I'll try." She was trying hard not to think of what they would find crawling around inside the dark recesses of the ventilation system, but her imagination was running overtime.

*Tell Rascal to wait.*

"Violet says to wait," Wynona repeated. She wished the three of them could still communicate, but her shield was too heavy at the moment.

The purple mouse scrambled to the floor and darted out of sight.

Rascal's eyes were lighting the whole hallway. "Where's she going?"

*Violet?*

*I'll find them and let you know where to come.*

Wynona repeated the message and she and Rascal awaited anxiously for word.

*You won't believe this,* Violet said a few minutes later.

"What?" Wynona responded out loud before wincing. *I really need to work on that.*

*You do. But right now you need to come listen to dwarf guy arguing with his HALF SISTER, about why they need to escape the circus.*

Wynona felt as if her jaw were about to hit the ground. She had a sneaking suspicion of what Violet was about to reveal and it made her feel ill. *Who, Violet?*

Violet sighed. *Ms. Fernsand. You were right all along about those eyes. They're definitely related.*

With a trembling voice, Wynona told Rascal everything Violet had said.

His growl was swallowed back, but Wynona could see how much effort it was costing him. "Up," he demanded.

Closing her eyes to concentrate, Wynona braced herself. She'd lifted her scooter a few times, surely she could handle a man. She grit her teeth when his weight hit her, but once she got the momentum moving in her favor, helping him to reach the ceiling wasn't as bad as she had feared.

"Let me go," Rascal grunted after pushing off the vent and pulling himself inside.

Wynona gasped, letting out the breath she'd been holding.

"Come on." Rascal was on his stomach, reaching his arms down.

Wynona started to reach up, then paused. "Hold on." Keeping her eyes open this time, she focused on lifting again, only this time, it was her own weight she was bracing for. "Whoa." Holding her arms out to the side, she slowly rose toward the opening and grabbed Rascal's hands as she shakily entered the dark space. "That was terrifying," she admitted after landing inside the vent.

Rascal chuckled darkly. "We'll practice later. Right now we have a job to do."

Wynona nodded, assuming Rascal could see her in the dark. On hands and knees, Wynona followed Rascal through a tunnel of dark, metal tubes. She'd never been claustrophobic and Wynona had never been more grateful. Even without a fear of small spaces, she was finding it harder to breathe the longer they were inside.

Rascal stopped and looked over his shoulder, a finger to his lips, then he pointed down.

Wynona nodded, trying to regulate her pulse, but it wasn't cooperating. Not every aspect of being a detective was her cup of tea. Once she finally got her loud breathing to calm down, she realized there were voices coming from below them. Frowning, Wynona laid down and put her ear to the dusty metal.

After a minute, Wynona raised her head, watching Rascal. His eyes lit up the space and were twitching from side to side, along with his ears, which had elongated. She might not have been able to hear what was going on, but Wynona was fairly certain Rascal was completely tuned in.

*Short boy is about to get his head taken off by the demon,* Violet said, obviously picking up on Wynona's frustration.

*Tag is there?*

*Yeah. He was with the water lady before Shorty arrived.*

Wynona huffed quietly. *Have they said anything about Mr. Nasille? And why did Officer Frostjaw kill Mr. Braxet?*

*Hold on...*

Wynona waited...and waited... She could hear the voices growing louder and louder and she suddenly realized the space was also getting warmer. "Oh no," she gasped.

Tag must be starting to lose it. If he went into full lava mode, she and Rascal were toast.

*Literally,* Violet offered unhelpfully.

*What's going on in there?* Wynona asked desperately. *We need enough evidence to convict Officer Frostjaw, but I'm afraid if we stay here someone's going to get hurt.*

Her hair was starting to stick to her forehead and her skin under her shirt felt damp. Looking at Rascal, she realized he was still too far into the conversation below them to be much help. His skin was rippling and she knew the wolf was barely contained at this point.

She didn't want to pull his attention away because his testimony would be absolutely necessary for them to put Officer Frostjaw behind bars. But something had to be done and she was the only one left to do it.

*Can you create a shield to keep you two protected?*

*What about you?* Wynona asked, her mind starting to panic.

*I'm fine. I'm in the far corner. Just take care of you!*

Wynona closed her eyes and called out her magic. She did it slowly, not wanting to draw any unnecessary attention. All they needed was for the crowd below them to realize they were being listened to.

Slowly, relief began to climb over her ankles and up her aching knees and thighs. She pushed it past her head and began to cover Rascal as well. She practically felt the moment his eyes snapped to her and he realized what was going on.

Taking a chance, she opened her eyes to a filmy purple, still set aglow with his golden orbs.

Rascal's nostrils flared and he nodded, but then went back to focusing down below.

With the heat pressing against her shield, but no longer scorching her skin, Wynona blew out a breath and allowed herself a moment to relax. For now they were—

"AHHHH!" she screamed. Her shield burst and something hot enough to brand her skin held onto Wynona's ankle. Without warning, she was falling, landing on her shoulder on the makeshift floor of Ms. Fernsand's dressing room.

The roar of a wolf sent tremors through her, but Wynona was too focused on trying to breathe. Black spots danced in her vision as the pain from her burned ankle and her shoulder combined to rob her of any normal bodily function.

*WYNONA!* a squeaky voice screamed in her mind. *Heal yourself! Do it now!*

Something soft brushed against Wynona's cheek and her eyes fluttered.

*Wolfy boy is going to kill them if you don't get up!*

Wynona blinked again. Her body shook as she finally managed to get some oxygen into it, but the pain filled groan that broke free nearly caused her to faint.

*NOW, Wynona! Heal yourself NOW!*

Not quite lucid, but understanding the panic in Violet's tone, Wynona held her breath, squeezed her eyes shut and sent a jolt of magic through her that jerked her body fully off the ground.

Her pulse was racing through the roof, but the burning in her ankle was gone and her shoulder no longer ached. Finally, conscious enough to look around, Wynona realized Violet had been right. A black wolf was facing down a lava flowing demon and a sneering dwarf, who was slowly backing up, his body blending into his surroundings, all while Cintrine stood in the corner sobbing and fading in and out of eyesight.

*Oh no,* Wynona thought.

*There are better words than that,* Violet retorted. *Someday, I'll give you a lesson, but right now, get off your fanny and get us OUT of here!*

## CHAPTER 27

Wynona scrambled unsteadily to her feet and put her hands in the air. "Everyone needs to calm down." She could feel the full blast of Tag's heat again. "Tag!" she shouted. "We're not here to hurt you! Pull back your heat!"

Tag snarled at the wolf, whose muscles were bunching in a way that worried Wynona. Rascal was about to spring and once that began, she wasn't sure she could stop anyone from being hurt…or worse.

"I mean it, Tag!" Wynona cried. "We're here for Frostjaw! He killed Mr. Braxet! We're here to take him in."

Tag hesitated, his intense glare dimming slightly. "You *killed* Braxet?" he thundered at the dwarf.

Frostjaw stopped moving, looking slightly like a deer that had been caught in a headlight. It only took him a moment to recover. He stepped forward, becoming more visible than his surroundings again. "Don't listen to her!" he shouted. "She has no proof of anything."

Wynona's eyes widened as she realized something. Tag didn't know. She had assumed the whole room was in on it, but Tag had no idea.

*He came in halfway through the conversation,* Violet explained. *His only goal is to protect Cintrine, I think.*

"Mr. Braxet was killed at the station," Wynona said, slowly inching her way to Rascal. "He was behind closed doors and no one could figure out how he was killed." Her brain was scrambling to put the pieces together and it meant she was grasping at straws, but she desperately needed Tag on her side. She couldn't handle the demon, plus keep Rascal safe and stop Frostjaw from getting away all by herself.

"Then how do you know it was him?" Tag ground out, his eyes darting between Wynona and Rascal.

Rascal took a step forward, his lip curled, and Wynona reached out, her hand landing on his back. She took a moment to send soothing magical vibes at him, but Rascal shook her off.

Frustrated, but trying not to show it, Wynona put her attention back on Tag. She needed to give him answers, but she was still struggling with them herself. "An officer, Daemon Skymaw, had been standing guard outside the door. He's a black hole, so no one in the area could use their magic."

Tag tilted his head, obviously caught up in the story, though he didn't take his eye off Rascal.

"Daemon...Officer Skymaw left for three minutes, came back and glanced inside the door to see Mr. Braxet still at his table alive and well." Wynona put her hand on Rascal again, clinging to his fur when he tried to shake her off. "A few minutes later, however, I showed up with Ms. Floura." Wynona raised her eyebrows when Cintrine gasped. "Do you remember Ms. Floura, Tag? Mr. Braxet's secretary?"

Tag nodded. "Yes."

Movement caught Wynona's eye and she realized Officer Frostjaw was trying to make a break for it again. "STOP!" she shouted, throwing her hand in his direction. She barely kept her magic from flinging across the room like a net. An explosion of power right now would only set the room into chaos. "If you're innocent, why are you trying to leave?" she questioned.

Tag frowned and chanced a glance over his shoulder. "Hold still,

Dwol. Or I'll stop you myself."

Officer Frostjaw came back to visibility and snarled. "You have no right to keep me here."

"I would hear her side of the story," Tag said in a heavy voice.

"She's lying! She's clearly lying!" Officer Frostjaw shouted back. "You can't believe anything a witch says!"

Tag stormed over and Wynona tightened her hand on Rascal's fur. With the demon's back to them, she had no idea if the wolf would take advantage of the situation. She let out a small sigh of relief, however, when he backed up slightly, standing more at her side. Apparently, he was willing to let her take the lead here.

Her shirt at this point was completely drenched in sweat and she wished that Tag would ease up on his heat the same way Rascal was backing off. The room felt as if it were about to spontaneously combust. She wiped the back of her hand across her forehead, grimacing at the wetness.

Tag grabbed Officer Frostjaw by the neck of his uniform and lifted the smaller creature into the air. "Hold still," Tag snarled, the two words a very clear threat.

Officer Frostjaw kicked and twisted, but finally nodded. He huffed and straightened his clothes when Tag put him down. "We'll bring you up for assaulting an officer," Officer Frostjaw tried.

"If you're not in jail for murder," Tag shot back. He turned to Wynona, his eyes crimson flashes of light. "Finish."

Wynona swallowed hard. "When Ms. Floura and I came to the door, Officer Skymaw opened it and Mr. Braxet was dead."

Tag scowled.

"It was made to look like a suicide, but things didn't add up." Wynona's chest was heaving, the heat making her head spin. "We realized that the only way someone could have murdered him was if they were already in the room." She pointed a trembling finger at Officer Frostjaw. "He slipped in while Daemon was gone, then waited to kill Mr. Braxet until Daemon had checked at his return. Because Mr. Braxet knew Officer Frostjaw, there was no sign of a struggle. In fact, he probably assumed Officer Frostjaw was there to bail him out."

Tag's frown deepened.

"Instead, however, he killed Mr. Braxet, then camouflaged himself behind the door." Wynona swayed slightly. "When the body was discovered, the room was flooded with officers. Officer Frostjaw was small enough that he was able to slip from behind the door and join the crowd without ever being noticed as coming from anywhere other than the door itself."

Tag turned back to the dwarf. "Is this true? You were here accusing Cindy of telling lies. Did it have to do with the murder?"

Officer Flashjaw gnashed his teeth. "I'm innocent. This is all hearsay! It'll never stand up in a court of law!"

"That's not true."

Wynona had almost forgotten Cintrine was still in the room. Wiping the sweat out of her face once again, Wynona looked over.

The water elf was still fading in and out from her spot in the corner, but there was a determined look to her jaw, which was currently aimed upward in a small show of defiance. "I wasn't a witness, but you told me you killed him. I'll testify against you."

Officer Frostjaw's face began to turn red and he ground his teeth. Stomping his feet on the ground, his hands clenched in rage, he began to shout. "I DID IT ALL TO PROTECT YOU! WE'RE FAMILY!"

Tag jerked again and Wynona realized the demon was out of the loop again. "Family? What do you mean family?" He reached for the dwarf, but Officer Frostjaw lunged backward.

"Don't touch me, you oversized bonfire! My father was never willing to admit he cheated on my mother."

Wynona's heart clenched. Tears were beginning to fill the dwarf's eyes.

"He never acknowledged his sins…" Officer Frostjaw's head slowly shook back and forth. "But I knew. I *knew!*" He turned back to Cintrine. "I found you! I brought you here! Gave you a place where you could be close and had others like you."

Cintrine stepped forward. "I'm a prisoner," she argued. "Do you have any idea what I had to endure when Mr. Braxet decided he wanted my attention?" Tears poured down her cheeks and she shook her head. "The only good thing has been meeting Tag. He's the only reason this has been worth it."

Officer Frostjaw screamed. A sound of true despair and heartache.

Wynona let go of Rascal and covered her ears. After wincing, Rascal darted around Tag and tried to pin the dwarf to the ground.

In the blink of an eye, Officer Frostjaw disappeared and Rascal's jaw snapped at air. The wolf backed up and his head whipped from side to side.

"Where is he?" Tag shouted, his heat flaring.

Wynona immediately turned on her magical vision, but she couldn't see him. "How is he doing that?" she called to Cintrine. "It's not magic!"

Cintrine put a fist on her mouth and sobbed. "It's not magic," she said brokenly. "It's part of being a dwarf. Like how I can disappear into my water. Dwol can disappear into the natural habitat around him. All dwarves can. It's how they survived in the forest for so many years."

Wynona spun in a slow circle. "So he's still here," she said.

Cintrine nodded. "He's corporeal. Just—" She cried out and held a hand to her face.

*Got him!* Violet cried. *Bar the door!*

Wynona scurried backward, throwing her body over the dressing room door. If Officer Frostjaw was corporeal, he wouldn't be able to get past her. "Tag! Look for movement! We need him caught." She quickly added, "In one piece!"

Tag and Rascal began to pace the room, while Cintrine stayed in her spot in the corner, still doubled over and crying.

Wynona tried her magic vision again, but she still couldn't see anything. Cintrine was right, it was part of being a dwarf, not a separate magical skill.

Rascal barked, then growled and began slowly prowling toward a corner.

Tag quickly followed and the two creatures created a blockade. Wynona blew out a breath, grateful it was finally over.

*Watch out!* Violet shouted.

Wynona's head whipped up just in time to see Tag fly backward, his heat climbing to deathly heights. A blur in Wynona's vision told her the running officer was coming her way, and he wasn't slowing down.

The couch to her left burst into flames just as she threw out a blanket of magic, hoping beyond hope that it would land on the racing creature. 'HOLD!" she shouted. She put up her magical vision again, watching the thick blanket land in an odd heap.

*Bingo,* Violet cackled. *Don't let him move.*

Wynona looked around. "We all need to get out of here or we're going to burn alive." Some of Cintrine's costumes were beginning to catch fire and the flames were hungrily licking at everything within reach. "Everyone out! Rascal, Cintrine, Tag!" Wynona jerked the door open behind her, nearly cursing when the burst of oxygen only caused the flames to grow. "Come on!" she urged.

Rascal was at her side, barking at Wynona to move.

"I know!" she shouted back. "Cintrine! Tag!"

"He's unconscious!"

Wynona peered through the flames, while pulling the blanket of magic tighter around Officer Frostjaw. She began to pull him toward the hallway.

"Wynona!"

Wynnona peered deeper. "Cintrine! Come on!"

"He's unconscious! He can't move!"

Officer Frostjaw fell with a thud and a cry.

"Help us!" Cintrine screamed.

At this point, Wynona could barely see Cintrine's blue head through the flames. There was no way to get to them without getting burned. "Rascal!" Wynona said quickly. "Pull the officer out."

Rascal began to shift back and Wynona knew if she didn't move, he'd try to stop her.

Throwing a shield over herself, she dropped to all fours and began to scramble through the room. She heard Rascal bellowing behind her and she sent a silent apology his way, but there was no way she could leave Cintrine and Tag inside. She also wasn't sure if she could put out the fire, not when they were in the bottom of the building. It wouldn't be the same as her old tea shop that had easy access to space and air.

Once she reached them, Wynona expanded her shield. Cintrine gasped, looking around. "What is this?"

"No time," Wynona gasped. "Let's get you two out of here." She brought her legs under her and crouched, trying to tug on Tag's body. He didn't budge and Wynona's hands were immediately burned. Hissing in pain, she pulled back and looked at Cintrine. "How are you not burned?"

"Water," Cintrine reminded her.

"Can you create water?"

Cintrine shrugged. "Sort of. I can use myself, in a way."

Wynona shook her head. "We can't use you." She grimaced. "Maybe I can create a shield to keep him from burning us."

"He's too heavy to move," Cintrine whimpered.

"How can we put out the fire?" Wynona shouted, fear starting to claw up her throat. She'd jumped into the rescue without thinking it through and now she was stuck. "Last time my sister and I choked it, but I…" Wynona gasped. She wanted to smack her forehead. She'd been throwing out blankets of magic without thinking about it almost every day. Why couldn't she smother the fire that way?

"Hang tight." Wynona spun and put her hands in the air. Taking the shield off of them, she thickened it, expanded it and threw it over the whole room.

"WYNONA LE DOUX!" Rascal shouted hoarsely. "If you're not burned to a crisp, I might kill you myself if you don't answer me!"

Wynona staggered to her feet. "I'm here," she said, swaying slightly. "But I'd rather you didn't kill me. I have a wedding to attend soon." Her face was crushed against Rascal's massive chest and her bones were almost snapped at his tight hold.

"Never again," he growled into her air. "Never again. Never."

Wynona wrapped her arms around his back and clung, not even trying to keep her tears from spilling down her cheeks. "I'm sorry. I couldn't leave them in here."

He growled, his head shaking. "I'm never leaving your side. Don't even ask, because the answer is already no."

*The heat got to him,* Violet grumbled.

Wynona leaned back and looked around. "Where are you?"

"In my pocket," Rascal muttered, pulling Wynona back in. "We can't keep doing this."

"I know." Wynona sighed, relaxing into his hold.

"I don't think you do."

"Excuse me," Cintrine interrupted. "But I still need some help."

Rascal growled. "She's right. We need to put Tag out, or he'll just restart the fire."

Wynona spun, Rascal not actually letting go of her. "I don't think one of my blankets will work this time," she said, swallowing convulsively to try and bring moisture to her throat, then glancing over her shoulder. "You secured Officer Frostjaw?"

Rascal's lip curled. "He's taken care of."

"Cintrine," Wynona said, coming back to the problem at hand. "I think you might need to handle this one. I don't even know what happened to him. How did a dwarf knock him out?"

"Tag's curse centers on his throat," Cintrine said through her tears. "It's a vulnerable spot. Dwol must have hit it."

Wynona sighed. "Let me see if I can…" She trailed off as she turned on her magic vision once again.

Cintrine put a hand on Tag's chest. Her jaw clenched and slowly, her arm began to disappear as she spread water over his body. Steam filled the space, hissing and making it hard to breathe once more.

Cintrine's arms were both gone and her core flashing in and out of visibility by the time she finished with Tag.

Meanwhile, Wynona's mind had been churning. "Rascal," she whispered.

"Hm?" He tightened his hold on her.

"I figured something out."

"What's that?"

Wynona waited until Cintrine looked up. "I think I can get rid of his curse."

## CHAPTER 28

"What do you mean?" Rascal asked, his hold on her tightening.

Cintrine's eyes narrowed in concern, but she didn't speak. Her limbs were slowly regaining their shape and Wynona was glad to see the elf wouldn't be scarred permanently from the encounter.

"Do you remember what we read in the grimoire?" Wynona asked softly.

Rascal nodded.

"About the yarn?"

"You mean the line about unspooling?"

Wynona nodded quickly. "When I looked at the curse with my magic vision, I realized that it looks like yarn. Sharp, pointy yarn, but still yarn. There's a thread-like quality to it, but with barbs that keep it attached to the person it's been cast. I had originally called it a vine in my head, but a thread works too."

"And how do you think you can get rid of it?" Cintrine asked.

Wynona pinched her lips and glanced over at Violet.

*Don't look at me. It's not my grimoire.*

Wynona rolled her eyes. "I don't actually know if the line I read about truly applies to curses, but it seems like it should."

"So…" Cintrine pressed.

"So it sounds like I should be able to…unwind…it from Tag's body."

Rascal's eyes widened and Cintrine's jaw dropped. "You can't be serious."

"The line said 'Piece by piece, until undone, unspool the yarn, the witch has won.'" Wynona flexed her hands. "When I was watching you bring down his temperature, it occurred to me that the curse looks like something that should be workable."

"Well, give it a try," Rascal encouraged.

Cintrine watched with fathomless eyes, but didn't interfere.

Slowly, Wynona dropped to her knees beside Tag's body. Rascal scooted closer so he was right next to her, and she was grateful for his support. She had no idea how much strength it was going to take to get rid of a curse, and she'd already spent a great deal putting out the fire and saving the three of them.

Her hand trembled as she began to reach forward, but Wynona grit her teeth, determined to help save the demon if she could.

"Wait!" Cintrine cried. "What if it hurts him?"

Wynona pulled back, feeling a bout of heavy guilt. "You're right," she said carefully. "I have no idea how he's going to react to this. We should wait until he comes to."

"Or maybe, doing it while he's unconscious is the best time, because he won't feel it," Rascal suggested.

Wynona raised her eyebrows at Cintrine.

The elf looked down and ran a newly formed hand over Tag's forehead and along the line of one of his horns. Her touch was so light and so obviously full of love-filled longing, it was almost painful to watch.

"What do you think?" Wynona asked softly.

"Maybe it's selfish of me," Cintrine whispered, her voice barely audible. "I just threw my brother to the wolves…" Her eyes darted up. "Literally."

Rascal snorted.

"And now I'm willing to put Tag through pain if it means we can be together." A tear slipped down the elf's face.

"If it makes you feel better," Wynona offered, "I think he would choose this. He obviously wants to be with you just as much as you want to be with him. Mr. Braxet is gone and now the only thing that stands in your way is this curse. I can't guarantee I can help, but the thought feels…true." Wynona waited. It really wasn't her decision to make, but something had clicked into place when she'd noticed the curse. It clung to Tag like a vine, and was eating him from the inside out. It was amazing his body had lasted as long as it had with all the scarring and cutting it caused.

Once again, Wynona found herself ashamed of her kind. She knew she wasn't the only witch who was on the lighter side, but the depth that some of the dark witches went to in order to gain power was nauseating.

"Do what you need to do," Cintrine said. When she looked up, her jaw was set and her eyes determined. She'd made up her mind.

Wynona nodded. On impulse, she reached up over her shoulder. "Violet?"

Rascal set the mouse in Wynona's palm and Wynona placed Violet on her shoulder. When the mouse's tail wrapped around Wynona's neck, she felt much more comfortable taking on the challenge.

Carefully, Wynona began to look for an end piece. Shaking her head when it proved fruitless, for she could neither see how the thread ended or began, she finally picked the branch closest to her and reached down.

It took a couple of tries to actually grasp the thread of the curse. The magic was slippery and seemed adamantly opposed to being shifted. Slowly, Wynona dug a thorn out of Tag's shoulder. When he groaned and shifted, she winced, but kept pulling. It was like taking a deeply rooted weed from the ground as she began tugging, pulling and eventually yanking at certain areas as they wound around his muscular body.

But slowly, much more slowly than Wynona would have liked, she found herself creating a pile next to herself. "Rascal," she rasped. "If you could find me something that I could wrap the curse around?" Wynona stopped to breathe before continuing. "I'm a little afraid that leaving it lying around will simply give it a chance to attach to something or someone else."

"On it." Rascal's heat disappeared and Wynona deeply missed him the couple of minutes he was gone.

It was a good thing her clothes were already soaked through with sweat and covered in ash because by the time Rascal got back, Wynona felt as if she had run a marathon.

Her breathing was labored and her fingers prickling with pain from the cursed thread. With each tug, a shock of electricity went through her skin and Wynona was beginning to feel as if her fingers were split and cracked, though they looked fine when she glanced down.

With one last tug and another long moan from Tag, Wynona pulled the last of the curse from his body and tucked it into the edge of the wooden rod Rascal had brought her. She wiped at her forehead with the back of her hand, then collapsed onto her seat.

"Gotcha," Rascal said, grunting as he pulled Wynona to her feet and into his arms. "Just lean against me," he murmured into her hair, his arms strong and secure in holding her weight.

"Thanks," Wynona slurred. Her energy was all but gone and she could barely keep her eyes open.

Violet's tail flicked. *I didn't think it was possible. But you did it.*

Wynona nodded, her eyes closed. "We need to find a way to get rid of that spool. I don't know how it'll react to being apart from Tag."

Cintrine gasped and Wynona managed to turn her head. Those brown eyes were large and filled with tears as Tag slowly blinked himself into the present.

"What happened?" he croaked. His hand came up to his face, and then the demon paused. Flexing his hand, he looked at it with narrowed eyes, as if he could see that something was different. "I…"

"Tag." Cintrine ran a hand down his face, drawing his eyes up to hers. "She saved you."

"She?"

Cintrine jerked her chin in Wynona's direction. "She broke the curse."

"Actually, I took the curse off," Wynona corrected, slumping deeper into Rascal's hold. "It's not actually broken and I'm a little worried about that."

"Perhaps I can help."

Wynona jumped, then hissed in pain. Every joint in her body felt as if she had run a marathon, but Bud's voice had truly startled her. Rascal helped Wynona turn to see an entire crowd gathered just outside the dressing room. Wynona's eyes widened and she snapped her jaw shut.

"Did you really think you could nearly blow up the circus without gaining anyone's attention?" Rascal whispered with a small chuckle. "They've all been standing out there like a bunch of ninnies, just watching you like *you're* the circus act." He gave a low growl after that comment. "Want me to send them away?"

Wynona shook her head. "He said he can help."

The kitsune waited with an eyebrow raised expectantly. When he realized he had Wynona's attention, he smirked and stepped closer. "First, may I say how magnificent that was to watch. I've never seen the like."

Rascal's growl was stronger this time.

Bud cleared his throat. "Second, I have a...chest...of sorts. It has the ability to block cursed objects." When Wynona gasped, the circus owner shrugged in feigned humility. "In my line of business, you often come across the unusual."

"I don't trust you to leave something like that with you," Rascal ground out.

"Agreed," Chief Ligurio said, coming up behind Bud. He gave Bud a look and the kitsune mockingly bowed before stepping back and allowing the chief inside. Chief Ligurio gave Wynona a once over. "You look paler than me."

Wynona managed a small twitch of her lips. "Thanks." Her knees buckled and Rascal swung her up into her arms.

"I'm getting her out of here," he told Chief Ligurio. "You need Skymaw if you're going to handle the curse. I'll explain everything tomorrow when I'm in the office."

Chief Ligurio opened his mouth, then shut it and nodded.

Wynona knew at that point she really did look horrible. Chief never broke the rules and here he was letting Rascal walk out without argument.

The next few minutes were a blur as Wynona was carried back up to the cars and loaded in Rascal's truck. Her head lolled to the side and Rascal was growling in frustration again. "Can you hold on just a few more minutes?" he asked her, his hands caressing her face in a way that was at odds with the anger flashing in his eyes.

Wynona nodded, her eyes slipping shut. "Yeah. I just need a minute to recover."

"Minute my paw," he muttered.

The door closed and then Rascal was climbing behind the wheel. "We need to make a stop on the way home," he said, reaching over to hold her hand. His thumb rubbed back and forth in a soothing motion. "Then we'll go back to your house and you can sleep as long as you need to, okay?"

"That's fine," Wynona murmured. She didn't know how long it had been before the truck stopped and Rascal was coming around to get her again. "Are we home?"

"No," he said. "But we need to go inside. Here we go." Rascal lifted her and Wynona laid her head in the crook of his neck.

"I'm tired," she slurred. Her body didn't want to obey her commands and Wynona didn't really have the energy to fight it. She hung from Rascal's arms like a limp herb. She had no idea what errand he needed to run, but it had to be important if he was dragging her like this. She knew how much he cared for her and wanted to take care of her. *I can't wait until we're married,* Wynona sent his way. Her wall was beginning to waver in and out and Wynona let it fall. She winced slightly as the emotions of several nearby animals hit her, but now that they were away from the circus it wasn't nearly as bad as it could have been.

Rascal kissed her temple. "Let's fix that right now."

"What?" Wynona brought her head up, then let it drop again. "I don't understand."

"I'm not taking you home and walking away," Rascal said, his tone low and unyielding. "Never again. I meant it, Wy. I'm done." He took a moment to talk to someone else before walking again. "I've shared you for years now and nearly lost you a dozen times. I won't keep waiting."

A hard chair landed gently under Wynona's backside and she swayed a little until Rascal held her shoulders to help keep her upright. He stood in front of her, his golden eyes blazing and his touch warm and strong.

"We're going to get married by a Justice of the Peace, so I can take you home and hold you as you recover and generally just be your slave until you're better." One side of his mouth curled when she huffed a tired laugh. "We can still have a party. A massive party if you want. Let Prim go wild, I don't care, but I won't walk away again, Wy." His smile fell. "Don't ask me to do it."

"Miss?" A timid voice came from the other side of the room and Rascal shifted so Wynona could see a creature watching the two of them with trepidation. He was older and slightly shriveled, but otherwise gave no indication of his species. Dark blue eyes went back and forth between Wynona and Rascal before settling on Wynona. "Are you being forced here against your will?" he asked. "I won't settle for coercion."

Rascal rolled his eyes and Wynona shook her head before swaying again. Rascal stepped closer and she leaned into his side. "No," Wynona whispered hoarsely. "No coercion. Just one more bump in our road to Happy Ever After."

White eyebrows bunched together. "Then you're sure you want to do this?"

Wynona nodded and Violet's tail twitched against her neck. Prim would probably kill her, but Wynona didn't care. Rascal was right. They'd waited long enough. He'd been more than patient and it was time to move on with their lives.

Who cared if her father was plotting in the background? Or if Celia was still upset about her tea reading? Lusgu could surely wait one more day before having his curse removed and Chief Ligurio would simply have to keep Frostjaw locked up until Wynona was well enough to come into the station.

"Please," Wynona said, managing to hold her head enough to look up at Rascal. "We've waited too long as it is."

Rascal's eyes flashed and he bent to give her a kiss so tender Wynona found herself tearing up by the time the judge began his speech.

*I'll hold you to that slave thing,* she teased him while they listened.

*It'll be my pleasure,* Rascal sent back.

*Once we're home, I'm out,* Violet grumbled. *If I have to listen to any more of this drivel, I'm gonna puke.*

Wynona sighed and rested against Rascal in contentment. For just this one moment…everything was perfect.

## CHAPTER 29

"Rise and shine, sleepyhead." An inviting, deep tone broke into Wynona's dream.

She stretched and moaned a little, not wanting to open her eyes. She'd had the most lovely dream…

A kiss on her forehead caused her to jerk and those eyes suddenly became very wide. "Rascal," she breathed.

He stood next to her bed, grinning from ear to ear. His eyes were warm and glowing, his hair stood up on end, his jaw was filled with stubble and in his hands was a tray with a steaming pot of tea and what looked like a bowl of oatmeal. "Well, hello, wife."

Wynona gasped. "Oh my word… it's true!"

Rascal chuckled, the sound sending a pleasant shiver down Wynona's spine. He set the tray down on the nightstand and then plopped next to her on the bed, his head propped on his hand. Reaching out, Rascal tucked a piece of hair behind her ear and Wynona felt a flush work its way up her neck and into her cheeks.

A sudden bout of bashfulness hit her and Wynona covered her face with her hands.

"None of that now," Rascal cooed, leaning up a little higher on his elbow. He pulled down her hands. "I could hear your voice and you sounded much better, so I decided it was time to wake you up and have you eat."

Wynona's stomach responded affirmatively and she groaned. "This is not how I planned to wake up on our wedding day."

Rascal laughed and climbed off the bed. "Actually, our wedding day was two days ago, Mrs. Strongclaw."

"Two days!" Wynona jerked upright, putting a hand to her forehead when her vision spun.

"You need to get your blood sugar up," Rascal said, handing her the bowl. "I would've made you pancakes, except..." He shrugged. "I don't know how to make them and decided to leave that disaster for when you were feeling better."

Wynona smiled. "Thank you," she said, taking the bowl. The heat of it felt good against her chilled fingers. She stretched her legs and her free arm. "I can't believe I slept for two days. But I have to admit I feel a lot better."

"As far as I can read, your body and magic should both be back at pretty much full capacity," Rascal added, perching on the edge of the bed.

"How can you tell that?" Wynona asked, taking a bite of her breakfast.

Rascal tapped his temple. "I can feel it. If you'll pay attention, you'll notice the soulmate bond has gotten a lot stronger."

Wynona frowned, then focused on her brain for a second. It took almost no time at all to realize she not only could feel the emotions of Rascal, but also his wolf. Not to mention, she could feel how hungry he was, how excited he was that they were now married and how concerned he was that she constantly seemed to put herself into danger. "And they say women are complicated," Wynona said breathlessly. "And you need to eat as well."

Rascal shrugged and stood. "You'll get used to that." He winked. "I'm always hungry." Walking to the door, he glanced over his shoulder. "Be right back."

When he disappeared down the hall, Wynona hurriedly shoveled the rest of the oatmeal into her mouth, swallowing as quickly as she could. Jumping out of bed, she rushed for the bathroom and hopped in the shower, shivering when the water was still cold.

She'd dreamed of being married her whole life and waking up after two days with bedhead, morning breath and dirt crusted under her fingernails was definitely *not* what she had planned.

It took nearly a half hour for her to feel witchy again and she managed to get herself to walk away from the hot spray to dry off. Grinning at herself in the mirror, Wynona wiggled her fingers and used a burst of magic to dress herself, style her hair and makeup and become presentable to greet her husband.

She paused with her hand on the doorknob. *Husband.* The word brought a giggle and a blush to her cheeks. How did she ever get so lucky to have Rascal waiting for her on the other side of the door?

*Waiting is right,* Rascal grumbled. *Care to come out and join me? You still need more food.*

Wynona rolled her eyes and opened the door.

Rascal leaned back against the headboard, his T-shirt flexed tight against his arms since he had them folded behind his head. His stockinged feet were crossed at the ankles as he waited for her.

Wynona smiled at the simple picture of domesticity. "Hi."

Smirking, Rascal quirked a finger at her.

Wynona walked over and sat next to him on the bed.

Leaning forward, Rascal cupped her face and kissed Wynona in a way she'd missed lately. They'd been so busy with the case, the tea shop, the wedding planning…all of it important and all of it pulling them apart from each other.

"No more," Rascal whispered against her lips.

"No more," Wynona agreed.

Time was irrelevant as they became lost in each other and if Wynona's stomach hadn't growled, she was positive they would have stayed there much longer. But she was still recovering and although magic could do a lot, it couldn't fix hunger, so hand in hand, the newly married couple walked to the kitchen and ate until Wynona was ready to be rolled to the police station.

"Let's get this finished," Wynona said. "Then we can come back and take care of Lusgu." She paused. "Is Violet with him?"

Rascal nodded and opened the front door, ushering her out. "She took off as soon as we got home. I'm sure she'll be back when she thinks the coast is clear."

Wynona climbed into her side of the truck. "I should send her a message. When should I tell her it's safe?"

Rascal leaned in for another kiss. "It might never be safe for her again," he teased.

Wynona laughed and smacked his chest playfully. "I guess it's a good thing Lusgu kept his portal linked to my home, then."

Scowling, Rascal grumbled under his breath and closed her door before walking to his side.

The trip to the station was filled with overly happy smiles and flirtatious winks, making the time fly by. All too soon, Wynona was holding Rascal's hand and walking inside the station.

For a moment, she half expected everyone at the station to come running to congratulate them, but then Wynona remembered...*no one knows. And I'm not wearing a ring to share with them.*

Rascal glanced down, his signature smirk in place. "Look at your finger."

"What?"

Rascal raised his eyebrows. "Look at your finger."

Wynona brought out her hand and looked down. Just as she thought, her ring finger only held her engagement ring.

Rascal pulled her to a stop. "Hang on." Reaching in his jacket pocket, he pulled out a box and took out another ring, grasping her fingers. "You were a little too tired at the ceremony for us to exchange rings," he whispered, slipping the extra band onto her hand. With a gentle touch, he brought her hand up and kissed her knuckles. "And we were a little busy this morning."

Wynona shook her head, a stray tear breaking free. "You're going to be the death of me," she whispered thickly.

"Hey," Rascal scolded. "That's my line."

Wynona held out her hand, allowing herself a moment to appreciate the added bling. There was no mistaking something new had been added and she couldn't wait to share it with Prim and Violet.

*It's so bright, I can see it through your mind,* Violet complained.

Wynona laughed through her tears, only to realize the station had grown very quiet. She looked around and noticed that almost every officer had stopped and was watching her and Rascal with wide eyes. "Not again," Wynona moaned.

"Deputy Chief," one creature said, coming up with a wide smile. "Congratulations, sir." The tall creature shook Rascal's hand with a hearty pump and then grabbed Wynona in a hug, nearly pulling her off the ground.

"Easy, Melion," Rascal growled. "Don't break the merchandise."

The officer boomed a laugh and stepped back for Wynona to be passed around to every other creature who wanted to offer their congratulations. By the time they reached the chief's office, he looked less than amused.

"Took you long enough," the vampire snapped.

"It was my fault," Wynona said, sliding into a chair. "I'll try to not come so close to dying next time."

Rascal snorted, putting a fist to his mouth to hide his laughter. It didn't work.

Chief Ligurio glared. "Well? Are you going to tell me how it all happened?"

Wynona turned to Rascal, offering him a chance to speak.

Rascal put a hand to his chest. "What? It's my turn? Is this how marriage works? I think I like it already!"

"Oh good grief," Chief Ligurio groaned, slapping a hand on his desk. "Someone speak so I can kick you out for a week, or until you two get out of the goo-goo stage."

Wynona laughed softly, but waited to let Rascal speak. She would have plenty to say when she had to tell about going into the fire without him.

"Then, Mrs. Strongclaw…" Rascal gave her a wink. "Ran into the fire with one of her purple shieldy things and Violet convinced me to wait in the hall. Said she could tell Wy was alright and that I should wait, rather than cause more possible damage." By the end of the explanation, Rascal looked less amused and Wynona couldn't blame him.

It would have been terrifying to watch him run into a fire like that.

"Purple shieldy thing?" Chief Ligurio grunted. "Is that a technical term?"

Rascal grinned. "One hundred percent."

The chief shook his head. "Wynona? What happened next? And how did you figure out it was Frostjaw in the first place?"

Wynona sighed. "I wasn't sure it was him, but we already told you how we figured out that the killer had to have been in the room and the only way to stay hidden would have been to be small and inconspicuous."

Chief Ligurio nodded.

"When I started getting Officer Frostjaw to talk, it was mostly out of desperation. I was guessing."

Chief Ligurio gave her a look. "And you just happened to guess right?"

Wynona shrugged. "I guessed enough to make him angry. Really, I wasn't getting very far until Cintrine decided to fight back. If she hadn't decided to stand up for herself, I wouldn't have had enough information to pin anything on him." Wynona's shoulders slumped. "I get the feeling that Officer Frostjaw felt like she owed him. I don't think she was involved in the murders at all, but she definitely was tired of being used." Wynona shook her head. "Officer Frostjaw brought her to the circus, probably trying to keep her safe. She did say her father wasn't in the picture. And then Mr. Braxet took a special interest in her, if only to keep Tag in line. Then her brother expected her to obey him like a servant because he was her brother. She's been manipulated and abused her whole life." Wynona clasped her shaking hands. "I just hope she's well enough to try and give Tag a chance. He seemed to truly love her."

"And now they have a chance." Rascal put his hand on Wynona's shoulder and gave it a little squeeze. "Because you took away his curse." Rascal frowned. "Speaking of, what happened with that?"

Chief Ligurio leaned back, looking smug. "After putting Skymaw back on duty, I had him bring it in and we disposed of it."

"I don't know what that curse is capable of," Wynona hurried to say. "I hope you have it somewhere where it can't attach to anything else."

"It's taken care of, Ms. Le–Mrs. Strongclaw," Chief Ligurio said with a wave of his hand.

"Oh!" Wynona jerked in her seat. "I just realized that he never confessed about Mr. Nasille. Did you ever figure out that connection?"

Chief Ligurio's smirk grew. "Perhaps that's classified."

Wynona folded her arms over her chest. "I'm a consultant. I get to have the information."

"Need to know basis."

"I'll tell you," Rascal offered.

Wynona smiled up at him.

"I can see where the rules will stand," Chief Ligurio grumbled.

"Yep. Now you see," Rascal challenged.

Chief Ligurio rolled his eyes. "He killed Nasille because the chauffeur knew Frostjaw was related to Ms. Fernsand and he confronted Frostjaw with some suspicions about Braxet's death. Frostjaw wasn't willing to take the chance Nasille would figure things out for sure."

"Wow." Wynona fell back in her seat. "So much deceit and death. Isn't there a way to shut that place down?"

Chief Ligurio sighed deeply. "I wish. But I'm hoping with Braxet gone, things will be above board. Or at least a little *more* above board than they were before."

"One can only hope," Rascal grunted.

Chief Ligurio steepled his fingers. "So now what? I'm assuming you want some time off?"

Wynona glanced up at Rascal. "I need to open the shop before we can take a trip."

"Count me out for the next month," Rascal said, not bothering to look at his boss.

"What?" Wynona cried. "A month!"

"Strongclaw," Chief Ligurio growled.

Rascal shook his head and turned to his boss with a fierce look. "I don't think a month is too much to ask before I'm willing to risk her life again. You understand that thought, don't you, Chief?"

Chief Ligurio's face softened and he eventually nodded. "A month it is." He cleared his throat. "Make it count."

Rascal took Wynona's hand and began to lead her away. "I plan to."

## CHAPTER 30

Wynona hesitated at her front door. It was her house, she shouldn't be nervous about this, but...

"You don't have to do this," Rascal assured her, his hands on her hips. "No one would ever ask it of you."

Wynona chewed on her bottom lip. "He'd never ask, but I'd always know." She cleared her throat, which felt uncomfortably dry. "I can't let him keep going like this. Not if I can help, but..."

"But you don't want to be knocked out for the next two days or go through the same amount of pain," Rascal finished for her. He sighed, spun her around and brought their foreheads together. "I won't tell him. He doesn't have to know."

"I know," Wynona said with a shake of her head. "That's enough." But Rascal had been right. She wasn't sure she wanted to go through that experience again. With each pull of the curse, she had felt her energy and health being drained from her body. It had cost her almost everything to get that curse off Tag. There were two curses on Lusgu and Wynona didn't know if she'd be able to manage them both in one sitting. The idea of doing this a third time made her stomach churn in knots.

"I just hope Fumio keeps his promise," Rascal growled. "If he tells everyone about what you can do, you'll have half the paranormal world at your doorstep."

Wynona shuddered and Rascal wrapped her in his arms. She gripped the back of his shirt, hanging on tightly enough that her knuckles ached. It had been several days since she'd helped put Officer Frostjaw behind bars. The grand opening to the shop had been yesterday and despite the hubbub of the case, it had gone off smoothly and generally been a wonderful success.

Day two had been almost as good. Though Wynona was tired, things had been much easier having Rascal at her side constantly. His month-long break from the precinct was definitely coming at a helpful time. She couldn't wait until they could use some of that time to get away from Hex Haven completely.

The plan was to give the shop a week, save Lusgu from the curse, and then take some time to themselves, leaving Lusgu and Violet in charge. It wasn't a perfect plan and a part of Wynona was worried about how uncursed Lusgu would handle everything, but Violet thought it was smart. She was sure she and Lusgu would have things running smoothly during Wynona's much-earned vacation.

Rascal pushed a hand into her hair, cupping the side of her head, and gave her a long, tender kiss. "Do you want to do this, sweetheart?"

Wynona let her eyes stay closed a little longer than necessary as she savored her husband's touch. "Yes. But I'm scared."

"If you want this, I'm here and I'll do all I can to help. If you don't want to go through with it, I'll defend your decision to my dying day. You don't owe anyone anything."

Wynona sighed and nodded. "I know. But I can't leave him like that. Not when I can help."

Rascal took a deep breath and straightened. "Okay, then. Let's get this over with. But I'm not leaving your side."

"You haven't left my side since we got married," Wynona teased.

"Best week of my life," Rascal teased back.

Smiling, Wynona stepped inside. *Violet? Can you bring him?*

*On it.*

Wynona went to the kitchen, Rascal in her wake. Rather than

using some of her magical energy, she began to make tea the old fashioned way, then paused and laughed. "I just realized I'm finally getting used to my magic." She smiled over her shoulder. "I considered this as making tea the old fashioned way."

Rascal grinned. "Took long enough."

Wynona stuck her tongue out and went back to pulling out the ingredients she wanted. Maybe if she got down a fortifying glass before she began, she'd manage to work through this curse-breaking without falling unconscious for days.

"Or at least having enough energy to heal yourself," Rascal grumbled. He was leaning against the wall, his arms folded over his chest, looking far too strong and delicious for Wynona's peace of mind.

A sudden quirk of his lips told her that he heard her thoughts and Wynona rolled her eyes. "Stay out of my brain."

"I'm not in your brain," he said, pushing off the wall and sauntering in her direction. "I don't have to be anymore." He crowded her against the kitchen counter, caging her in with his arms. Slowly, he ran his nose along her cheek, then traced down her jawline. "Perks of being soulmates," he whispered.

Wynona shivered, locking her knees as they began to go weak from his attentions. She was so glad Rascal had dragged her to the courthouse when she was half conscious. Best decision ever.

The pantry door opened at the same time the front door did and Wynona nearly hit the ceiling.

"Hello!" Prim's voice called into the house.

Lusgu grunted and slammed the pantry door behind him. "Didn't realize I was walking into a crowd," he muttered.

Rascal pinched his lips, not moving away from Wynona for a second. "When we get back from our honeymoon," he ground out, "we're getting a different house."

Wynona laughed softly and brushed his longish hair away from his forehead. "I like my house."

"It's too crowded."

Still smiling, Wynona pushed lightly on his chest and Rascal grudgingly moved back and stepped to the side, falling easily into his police stance.

Prim stood in the doorway of the kitchen, her cheeks red and her hands on her hips. "I'm going to ignore how cute that was in favor of being angry," she snapped.

Wynona jerked back. "I...what?"

"How dare you get married without me!" Prim shouted, throwing her arms in the air. She was still in her fairy form and Wynona had a hard time being intimidated by the tiny creature that only reached her waist. But the huge black hole behind Prim was a completely different story.

His face appeared as if it had been carved out of stone. No emotion shone in his black eyes, whether good or bad as he stared at Wynona.

A hand fluttered to her cheek. "Prim...Daemon...I..." Wynona's eyes filled with tears. "Please, understand. It all happened so fast and I..."

Prim tsked her tongue. "You better be showing me that ring and I better be getting to throw you the party of the century, or I'm walking and never coming back."

Relief flooded Wynona and Rascal growled.

Prim giggled and stepped farther into the room. "Ah...give it up, Wolfy, she's your wife now. You can't hurt the best friend."

Wynona shook her head. "You nearly gave me a heart attack," she scolded.

"Empty threats," Lusgu grumbled.

Prim rolled her eyes at the brownie. "Stuck with me now more than ever, Louie!"

Lusgu sneered, but Rascal laughed. "That might be better than Lu."

Wynona held up her hands. "Enough, everyone." When the fighting had stopped, she turned to Daemon. "Officer Skymaw," she said, purposefully reminding him of his station. "Are you doing alright?"

Daemon was still standing like a statue in the doorway and he tilted his head slightly at her question. "Did you really take that curse off the demon?"

Lusgu gasped, but Wynona kept her eyes on the black hole. "I did."

"Could I have been doing that this whole time?" Daemon's throat moved as he swallowed and Wynona finally realized the officer was feeling ashamed.

She'd performed a miracle using a skill only she and he had, and he was worried about all the creatures he could have helped if he'd thought about it. "I don't think so," Wynona stated slowly.

Daemon's shoulders relaxed slightly.

"Have you ever been able to touch the magic before?"

He shook his head. "Not that I know of. See it, yes. Stop it, yes. But manipulate it? No."

"I believe my ability to pull off the curse has something to do with a prophecy I found in my grandmother's grimoire."

Prim squealed. "You're kidding, right?" She slapped her forehead. "Girl, you have the most complicated existence of anyone I've ever known."

Wynona shrugged, then leaned into Rascal when he wrapped his arm around her waist. "I didn't ask for it."

Prim shook her head and walked over to give Wyonna a hug. "I wouldn't trade who you are for anything," she whispered. "You're perfect. And I'm going to throw you the biggest, bestest party this city has ever seen."

Wynona cleared her throat and gave Prim a look. "We'll talk about that later." She looked back up at Daemon. "Feel better?"

He blew out a breath and ran a hand through his hair. "I suppose I should have started this conversation with a thank you and a congrats, but I—"

Wynona stopped him. "I get it," she said softly. "I'd have felt the same way."

Rascal snorted.

Giving him a mock glare, Wynona looked down at Lusgu. "When we were at the circus, trying to pin the murder on Officer Frostjaw, I had a realization."

Lusgu's body was stiff as a board.

"A demon there had a curse and I could see it, just like I can see yours, and I realized..." Wynona swallowed. "I realized it was like a thread. A poky thread, but still, the words of the prophecy came back to me about 'unspooling.'" She shrugged. "I gave it a try and was able to pull the curse from him."

"What happened to it?" Lusgu responded, his voice tight and strained.

"I wound it around a piece of wood," Wynona answered, then turned to Daemon. "I hadn't planned to have an audience for this, but I'm glad you're here. I can't neutralize magic the way you can and I still don't know what a curse will do if left to its own devices."

Daemon glanced at Lusgu, then nodded at Wynona. "I'm here to help. I owe you two everything."

Wynona could hardly hold back her tears as she turned to her janitor. A creature she viewed as a part of the family, despite his grumpy nature. "Lusgu. Would you like me to take off your curse?"

Lusgu opened his mouth, but the front door opening stopped them all.

Celia sauntered in. "Well, hello…" she purred, eyeing the group. "What's all this about? And why wasn't the sister invited?" She pinned Wynona with a glare. "I do believe I heard a rumor I knew couldn't possibly be true."

Prim huffed. "Your sister got married without any of us. Get used to it, Sissy."

Celia glanced down, not the least bit impressed. "Call me that again and I'll send a hurricane through your greenhouse."

"Nope!" Wynona shouted. "Don't even start! I'm not playing referee today. If you all can't get along, then I'm kicking you out. I have enough on my plate without you all acting like toddlers and I'm about to do something that's going to take all of my concentration. Either help, or move it, because so help me, I can't take it anymore."

The group stood in stunned silence for a moment before Celia clapped slowly. "Well, well, well…it's about time you came into your own." She eyed Rascal. "Maybe marriage isn't quite as bad as I thought it would be."

Rascal smirked but didn't respond.

Wynona found herself very grateful he didn't pursue the fight. "So? What'll it be? In or out?"

A chorus of "in's" rang through the room and Wynona nodded before turning her full attention back to Lusgu. "I never did hear your answer to the question."

Lusgu's eyes were glittering in a way Wynona had never seen them shine before. He stood straight, his shoulders back and his head high. "I'd be forever in your debt. But I have one request."

Wynona nodded. "Name it."

"If it all goes well, I'd like to be the one to tell Rayn."

Wynona couldn't help the smile on her face. She knew there was something between those two, despite the fact that Dr. Rayn had gone back to her house in the forest. "I don't think anyone would take that from you."

Lusgu nodded. "Then what do we need to do?"

## CHAPTER 31

The room was uncomfortably quiet as Wynona began her work. As if they were each holding their breath, unsure of the outcome. If Wynona's heart hadn't already been about to burst through her chest, the heavy tension in the room would have squeezed it into oblivion.

Violet's tail flicked against her neck. *One step at a time, Wynona. Just get started.*

"Easier said than done," Wynona whispered back. She was currently walking around Lusgu, looking for a piece to begin with, but the curse around Lusgu was much sleeker than the barbed wire around Tag. "We're going to start with the one that stops you from speaking," Wynona said softly.

Lusgu nodded. He, at least, looked unafraid.

Wynona wasn't sure if that comforted her, or made it worse that he was putting on a false front. She didn't want to hurt him, but she did want to help. One would more than likely not come without the other.

Her fingers were like ice as she tugged at a strand of the curse just below Lusgu's ear.

He flinched, but held his silence.

"Sorry," Wynona murmured. The chain was much more substantial than Tag's and Wynona could already tell it was going to drain her further than before.

Rascal growled at her thoughts.

She gave him a wan smile and went back to the curse. Using one finger, she ran it under the magical thread until she found a linked beginning. "I need to untie this…then I think we can begin."

"Tell us what you're seeing," Celia said, her voice tangible with curiosity.

"There's a thick…thread or chain…for lack of a better word," Wynona explained. She used her nails to dig at the knot. "I'm working to find a beginning so I can unravel it from Lusgu's neck, but this one has been tied off. Tag's wasn't quite so complicated."

Lusgu's throat moved as he swallowed.

"Ah-ha!" Wynona cried in triumph, then yelped when the end of the thread shocked her.

Rascal was there immediately, reaching out to steady her.

"It's okay," she assured him. "I'm fine, just surprised." She rubbed her fingers, noting that Lusgu still wouldn't look at her. "I need that piece of wood now."

Rascal grudgingly handed over the stick they had decided to use.

Until Wynona knew more about the curses, she figured wood was probably her best bet, since it wasn't living and shouldn't affect the curse in any way. Careful not to touch the very tip of the curse again, she began to slowly wind it into a spool. The process was tedious and the curse was far longer than Wynona would have predicted.

By the time she finished, she was trembling and her fingers felt raw. "Daemon?" Wynona held it out. "Can you?"

Daemon gave her a sympathetic look, gingerly took the spool and concentrated for a moment until the glow of magic faded. "It won't last," he explained. "Only while I'm using my powers."

Wynona nodded, wiping at her forehead. She smiled when Rascal handed her a cool glass of water, gulping it down with a decidedly unladylike manner.

"Can you try healing yourself now?" Rascal asked. "Before you do the second half?"

Wynona pinched her lips. "I'm afraid to use the magic on that and not have enough to handle the big curse."

"Do it," Lusgu said, causing everyone to jerk toward him. His voice had gone from low and gravelly to baritone smooth, almost silky in nature.

Wynona's eyes widened. "What did you say?"

The brownie's lips quirked. "Heal yourself. It will be better for everyone in the end."

"Please tell me that some old crone cursed you because she was jealous of your singing voice," Prim said with a laugh.

Lusgu scowled. "I don't sing."

"You should," Celia said with a smirk.

Wynona caught Rascal rolling his eyes in her peripheral vision and she laughed a little before coming to a realization. "Did it hurt to talk?"

Lusgu's mouth snapped shut and all humor fled. He didn't answer.

Wynona hung her head. "I'm so sorry."

Lusgu shrugged, but stayed silent.

Rascal put a hand on her lower back and Violet nuzzled under Wynona's ear. *Get your energy back and let's take care of this once and for all.*

Wynona nodded. Closing her eyes for a split second, she used her magic to take away the aches, pains and weakness in her body. Just like she'd predicted, however, she could feel that her magical supplies were lower than she was comfortable with.

*We'll deal with that later,* Violet said. *I'm here and can lend a hand, and so can Celia if it comes down to it, though she'll probably act like a diva about it.* Violet sniffed and Wynona couldn't help but smile a little. *But I think she's curious, so we'll use that to our advantage.*

"Why does it sound like we're going to war?" Wynona asked her familiar.

Violet gave Wynona a deadpan look. *Everything is war. Where have you been the last two years?*

Laughing softly, Wynona walked back to Lusgu, grateful her joints no longer ached, but still worried. This thread was infinitely thicker. In fact, it was more like a chain than a thread. "A stick isn't going to cut it," Wynona murmured absently as she walked around the brownie.

"What about a bucket of some sort?" Daemon asked.

"A bucket?" Prim scrunched her nose. "Whatever for?"

"This one is too thick to wind," Wynona responded, indicating Lusgu. She stopped in front of the brownie. "I have a feeling this is going to hurt. Badly. Are you sure you want to try? I don't even know if I'm strong enough to pull it off."

Lusgu clenched his jaw and nodded.

"How long have you been cursed, Lusgu?"

His black eyes glittered in anger. "Too long."

Sighing, Wynona nodded and knelt down. Without allowing herself to think on it further, she reached out and grasped the chain. Pain immediately shot up her arm and Wynona grit her teeth. Violet was right. Everything was war.

A plastic tub landed at her side and Wynona began the arduous task of unwinding what felt like miles of chains from Lusgu's tiny body. His face was contorted in torture with each pull and Wynona noticed that he was bleeding from several locations, as if the curse had been attached to his skin.

Her chest heaved and her body felt on fire. Instead of just her hands, which had struggled with the previous curses, this one was pulsing through Wynona's entire system. Every tug felt heavier than the one before, but slowly, the chain in the bucket began to build up.

Wynona's head was buzzing so badly from the magic she was dealing with that she had no idea what was going on in the room around her. She couldn't hear Rascal anymore and she was struggling to keep her arms moving.

Violet's tail tightened. *Let me help.* She sent a few pulses of magic through Wynona, enough to have her opening her eyes.

"Thanks," Wynona whispered hoarsely. A few more minutes went by and Wynona could finally see the end. Another four to five feet was wrapped around Lusgu's legs, but she could barely stay upright.

*Get your lazy sister over here to share some of her magic.*

Wynona shook her head. Celia would never go for it.

*Do it, Wynona. You won't finish otherwise and who knows what the curse will do if left like this.*

Wynona leaned back on her heels. It took a few blinks to make everyone in the room not look blurry. "Celia?" she croaked.

Celia lifted her chin.

"Will you..." Wynona coughed and gasped for breath.

"She needs your magic," Rascal ground out. His hands hovered over Wynona's shoulders.

"Don't touch me," Wynona warned him. "I don't know what will happen."

"Oh sure..." Celia drawled. "But it's fine if I do."

"Celia, I..." Wynona coughed again.

Celia pinched her lips and she glared at Lusgu. "This had better be worth it," she snapped. Marching over, she put a hand on Wynona's shoulder.

A surge of magic went through Wynona's chest and she obeyed as quickly as she could, trying to capitalize on the energy before it waned. Crawling on hands and knees, Wynona continued her tugging, even knowing each pull was hurting her and Lusgu. They were so close. She just couldn't stop.

Finally, the last loop lay around his ankle.

"Hang on, Lusgu," Wynona rasped. "This is going to be the worst part, I think." Climbing clumsily to her feet, Wynona grasped the curse with both hands and braced herself. Thin arms came around her and she startled, looking over her shoulder.

Celia made a face. "Someone has to keep you from killing yourself," she muttered. "I still want that tea reading, after all."

Her strength warmed Wynona more than the magic flowing between them and Wynona nodded gratefully. "One...two...three!" The two women fell to the floor as Lusgu bellowed in pain and collapsed.

Wynona couldn't move. Her body shook with residual magic and her skin felt as if she were being burned from the inside out.

Voices were screaming and shouting and she couldn't respond to any of them. A heavy thud to her left and a deep growl told Wynona Rascal was there. His hand landed on her forehead.

"Hold on," he ordered. "You're going to be fine." His thumb rubbed against her skin and Wynona didn't have the energy to tell him how much it hurt with her raw nerves trying to out-do each other.

She gasped when the heavy weight of the chain in her hand disappeared.

"I've got it," Daemon told her, referring to the curse. His voice was strained and she knew that he was struggling to keep the magic contained.

"What…are…"

"Don't," Rascal interrupted. "Don't talk. We'll figure it all out."

"Out of my way."

Rascal's head jerked up and his eyes flashed with a warning. "If you think I'm letting you near her, then you better think again."

"I can heal her," the smooth voice said. "Let me in."

Rascal's skin rippled and Wynona knew he was about to lose it to the wolf. But she had no way of stopping him.

*Trust him,* Violet said, her voice uncharacteristically soft.

Rascal's head jerked down to the mouse. "Why?"

"I owe her everything," the male voice said again. "And her work isn't done yet."

Rascal's hands flexed and he looked at Wynona, obviously torn with indecision.

*Rascal,* Violet said again. *Trust me.*

Shaking with anger, Rascal stood and backed off.

Wynona's eyesight was blurry and still slightly purple around the edges. The weight of the curse was gone, but her body was still suffering all the ill effects of having handled and dealt with a magic so dark. She shook against the hardwood floor, her body screaming in pain and her brain crying for relief of any kind.

A dark shadow landed over her and she couldn't tell who it was.

She'd never seen the man before as he laid a cool hand on her forehead. Unlike Rascal's warm touch, there was a slight abetting to the pain when the man's hand reached her skin and Wynona sighed without meaning to.

"That's it," the voice cooed. "Relax."

Slowly at first, then with increasing speed, Wynona found her body relaxing. Contorted muscles stop twitching and pain eased. Her joints felt normal again and soon her breathing had calmed down as well.

When the hand came off her forehead, she blinked, not having realized she had closed her eyes, and took in a deep breath. "Thank you," she whispered.

The man stood and held out a hand for her.

Wynona allowed him to help her to her feet, then immediately leaned into Rascal when he wrapped his arms around her, but she couldn't quite take her eyes from the newcomer. "Who are you?" she asked.

The man smirked and adjusted the cuffs on his perfectly tailored suit. He stood taller than Rascal, but with a thinner build, though there was no denying the power that emanated from every pore of his being.

Confidence, even arrogance, were written in every line of his face as he turned black eyes that felt oddly familiar to Wynona.

"I suppose introductions are in order," the man said, that grin still tugging at his mouth. He inclined his head slightly, as if he were royalty come to visit. "I never expected to greet not only one, but two family members at the same time." His eyes went from Wynona to a gaping Celia and back. "Hello, my dear nieces. I'm your Uncle Arune."

# COMING NEXT

Eager for more answers?
You definitely don't want to miss
Wynona's next adventure!
Check out "Earl Grey with a Hint of Murder"!

Made in the USA
Monee, IL
05 February 2023